TEARDROPS IN THE MOON

by

Tania Crosse

Magna Large Print Books
Long Preston, North Yorkshire,
BD23 4ND, England.

British Library Cataloguing in Publication Data.

Crosse, Tania
    Teardrops in the moon.

    A catalogue record of this book is
    available from the British Library

    ISBN   978-0-7505-4044-5

First published in Great Britain in 2014 by Robert Hale Limited

Published in Large Print 2015 by arrangement with
Robert Hale Limited

Magna Large Print is an imprint of Library Magna Books Ltd.

Printed and bound in Great Britain by
T.J. (International) Ltd., Cornwall, PL28 8RW

DEDICATION

In memory of
Dorothy Lumley
Agent and friend
1949–2013

And, as ever, for my husband, for always
being at my side.

The BRADLEY Family Tree in 1906

```
                                    1867
Rebecca Westbrook (betrothed to)  Tom Mason   m.   Captain Adam Bradley
1847 –                            1845-1867  │    1837 –
                                     │   ┌────────┴──────────────────┐
          1892                       │   │                           │
Chantal Pencarrow  m.  Toby (Bradley)│   │                           │
1865 –             │   1868 –        Charlotte m.  a sea captain    James
                   │                 1873 –    │                    1875 –
              Michael                          │                    married
              1895 –                        children                 with
                                                                   children
```

The FRANFIELD Family Tree in 1906

```
          1885 (1)                 1895 (2)
Ling Southcott  m.  Barney Mayhew   m.   Dr Elliott Franfield
1868 –          │   1865-1892      │    1863 –
                │              ┌───┴───────────┐
          Arthur (Artie)      │               │
          1893 –            Mary           William
                           1895 –          1901 –
```

The PENCARROW Family Tree in 1906

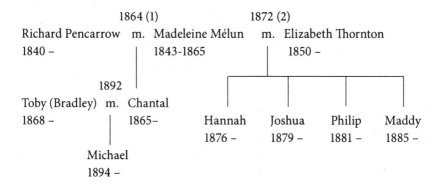

```
                1864 (1)              1872 (2)
Richard Pencarrow  m.  Madeleine Mélun   m.  Elizabeth Thornton
1840 -              |   1843-1865             1850 -

        1892        |
Toby (Bradley)  m.  Chantal
1868 -           |  1865-        Hannah   Joshua   Philip   Maddy
                 |               1876 -   1879 -   1881 -   1885 -
        Michael
        1894 -
```

The WARRINGTON Family Tree in 1906

```
              1876 (1)               1879 (2)
Rose Maddiford  m.  Charles Chadwick   m.  Seth Warrington
1854 -           |   1839-1878              1847 -

             Alice
             1877          Henry (Hal)  Katherine (Kate)  Marianne
             d. 3mths      1884 -       1887 -            1889 -
```

PROLOGUE

The man hesitated briefly at the top of the gangway, his shifty eyes scanning Plymouth's quayside. No sign of any police officers then. So, none of the American authorities in any of the places he was a wanted criminal – New York, Boston, Chicago – had discovered that he had embarked from Manhattan on a passenger ship bound for England and wired ahead for his arrest, for he was sure the British police would have cooperated.

One side of the fellow's mouth curved into a smirk. He hadn't spent a lifetime of crime without learning a trick or two. When he had sailed from this very spot over twenty years ago, he had evaded the local constabulary even though every man jack of them had been after him. Then as now, he had travelled under a false name with forged documents, even fooling the immigration authorities on New York's Ellis Island. In fact, he had never used his proper name since and certainly didn't intend to do so now he was home. The law had too long a memory, and he had left England for the same reason he had left America: it was too dangerous for him to stay.

He could have gone far away in that boundless continent of course, perhaps to San Francisco, although the massive earthquake there two years previously was somewhat off-putting. He'd heard though, of a small but thriving mining town called Silverton up in the Colorado Mountains. Apparently there were over forty brothels along what was known as Notorious Blair Street, so there'd surely be a way for someone like him to set up a rival business!

The thought was appealing, but the thing was, he was getting too old to start again in a completely strange place. Into his fifties now, he'd had enough of armed robbery, protection rackets and gangland feuds and murders. He just wanted a quiet life, existing nicely from his ill-gotten gains. He was tired of constantly looking over his shoulder, carrying a pistol about his person, afraid to walk down a dark street at night in case he found a knife stuck in his ribs. And the only place he felt he could achieve that peace was back home in Devon.

Now though, as he moved down the gangway with his fellow passengers, he wasn't so sure. Maybe he hadn't outwitted the authorities after all. Perhaps there were plain-clothes officers waiting for him just yards away. Or worse still, envoys from rival New York gangs lurking behind the barrels and other merchandise stacked on the quayside.

His eyes swivelled furtively as he crossed the cobbles, suitcase in one hand, turning up the collar of his coat with the other. No one appeared to be following him even when he used a shop window as a mirror to check behind him. But as he caught his own reflection in the glass, he began to relax. His own mother wouldn't have recognized him; he wondered disinterestedly if she was still alive.

The port hadn't changed. The backstreets and alleyways were exactly the same, a labyrinth where you could easily lose a pursuing copper. He hoped his old fence was still there. He had converted as much of his money as he could into jewellery, sewn into the lining of his coat together with the stolen diamonds. He should be able to live comfortably for the rest of his days; perhaps he had something to thank that stuck-up bitch, Rose Chadwick, for after all. Preferred that bloody convict to him, she had, the devil who'd escaped from Dartmoor prison and hidden in the stable. Well he'd got his own back by telling the authorities, hadn't he, and been paid handsomely for his troubles. But when that fool of a husband of hers had died – curious business that – the first thing she had done was to give *him* the sack!

Well, maybe it had been for the best. If it weren't for her, he might still have been an impoverished stable-hand. So, although the idea of getting even with her still appealed,

11

he ought to let bygones be bygones. She'd be about the same age as him. Could even be dead by now. Provided his fence was still there and he could convert his haul into cash, he would be happy just to enjoy the fruits of his crimes for the rest of his life.

He pushed open the door to the pawn-shop. It was like stepping back in time. Not a thing had changed, the same scratched counter, the same crammed shelves, same dank, musty smell. And the man dressed in what he swore were the same moth-eaten, filthy clothes, got to his feet. He was more stooped, his hair now grey and wispy, but it was him all right.

'Can I help you?' he asked gruffly.

The traveller's lips stretched into a sly smile as he removed his hat and placed it on the counter. Then he wallowed in the shop-keeper's dumbfounded surprise as he peeled off the false eyebrows and beard, and finally the wig.

'Remember me?' he purred.

The old chap's jaw snapped shut and his bloodshot eyes bolted from his head. 'Bloody hell, Ned Cornish as I does live and breathe.'

Marianne Warrington had sensed all morning that something was going to happen. There had been an excitement about her elder sister, Kate, that only Marianne recognized, a tilt of her beautiful, dark head, a flash of her intense, violet-blue eyes. It made Marianne feel uneasy, as all their lives the two sisters had confided everything to each other. Absolutely everything. So why was this different?

The whole family – Marianne, Kate, their elder brother, Hal, and their parents, Seth and Rose Warrington – had all climbed into the wagonette. They were driving from Fencott Place, their own remote home on Dartmoor, to visit some long-standing friends. The Pencarrows lived on another part of the moor at a somewhat grandly named farmhouse, Rosebank Hall. They were yeoman farmers who also rented out a handful of smaller farms nearby.

As a young man, Richard Pencarrow had taken himself off to France following a vicious argument with his father. He had settled in the north-east of the country, but his happiness had been short-lived when his young French wife had died, leaving him to bring up their little daughter, Chantal, alone. Events in the Franco-Prussian War had forced Richard to return to the family home where he had met his second wife, Beth, and they had produced four children: Hannah, Joshua, Philip and Madeleine. Only Hannah had been born when Rose had made Richard and Beth's acquaintance under the most harrowing of circumstances,

13

but as the two families became such firm friends over the years, it was inevitable that the children all grew very close as well – although less so with Chantal who was that much older and was now married with a son, Michael.

And so, when later that morning, the Warrington family had arrived at Rosebank Hall, there were all the usual greetings and chatting as everyone who knew each other so intimately, met up once again. Marianne had waited, wondering and uncertain about Kate's secretive mood, and now, as Kate went to stand by Philip Pencarrow, she sensed that the time had come.

She watched as the young man glanced nervously about him.

'Can I have...' he began, but his voice was no more than a croak that nobody except the two sisters heard. He sucked in his breath in an effort to summon up his courage, but when Kate smiled up at him, it seemed to Marianne that his confidence rallied.

'While we're all together, can I have your attention, please?' Philip tried again. This time, the convivial conversation between the members of the two families gathered on the lawn gradually ceased, and all eyes turned expectantly to the young couple. It made Philip look even more apprehensive, but he seemed determined to continue. 'Kate and I have an announcement to make,' he went on more boldly now. 'We're to be married.'

It was only a few seconds before a ripple of happy exclamations echoed among the excited faces.

'Congratulations!'

'Oh, that's wonderful news!'

It appeared to Marianne though, that the smile was nailed on Philip's face as everyone came up to hug him and his new fiancée. There was something else, she was sure, that he wasn't saying. Something he was ashamed of.

'Aren't you supposed to ask my permission first?'

Marianne could see that her father, Seth Warrington, was attempting to sound stern, but his dancing hazel eyes gave him away.

'For heaven's sake, Dad!' Kate grinned exuberantly. 'We're not in the Victorian era any more. It's 1906, not 1850! Besides, I knew you'd say yes. Especially as I'm expecting Philip's child.'

'What!'

A sudden, shocked silence extinguished the cacophony of jubilant voices. Stunned, Marianne remained speechless, as wordless glances were exchanged and Philip looked as if he wanted the ground to open up and swallow him.

'Good God, Philip.'

It was his father, Richard, who spoke first. Age had not bent his tall, broad back and he still topped both his sons by a good inch. A hard-working hill-farmer all his life, in his sixty-seventh year he was just as strong and active as in his youth. Marianne knew he was as steadfast and loving a father as her own. But she also knew he was likely to react like a flash of lightning to the news. She was not mistaken.

'I thought we'd brought you up better than that,' Richard growled, his eyebrows swooping darkly. 'Chantal and Hannah both waited years to marry the men they loved, and—'

'I can't help what my sisters did,' Philip broke in, colour spreading into his cheeks. 'And I *have* waited years, too! I think I've loved Kate all my life, so waiting until she's nineteen has been a long time.'

Marianne saw his desperate expression seek the petite woman standing at his father's side. She guessed he was expecting his gentle, caring mother to understand, but he must still have been relieved to see Beth squeeze her husband's arm.

'What's done is done, Richard,' she said softly. 'And we've thought for some time that they'd marry and have children sooner or later, didn't we?'

'Pity it wasn't in that order,' Richard grumbled. But as he gazed down into his wife's melting, amber eyes that still did something to his heart even after all the years they

16

had been together, his anger obviously wavered. 'I suppose if they see the vicar and get married as soon as possible–'

'That's right.' Kate and Marianne's mother, Rose Warrington, stepped forward, positively glowing with delight. The only difference between mother and daughters was that Rose bore faint laugh-lines about her eyes and her raven hair was threaded with silver here and there. 'And since when did we ever give a fig about scandal?' she went on, turning mischievously to her husband. 'If Seth and I don't mind as Kate's parents, then you really shouldn't worry, Richard, dear.'

'And Philip wasn't entirely to blame,' Kate added in her usual self-assured, matter-of-fact tone. 'I was there, too. And we do love each other utterly.'

'Just as well,' Richard came back. 'And where do you propose to live when you're married?'

'Here at the farm. If you'll have us,' Philip replied hesitantly. 'Or we could rebuild the cottage. I know you and Josh will need me here more than ever now we have Moor Top back on our hands. Or we could live at Moor Top ourselves.'

By the look on his face, Richard was admitting to himself that he was impressed. Marianne knew that Moor Top was the second of the Pencarrows' tenanted farms that had recently been vacated, but it was somewhat of a white elephant. Isolated and exposed, it was farming at its most gruelling, and unlike his brother Josh, Philip was not a born farmer. As for the cottage, it had been in ruins since an explosion there nearly thirty years previously. And yet Philip was willing to sacrifice his home comforts at Rosebank Hall for the sake of his love for Kate.

'Well, I won't have you living at Moor Top,' Richard answered fiercely. 'You know your mother and I were forced to live there once and ... well, it has too many bad memories. And as for rebuilding the cottage, I'm not sure it'd be worth the effort. But you and Kate are welcome to live here with us, aren't they, Beth?' he asked, addressing his wife who nodded back with a beaming smile. 'Kate's part of the family already, so it won't be that different, will it? So...' He held out his hand to his son who clasped it in grateful relief, and there were hugs and merry chatter all round.

No one seemed to notice that Marianne was the only person not to join in the felicitations, standing back while everyone else milled about the happy couple. Marianne remained apart, biting her lip. She was two years her sister's junior, but she and Kate might have been twins in both looks and personality. The only passion Kate did not share with her was her love of horses, even though the family ran a successful stud-farm at their own isolated home. It never seemed to matter, though. In every other way, Kate was Marianne's soul-mate. They had always shared everything, every whispered secret, every midnight feast, every madcap, reckless escapade.

But now...

Marianne felt betrayed. Not by Kate because this sister she worshipped was part of herself and could never be anything but loved. But by the fact that something had come between them. Growing up, love of a member of the opposite sex, and now a *baby*, for heaven's sake.

Marianne turned her back on the little crowd and gazed out across the valley. The lawn at the front of Rosebank Hall overlooked the pretty combe above the village of Peter Tavy on the western fringe of the moor. It was a beautiful spot. Whenever Marianne stood there, she fancied she could reach out and touch Great Combe Tor, the high outcrop of granite on the far side. She couldn't of course, and neither could much of the infinite, high moorland be seen from that point. And that was where Marianne longed to be now, galloping across the heather and wild grasses on one of the family's fine horses, the wind in her hair driving out all care.

She felt lost, as if half of her had suddenly fallen away. How would she manage to be herself again without Kate constantly by her side? She did not blame Philip. He was a kind, caring fellow, like another brother almost, so how could he now become her brother-in-law and take on a completely different role in her life? The change was unimaginable. Unacceptable.

Marianne felt her heart rip. When had her sister and Philip become lovers? When had they found the opportunity to perform that mysterious, wonderful and yet frightening act that led to babies being born? She could never imagine she would want to engage in such a thing, even if she were madly in love with someone and it was, so her mother had explained, the culmination of the sanctity of marriage.

Except that Kate had not waited to be married first. Making love might be the natural thing to do, but the idea filled Marianne with disgust. Kate had toppled from her pedestal, leaving Marianne floundering in a sea of bewilderment. You had to be careful when you were pregnant, not climb trees or scramble to the crest of sheer, towering rockfaces, run and jump across rivers and bogs. And when the baby came, it would be no better. Beth would be only too happy to mind it for a few hours; she was the village midwife, after all. But Kate would always be anxious to get back to it, and never again would she and Marianne enjoy that sense of abandonment together. Oh, it was intolerable, and Marianne suddenly felt tears collecting in her eyes.

The tap on her shoulder startled her from her misery. She turned, and there was Kate, her face radiant with joy. It was like looking in a mirror, they were so alike, and yet not any more. Kate was no longer who she had always been, and part of Marianne died.

'Oh, don't cry!' Kate exclaimed in horrified concern. 'Aren't you pleased for me?'

'Of course I am!' Marianne lied. 'These are tears of happiness.'

'Are they? Oh, thank you–'

'It's just that, I don't know–'

'We're not children any more,' Kate finished for her. 'I know. It's really weird, isn't it? But this won't make any difference to us. It'll be your baby, too. You can help me wash and feed it, just like we used to with our dolls, only this will be real. Oh, Marianne, I'm so happy!'

All at once, Kate folded her younger sister in her arms and hugged her so tightly that Marianne could hardly draw breath. She gazed over Kate's shoulder back towards the farmhouse. The other members of the two families were chatting away, already making plans, no doubt. But Marianne felt alone. An outsider. She would pretend to be happy, of course she would. And she would support her sister in every way. But in that moment of embrace, Marianne made a silent vow. She would never allow herself to fall in love and have children. Her life would be dedicated to the superb horses her parents bred, and the love of her life would be the savage beauty and endless wilderness of the place that was the cornerstone of her soul. She would live and die on Dartmoor, and nothing or no one would ever come between them.

CHAPTER ONE

'Oh, when *will* you let me learn to drive?' Marianne called out, exploding with frustration, as her father brought the Napier to a stop at the front of the grand family home known as Fencott Place. 'I'm nearly twenty-five, for Heaven's sake! Surely I'm capable—'

'Now then, young lady,' Seth admonished, switching off the engine and climbing out of the elegant motorcar. 'Don't start that again. And you know it's your brother's machine, not mine, so it's him you need to persuade.'

'He lets *you* drive it.'

'Perhaps he trusts me more. Keep saving your allowance and when you can afford your own vehicle, I'll be happy to teach you.'

'But that could take forever!'

'It will if you keep buying new saddles when we have perfectly good equipment in the tack room. Now, I'm just going to see if your mother's ready, and then we're going to meet Adam and Rebecca at the station. If you want to come too, why don't you saddle up Pegasus and ride there?'

Marianne's petulantly bunched lips slackened and then spread into a grin. Not that she needed an excuse to ride her beloved horse. 'I'll race you,' she challenged. 'And I bet you I'll win!'

'I expect you will,' Seth grimaced. 'The road is so full of potholes, I can barely crawl along if I don't want to damage the car. I'll be glad when they put tarmac down on the roads over the moor. Not that I suppose that will happen for many a long year. And I can't imagine they'll do this stretch, anyway.'

He shook his head with a half amused, half exasperated sigh. Marianne was so like her mother. She hadn't waited for him to finish speaking, but had dived around the side of the house towards the stables. She dressed habitually in a riding habit so there was no need to go indoors to change. Instead, she went straight out to the field where Pegasus was grazing with his companions. He came straight up to her, knowing that a mad dash across the open moor might well be on offer, and followed his young mistress expectantly through the gate and along to the stable yard without her having to lead him.

'You'm off for a ride, Marianne?'

'Yes, Joe.'

She turned to the groom, pleased to see a happy gleam in his eyes, as he had always looked so sad since his wife, Molly, had died the previous year. Marianne's mother, Rose, had been close friends with Joe and Molly since youth, which was why there was no doffing of caps or deferential speech. But that was how Rose had always run her household, treating her so-called servants as members of the family, and Marianne would not have done things any differently herself.

'You know Uncle Adam and Aunt Becky are coming to stay?' she went on casually, slipping the bit of the bridle into the stunning dapple grey's mouth.

At this, Joe actually grinned. 'Cap'ain an' Mrs Bradley? Yes, of course I knows. Talked of nort else the past two weeks has your mother!'

'Well, Mum and Dad are picking them up at the station in the Napier and I'm going to ride alongside. Or rather, I'll get there first as I'm sure Pegasus would like a good gallop.'

'You be careful now,' Joe warned, pulling in his chin. 'Mad as a hatter you be when you'm in the saddle, just like your mother. An' I wouldn't want ort to happen to you *or* Pegasus.'

'Don't you worry. I'd never do anything silly where any of the horses are concerned, and especially not dear Pegasus.' And she gave the animal a smacking kiss on his nose to prove it.

'Mind you doesn't,' Joe nodded with an amused smile. 'I'll get that fancy new saddle from the tack room for you.'

'Would you, Joe? That's very kind.'

Five minutes later, she swung herself into

the saddle. 'No, dogs, not this time,' she told the two Labradors who were gazing up at her expectantly, and then she was clattering round to the front of the house on Pegasus's back. The car was still parked there, but Marianne was not prepared to wait. She urged Pegasus into a trot along the sweeping drive, but as soon as they passed through the gates in the high brick wall, she turned him across the open, windswept moor towards the prison settlement of Princetown. She did not take the direct route along the road however, but crossed over to the parallel track that had once led out to the long-defunct Eylesbarrow Mine. The ground was softer and would be safer for her steed's finely sculptured legs, for despite Joe's words of caution, neither she nor her mother would ever take a risk with any of the horses.

She gave Pegasus his head, feeling the power of the magnificent creature beneath her and crouching low over his strong, out-stretched neck. Her own body echoed the rippling movements as if she and the horse were one, the ground flying beneath them in a blur. They slowed only to navigate the occasional stone embedded in the track, and it only seemed minutes before they had eaten up the two miles or so into Prince-town.

They trotted into the heart of the small, isolated town. People were going about their business, mainly the families of warders who were obliged by the terms of their employment to live within sprinting distance of Dartmoor's grim prison. But Princetown was also the main centre for the hardy farming community scattered across that part of the bleak, hostile moor. The warm weather had brought women out to shop in the various establishments, Bolt's Store on the corner and other shops scattered elsewhere. Further along the road towards the prison was the attractive building that housed the Co-operative store. Attached to it was a small, single-storey newsagents, W. H. Smith, but Marianne was not buying a newspaper today. It would only be full of the worrying situation in Europe and just now, she would rather not think about it.

Instead, she turned off onto the road to the railway station. As they approached the long, low building that housed the waiting rooms and the ticket and station master's offices, she glanced back over her shoulder. She tossed her head, bringing Pegasus to a halt and swinging her leg fluidly over his neck to dismount. No sign yet of her parents in Hal's precious motorcar. What did she care? Give her a horse any day! But she knew that she did care very much indeed. She wanted to do anything a man could – and one day she would prove that she could do it better, too!

Tying Pegasus's reins over the railings, Marianne skipped through onto the platform and peered down the track that snaked its way down over the moor to join the mainline at Yelverton. She was sure her parents would arrive in the Napier at any minute to greet their dear friends, Captain and Mrs Bradley. Rose had originally been introduced to them by Richard and Beth Pencarrow, and all three families had, over the decades, become as one.

As she waited for Adam and Rebecca to arrive, Marianne reflected on how inordinately fond she was of the aging couple. They had acted as surrogate aunt and uncle to Marianne and her siblings in their childhood, and the love that had passed between them had not diminished with time. Kate and Philip had even named their son for Adam, something that had brought an emotional tear to the captain's eye when they had asked his permission to do so.

At the thought of her sister, Marianne's heart jerked. What was it to Rosebank Hall? Ten or twelve miles? She could easily ride over for the day and did so frequently. But if she was allowed to *drive* over in the motor-car, she could get there so much more quickly despite the uneven surface of the roads since she could not keep Pegasus at a flat out gallop all that way. And then she could spend longer with Kate.

'Miss Marianne! You meeting someone off the train, your brother, perhaps?'

The station master's voice drew Marianne from her thoughts and she turned to smile at the uniformed fellow coming towards her. 'Yes, but not Hal. Captain and Mrs Bradley, my parents' friends. They're coming to meet them in the car, but I rode on ahead.'

'You and that horse!' the man chuckled, shaking his head. 'Remind me so much of your mother, you does. Huge great thing she used to gallop all over the place on, she did, when she were younger. Black as night it were, and a temper on it to match if you wasn't careful. Us was just tackers back then and terrified of it. But it were like a lamb with your mother.'

'Gospel he was called,' Marianne grinned back. 'Mum's favourite horse ever, she says. Tested all her riding skills to the limit, and you know what a superb horsewoman she is.'

'And you'm a chip off the old block from what I sees. But I suppose you'd expect it with your father being such a horseman, too, and your business being in horses and all.'

'It doesn't necessarily follow.' Marianne shrugged. 'My sister's not that keen on horses.'

'But your brother be. When's he back from London, then? Or has your father already fetched him from Plymouth or Exeter Station in that there motorcar contraption?'

'No. He's still in London. On business for Dad.'

'Oh, yes?'

The man raised an inquisitive eyebrow but Marianne said nothing. She knew her parents weren't keen on people knowing that their money came not so much from the stud-farm, successful though it was, but from global investments inherited from Rose's first husband, Charles Chadwick. So Marianne was not going to discuss such matters with the station master, kindly though he was.

'Here comes the train!' she was relieved to cry as a wisp of white smoke appeared above the bend, followed a few seconds later by the shiny green engine whose black and copper chimney gleamed proudly in the sunshine. The glorious sight of the fine machine on the long, straight home-run into Princetown after its tortuous climb to conquer the moor never failed to set her blood pumping. With its fire and steam and strength, it was like a living creature to Marianne, a little like a gigantic horse. And now it was bringing dear Adam and Rebecca to visit.

'Ooph, just in time!' Rose panted, running up behind her daughter, her face radiant and not looking anything like the sixty years she was about to celebrate. Elegant in a mid-grey suit of good quality, yet serviceable cloth that was fitted into her still trim waist, Marianne often hoped she would have as good a figure when she reached that age.

Now though, she turned her attention back to the mighty engine and its two coaches coasting into the station. The great coupling rods that drove the huge wheels gradually slowed, the driver having such perfect control that the train inched to a halt without the slightest grinding of brakes. A mere breath of white steam wafted across the platform and an instant later, came the distinctive clunking as carriage doors were unlocked and pushed wide open.

'Half past three, dead on time,' Rose announced. 'And there they are. Becky! Adam!'

Marianne waited, grinning ecstatically, as both her parents hurried past her to greet their old friends, for it was only right that they should be the first to welcome them. Captain Adam Bradley was still tall and broad-chested, as distinguished as ever in spite of his white hair being thin and wispy on top, while his wife was like a doll beside him, not as slim as Rose, but hardly plump. She broke away from Rose's embrace and came towards Marianne, smiling broadly.

'Marianne, my dearest!'

'Aunt Becky! Did you have a good journey?'

'We certainly did. Did Rose tell you we

31

spent a couple of days in Bath on the way? I would never want to live in a town, but Bath is so very beautiful.'

'I don't like even *visiting* towns. Apart from Tavistock, of course,' Marianne insisted, hugging her tightly. 'Uncle Adam! How are you?'

'My dear child! Let me guess. You rode here on that handsome animal of yours, I'll be bound.'

'I did indeed! Well, Hal still refuses to let me drive his motorcar,' she complained with a mock pout. 'But I'll learn to drive one day, I promise you.'

'Knowing you, I'm sure you will!' Adam gave a light laugh. 'Now, if you'll excuse me, I need to find the porter and see to our luggage.'

'I'll come with you,' Seth offered. 'I know the young lad well.'

Marianne smiled to herself, falling into step beside her mother and Rebecca as they made their way to the exit. Happy chaos would reign at Fencott Place, Rose in her element since Adam and Rebecca only visited from their estate in Herefordshire once a year now, and when they were together, Rose and Rebecca sparked delightedly from each other like two firecrackers.

'I'm surprised you didn't ride here, too, Rose,' Rebecca observed with a teasing light in her sapphire eyes. 'Or are you becoming more sedate now you're about to turn sixty?'

'You must be joking!' Marianne giggled back, since the idea of her mother taking life easy was, quite frankly, ridiculous. 'She rides out with me virtually every day. Except for the last few days because she's been dashing about the house like a whirlwind making sure everything's perfect for your stay.'

'Oh, but you shouldn't–'

'Yes, I should! I *love* having you to stay! So, tell me, how are you? Truthfully, mind,' Rose concluded, serious for once.

'I'm very well. Adam's slowing down a little, but he *is* seventy-seven, so what can you expect? Hasn't been to sea in two years, not even on the *Emily*. And he still swears he'll never set foot on a steamship, even though he had three of the things built, as you know.'

'Toby still hasn't been able to persuade him, then?' Rose asked, referring to their son who was also a sea captain and was in fact married to Richard Pencarrow's half-French daughter, Chantal.

'No.' Rebecca gave a chuckle. 'I think Michael might one day, though. Grandchildren can sometimes be more influential than sons.'

'Michael's training still going well, then?'

'Certainly is. He's only twenty, of course, so he's a long way to go yet. But he'll get his master's ticket eventually, so that'll make three generations of sea captains in the family.'

They had reached the end of the platform and came to a halt as they watched the two men overseeing the loading of the luggage into the car. Marianne sensed a change in Rebecca's mood, as if she was hesitating. Rose must have felt it too, as Marianne saw the faint lines on her mother's forehead deepen.

'My dear Becky, is anything wrong?' Rose asked anxiously.

Marianne noticed Rebecca bite her lip and glance towards her husband. 'Well ... don't say anything, but Adam gave us a fright a few months back. But the doctor's put him on something for his heart, and he's been fine since.'

'Oh, Lord–'

'Shush. And promise you won't let on I've told you,' Rebecca pleaded. And then she turned her vivid smile on Adam as he held open the door of the Napier.

'I expect you two will want to sit in the back and natter away like two jackdaws,' he smiled fondly.

'Why, of course!' Rose agreed with even more unashamed gusto than ever – to conceal her shock, Marianne surmised.

'And will you be following us, Marianne dear?'

'Er, no, not yet, Aunt Becky,' Marianne answered after a moment's reflection. 'I need to give Pegasus more exercise yet.'

'We'll see you later on, then.'

Marianne nodded, forcing a smile to her lips while she absently stroked Pegasus's beautiful face. Feeling his silky hair beneath her fingers was like a soothing balm to her own heart which had begun to patter nervously at Rebecca's news. Dear Uncle Adam. He had always been like a rock in her life, the eldest of all her parents' friends, a solid and dependable patriarch. With influential connections in his native London, he was so strong and godlike in Marianne's eyes, and yet he was kindness itself. He was a constant, and she could not imagine her world without him.

She watched her father drive the motorcar smoothly away from the station, her throat choked. Adam and Rebecca's visit always presented a joyous occasion, even more so this year as they would be celebrating Rose's sixtieth birthday. The concept that all these people she loved were entering old age had never crossed Marianne's mind before. Or if it had, she had dismissed it out of hand. But now it hit her like a sledgehammer.

There was only one way she could open up her mind to the cold reality of acceptance. That was why she had replied instinctively that she needed to give Pegasus a longer ride, and she swung herself back into the saddle. The familiar sensation of the warm, vigorous creature beneath her was immensely comforting, and she turned his head to retrace their steps through Princetown and back across the open moor the same way they had come. Except that this time, they did not turn off towards Fencott Place, but followed the track even further out across the wild, empty moorland.

The gentle summer breeze lifted Pegasus's white and silver mane as he broke into a gallop, his hoofs pounding rhythmically on the soft earth. The air rushed against Marianne's cheek, driving out her melancholy thoughts, the pure joy of freedom and speed and being at one with nature pouring into her heart and settling the unnerving shock of Rebecca's revelation. It was not until they reached the ruins of Eylesbarrow Mine that Marianne felt at peace, and she reined Pegasus in, slowly drawing him to a halt.

She gazed all around her, twisting about in the saddle. The ancient landscape was relatively flat here, totally exposed and rolling gently so that she could see for some way in every direction. As ever, she felt herself overflow with profound emotion, an ethereal sense of timelessness and awe. Dartmoor was eternal, born in the mists of time before man had walked the earth, dark and mysterious, and would be there long after

Marianne herself had gone. The feeling that no matter what happened, her soul would forever remain part of the moor, wreathed her in a strange and overwhelming comfort.

Refreshed and steady once more, she urged Pegasus forward again, turning almost back on themselves down a track on the left that led down to the remote upper valley of the River Plym. It was scarcely a river here, more like a stream, the ground uneven and boggy. They did not pass another living soul, not even a sheep or wild pony, and Marianne kept Pegasus at a walk, relishing the utter quiet broken only by the dull plod of his hoofs. It was not until the track lifted out of the valley again that she let him increase his pace on the firmer ground, eventually following a sharp bend and cantering downhill towards Nun's Cross Ford.

Another mile or so and they would be back at Fencott Place. Marianne could imagine her parents, Adam and Rebecca in the grand drawing room under the glorious portrait of her mother – or, being such a balmy afternoon, more likely enjoying the fine views from the terrace at the back of the house. Each would be quaffing their favourite tipple before going upstairs to wash and change for dinner.

It was so unexpected, happened so quickly, that she had no time to react. Pegasus skidded to a halt, front legs stiffened and hind quarters bunched beneath him. He let out a petrified squeal, rearing up and twisting sideways so that Marianne was propelled out of the saddle. There was no room for fear, just a strange detachment as she flew through the air and landed with a thud on the track. A malevolent hiss wheezed in front of her, and she raised her head to see the forked tongue flicker towards her before the distinctive zigzag markings of an adder slithered away into the deep heather.

Marianne did not move for several seconds. In her entire life on the moor she had never had such an encounter. She gulped hard, catching her breath and slicked with sweat. She knew she wasn't hurt. Thank goodness she had not landed on a stone or boulder that could have broken a bone or knocked her unconscious. But the shock of the fall and coming, quite literally, face-to-face with the venomous snake, had momentarily stunned her. Pegasus snorted in distress, snapping her to her senses, and she scrambled to her feet. He was dancing in a circle, stamping the ground and his eyes rolling. Oh, no! He hadn't been bitten, had he?

Marianne caught the reins, crooning softly and stroking the horse's neck. He made a noise in his throat like a gurgling whinny and shook his head so that the bit jangled about his mouth. A mighty shiver trembled through him and his withers twitched several times, but he seemed calmer now and Marianne led him forward, eyes fearfully observing each leg. No sign of a limp, thank goodness. She nonetheless inspected each limb in minute detail before she was satisfied. But just in case, she would not ride him home, and would warn Joe to keep a lookout. A bite to an animal the size of a horse should not be dangerous, of course, unless it happened to be on the face where it could cause complications. But Marianne would not want Pegasus to suffer the discomfort of a bite when there were things that could be done to lessen the pain.

She led him forward, cursing herself for not noticing the adder before he did. It did not appear that any harm had been done, although Marianne's own shoulder was starting to ache from where she had fallen on it. She would be bruised for several days, but she would not reveal that she had come off Pegasus's back. Her parents would be deeply concerned by the news over Uncle Adam, and she would not want to worry them further. Besides, her pride would not let her admit that she had been unable to keep her seat, and her father might forbid her to ride out alone ever again. She clamped her jaw stubbornly – for she certainly was not having *that!* If she was not allowed to drive a motorcar, she was not going to have her wings clipped when it came to riding horses as well!

CHAPTER TWO

'So, when will Hal be back?' Rebecca asked over dinner that evening.

'Soon, I imagine,' Seth answered. 'I would have gone myself, but my chest was playing up last week. Hal's not really a business-man. His head's too full of horses. But he'll have to take over that side of affairs when I'm gone, so I thought he might as well start now.'

Marianne's hand jerked as she lifted a spoonful of soup towards her mouth. It was the second time that day her attention had been drawn to the fact that her parents' gen-eration were in the autumn of their lives. Although her dear father was ten years Uncle Adam's junior, the devastating circumstances he had unjustly suffered in his earlier life had left him with a weak chest which was mani-festing itself more regularly of late.

'You're better now, though, aren't you, Dad?' Marianne said, trying to conceal her concern.

'Indeed I am. But I'm sure a week in Lon-don's smoke wouldn't have done any good. And I'd have been all alone in your mother's little house if I'd happened to get worse. Hal has sent me a couple of telegrams to keep me informed, as you know.'

'Difficult times, though,' Adam put in gravely. 'Hard to know what's best for investments with the situation in Europe as it is.'

'Exactly so. Perhaps we shouldn't have sold those shares in the gold and diamond mines. They brought in a good return, but you know I'd been protesting against conditions for the workers for years, and when they still weren't improved, well, we didn't feel it was morally right to keep them, did we?'

Seth sought his wife's hand and squeezed it tightly. Rose gave a deep nod of agreement and Marianne caught the loving glance they exchanged. Her parents shared a wondrous relationship, one she was convinced she could never replicate. Besides, she had never encountered a member of the opposite sex who had remotely appealed to her. Instead she spent her time caring for horses. Horses were simple. She valued her independence too much to share her life with another person – and she certainly did not want to be tied to a child like her sister Kate had been from such a young age!

'Well, who knows what's in store for any of us if there is a war,' she was aware of Adam saying now.

'I think it's more likely a case of *when* rather than *if*,' Seth pronounced gravely. 'Personally, I can't see the situation resolving itself without a massive conflict.'

'Unfortunately I have to agree with you,' Adam concurred.

'Oh, men always assume the worst, don't they?' Rebecca said lightly, but Marianne could tell by her tone of voice that she was attempting to hide her own fears.

'Just being realistic, my dear.'

'Well, I just hope you're both wrong,' Rose stated. 'The idea frightens me too much.'

Marianne's eyes travelled over the sombre faces of the four older adults enjoying the first course of the sumptuous supper prepared by their housekeeper-cum-cook, Patsy. It seemed incongruous that they were discussing such serious matters over such a fine repast.

'I don't think we should spoil Uncle Adam and Aunt Becky's first evening with all this depressing talk of war!' Marianne announced, although she knew it was merely sweeping the dirt under the carpet. The subject was bound to be brought up again – only not that evening, she hoped!

'Ah, the sensible voice of youth,' Rebecca approved, and Marianne was relieved to feel she had an ally in her aunt. 'We're here to visit our dear friends and celebrate your special birthday, Rose. I do assume Hal will be back in time for the big day?'

'He'd better be, or I'll want to know the reason why, elder brother or no!' Marianne declared. 'Mind you, there's a certain young lady who I believe may be detaining him in London.'

'Oh, yes?' Rebecca was all ears.

'Our stockbroker's daughter, would you believe.'

'Do I detect a note of disapproval there, Seth?'

'Not disapproval. She's a lovely young woman. But she strikes me as a born city-dweller, while Hal lives for the countryside and the horses. I can't see her wanting to come and live in the middle of Dartmoor.'

'Adam left London for the country,' Marianne noticed Rebecca put in a little defensively.

'I left London for the *sea*,' Adam corrected his wife with an indulgent smile. 'And *then* for you, remember? If it hadn't been for inheriting the estate from my disreputable cousin, we'd probably still be living at Morwellham rather than in deepest Herefordshire.'

'We will visit the quay while you're here, won't we?' Marianne asked excitedly.

'But of course!' Rebecca declared. 'How could we possibly come all this way and not go to Morwellham? 'Twill always be my spiritual home. So much happened there.' She broke off, and her eyes dropped wistfully. ''Tis so different nowadays, mind. Half the buildings are empty, and the few people who do live there are farm workers, rather than all the miners and quay labourers who far outnumbered them in my day. And it makes me so sad to see my parents' cottage without them living in it any more. But I should still love to go. I can take some flowers to my parents' graves at Gulworthy on the way. If 'twill be agreeable to you all?' she concluded.

'We shall look forward to it,' Rose told her with genuine feeling. 'I'm sure Seth will be happy to drive us there, won't you, my dear?'

'I just think it was so romantic the way you and Uncle Adam met at Morwellham,' Marianne put in dreamily. 'The harbour master's daughter and the sea captain, just like something out of a novel.'

''Tweren't so romantic at the time, as I believe you know.' For once, Rebecca appeared a touch embarrassed. 'But we ended up with the happiest marriage anyone could wish for. Just like your mother and father. So...' She dipped her head towards Marianne and lowered her voice to a conspiratorial whisper. 'Anyone on the romantic horizon for you yet, may I ask?'

'Ask away!' Marianne laughed, not the least perturbed. 'I intend to remain a spinster all my life and concentrate on making this the finest stud-farm in the whole country.'

'Well, my girl, I hope everything turns out

well enough for this dear country so that you are able to. But the way things are going at the moment—'

'Oh, Dad!' Marianne remonstrated, irritated that talk of war was creeping into the conversation yet again. 'Stop being so pessimistic. I reckon you only think like that because you were in the army yourself once.'

'That was totally different. I was a young man then, defending the Empire out in India. I was never involved in anything beyond a few skirmishes.'

'Well, that's probably all this will amount to. *If* it amounts to anything. And when it's all over, perhaps I can do some travelling, too. You were so lucky being able to see *India* of all places! It must be so exotic.'

'Sadly, I do seriously believe the situation will end in rather more than a few skirmishes. So you'll probably have to put your plans on hold for a while, young lady, and find some other way to occupy yourself.'

'Oh.' Marianne's voice landed disappointedly. The idea of visiting strange, faraway countries had momentarily fired her with enthusiasm, and she felt somewhat peeved at her father's attitude. 'You make it sound as if I waste away my days all the time. But you know how hard I work with the horses. I can train a horse as well as you or Mum or Joe. Well, almost, anyway.'

'I know you can,' Seth admitted, 'when

you're not out on the moors with Pegasus.'

'He needs the exercise. And Mum comes with me most days on Hermes. Tell you what Mum and I could do, mind. How about we organize another Suffragette rally?'

'God forbid, that seems of little importance just now. You know I'm all for votes for women, and I supported you both last time. But under present circumstances–'

'That was such fun, wasn't it?' Marianne interrupted him. 'Mum driving round Tavistock in the landau with a huge *Votes for Women* banner and leading a whole procession of protestors. It was in all the papers!' she concluded proudly.

'Yes, but we were entirely non-militant,' Rose insisted. 'No breaking windows or anything like that. But it was five years ago, and I don't think I'd have the energy for something like that nowadays.'

'Well, I think we should concentrate on your birthday for now,' Rebecca declared, neatly changing the subject. 'Kate will be coming over, won't she, with Philip and little Adam?'

'Not so little now. He was seven at the beginning of the year. Richard and Beth will be coming, too, of course, but Joshua says someone needs to be at the farm all the time, and his wife wouldn't want to come without him. Chantal's in London and as you know, both the younger girls are married now and live away, so they won't be coming. But do you remember Elliott and Ling Franfield?'

'How could I not?' Rebecca nodded with a merry smile, making Marianne feel more relaxed now that they were discussing happier matters. 'Adam let them sail with him to France on the *Emily* for their honeymoon, if you remember. And before that, Ling and our Toby were quite friendly. What a pity he's just set sail to America and won't be back in time for your celebration. I'm certain he'd have liked to have seen Ling again after all these years.'

'Yes, it is a shame,' Rose agreed. 'I should have liked all the children and grand-children of all our close friends to have come, but it's impossible for everyone to be free at the same time.'

'We'll have a wonderful time anyway, Mum!' Marianne assured her. 'Patsy's already made an enormous fruitcake that she's going to ice, and I'm going to help her in the kitchen.'

'We all can!' Rebecca clapped her hands in delight. 'That'll be such fun! I can make scones if you like. They were always my speciality.'

'Well, if you ladies are going to be discussing menus,' Seth interrupted, 'perhaps Adam and I will leave you to it after we've finished eating. We can have a more worldly talk in the drawing room. Over a good vintage brandy, if you'd like, Adam?'

'Ask a silly question,' his good friend grinned back.

'And you two can put the world to rights,' Rose teased, 'while we have much more fun!'

She glanced triumphantly around the table, catching her daughter's eye. Marianne returned her happy smile. Making arrangements for her mother's party held far greater appeal than contemplating the prospects of a threatening war!

But ... the contentment on her face suddenly slipped away. For what if her father and Uncle Adam were right...?

'It certainly is so very beautiful here,' Marianne sighed blissfully a few days later as she stood with her mother and Aunt Becky on the river bank at Morwellham Quay. 'And so very peaceful.'

'Too peaceful.'

Marianne lifted an eyebrow. She had detected a hint of sadness in Rebecca's voice, but she knew this lively, surrogate aunt of hers would not be downhearted for long. Nevertheless, she sensed that the older woman was going to expand on her thoughts. She waited patiently while Rebecca turned her back on the river and Marianne watched her deep blue eyes move over the quiet village nestling at the foot of the towering, tree-covered ridge behind.

'So hard to imagine this was once a thriving river-port.' Rebecca's voice was a rueful whisper. 'Tons of copper ore would be piled on the quayside around the great dock waiting to be loaded onto ships for South Wales when they'd unloaded the coal. There were dockers and quay workers shouting instructions to each other, the rumble of carts and the overhead railway from the mine, sailors, miners, farm workers, copper agents and sea captains. Especially as the harbour master's daughter, I knew so many of them. And then there was my dear Tom at the cooperage.'

Marianne met her mother's glance at the crack in Rebecca's voice. They both knew the story, of course, but they also knew that Rebecca sometimes liked to speak of her past, as if talking of it still helped even after all those years.

'Uncle Adam doesn't mind a bit when you put flowers on Tom's grave as well as your parents', does he?' Marianne said gently.

'No, he doesn't.' Rebecca flashed an adoring smile towards the sleepy inn where Adam and Seth had gone to enquire if they could purchase a cooling glass of ale. The inn provided refreshments when day-trippers from Plymouth arrived on paddle steamers on summer Sundays when the tide allowed – leisure craft being the main vessels to visit the river-port for well over a decade now. But this was a weekday and they weren't sure if the inn was open.

'When Tom died, Adam rescued me,' Rebecca went on. 'I was so young and lost in grief. But Adam was so understanding. A tower of strength. And he's always treated Toby as his own son, no differently from Charlotte and James. So when he lost his hand in that dreadful accident, it just seemed so unfair.'

Her mouth, only faintly lined with the telltale signs of age, twisted slightly, and Marianne took one of her hands.

'Please don't upset yourself, Aunt Becky.'

'Let's go and get that picnic out of the car,' Rose suggested. 'I'm as hungry as a horse!'

'You go on up,' Marianne said diplomatically. 'I'm sure you two would like a good old gossip without me in tow all the time. I'd like to sit here by the river for a few minutes. The Tamar looks so lovely with the tide up.'

'Don't be too long, mind, or we'll have eaten everything.'

'With the feast dear Patsy packed into the hamper?' Marianne laughed back.

She turned back to the river, listening to her mother and Aunt Becky's fading chatter as they walked away, and then she flung herself onto the grass. The strong June sunshine was glittering on the water, refracting into a million spangles of dazzling brilliance, and

Marianne tried to imagine Uncle Adam's favourite ship, the *Emily*, slowly appearing around the meander in the river, her tall mast visible above the trees before the rest of her came into view. What a sight it must have been, with so many sailing ships carefully navigating the Tamar's treacherous currents on the incoming tide.

Marianne released a nostalgic sigh. Virtually every one of the dozens of mines that littered the region was long gone. And it wasn't just from the upper reaches of the Tamar that the large sailing ships had disappeared. Steamships were taking their place everywhere, rigged vessels like Uncle Adam's beloved *Emily* becoming an ever increasing rarity.

But life never stood still, Marianne reflected wistfully. She herself was grown up, her sister and soul-mate a devoted wife and mother for many a long year, and her parents growing old far more quickly than she cared to contemplate. You couldn't stop time moving on, and there were certain things you were powerless to influence, too. Like this war her father and Uncle Adam were convinced was inevitable.

Marianne plucked a blade of grass from the river bank and twisted it in her fingers, an unwelcome uneasiness settling in her heart.

CHAPTER THREE

'A telegram for you, Captain,' Patsy announced, holding out a silver tray to the old man as they all sat around the breakfast table.

Marianne glanced up from buttering some toast to catch the look of trepidation that passed between Adam and Rebecca. A telegram. She supposed that when your daughter was married to a sea captain and you had both a son and grandson at sea, you must instantly think the worst. Marianne could see the fear on Rebecca's face as she opened the telegram for Adam since it was something he couldn't manage with his one hand. Adam searched in his breast pocket for his spectacles, but as soon as his eyes had scanned the print, his mouth widened into a smile.

'It's from Michael,' he explained, his face brightening at the communication from his grandson. 'They've docked in Plymouth several days ahead of schedule and he's staying with Sarah and Misha. So he can make the party after all, if he's still invited.'

'Bless him, of course, he is!' Rose exclaimed at once.

'Then, if you'll excuse me,' Adam said, getting to his feet, 'I'll give the telegram boy a reply if he's still waiting.'

'Yes, he is, Captain,' Patsy informed him.

'Oh, that's super news!' Rose went on exuberantly. 'And I expect you can't wait to see your sister again either, Becky.'

'No, I can't. I haven't seen Sarah since she and Misha came to stay with us at Christmas, so 'tis so kind of you to invite them as well.'

'Not at all. The more the merrier for my big day.'

'And I love to hear Uncle Misha talking about Russia,' Marianne enthused, 'even if they weren't always happy times for him.'

'Russia would be our ally against Austria-Hungary, of course, if the situation deteriorates.'

'Oh, can't you forget about that for the moment, Dad?' Marianne demanded in exasperation. 'It's Mum's birthday the day after tomorrow.'

'And I think 'tis time you forgot about calling us aunt and uncle.' Rebecca nodded her head emphatically. 'You're all adults now, and 'tis not as if we're proper family anyway.'

'Hmm. Adam and Becky.' Marianne tried the names thoughtfully on her tongue. 'All right. But it'll take some getting used to. And I shall always love you both as much as if you were my real aunt and uncle.' She jumped up to lace her arms about Rebecca's shoulders and then, as she danced towards the door, surprised Adam with a peck on the cheek as he came back into the room. 'I'll go and find Hal. He's helping Joe muck out the stables, I think. I'll tell him he's to call you Adam and Becky from now on, and the good news about Michael. It'll be so nice to see him again. It must be five or six years since we saw him last.'

With that, she flitted out of the room, purloining a slice of sausage from her father's plate as she went and popping it into her rosebud mouth. Seth rolled his eyes, while Rose and Rebecca instantly burst into mirthful laughter. For Marianne was so very like her mother!

'Isn't this a wonderful day, Mum? And you look absolutely radiant!'

Marianne held her mother at arms' length. A new silk gown in shimmering purple fitted Rose's slender waist to perfection and was trimmed about the heart-shaped neckline with fine, gauzy lace. Rose had wanted a fusion between a day frock and an evening dress for her garden party, and so was not sporting the high collar that most of her female guests were wearing. But when had her mother ever paid any heed to convention, Marianne asked herself? It was why

Marianne loved her so much.

'The amethyst goes perfectly with the dress, doesn't it?' she went on admiringly.

'Always liked this necklace, haven't you? Your father bought it for me when you were born, so I reckon I should leave it specifically to you in my Will.'

'Oh, Mum, don't talk about such things on a day like this. We're supposed to be celebrating.'

'And celebrate we shall! Come on. Let's make sure everyone's helping themselves to enough food and drink.'

Marianne darted forward to mingle among their guests, only too pleased to put her more morose thoughts aside. There were so many people gathered under her mother's magnetic wing, and Marianne knew most of them so well. The only person who appeared almost a stranger to her was young Michael Bradley, Adam and Rebecca's grandson. He had come on the train from Plymouth the previous day with his great-aunt Sarah and great-uncle Misha, and Seth had driven to the station to collect them. When everyone had piled out of the car in front of the house, Marianne would never have recognized the tall, slightly built figure that stood back reservedly while the older adults greeted each other heartily. As they then moved towards the house, Marianne was left face-to-face with this apparently shy but stunningly handsome young gentleman. In no way did he resemble the awkward boy she recalled from so many years before. Back then, she already considered herself an adult while he was a mere child. But now...

Marianne couldn't understand why her heart had suddenly started bouncing about in her chest in the most curious fashion, and she could not move her gaze from Michael's face. Curls as raven dark as her own hair capped his well-shaped head, and a rogue lock fell impishly over his broad forehead. Eyes as black as coal but with a slight slant gave him the look of a gypsy, and yet his demeanour spoke of quiet sophistication. He held himself well, shoulders and back straight, waiting for the appropriate moment to speak.

'Miss Marianne,' he said at length.

Marianne felt her heart give another thump. 'Michael,' she murmured in return, and then tossed her head in amazement. 'Good heavens, I should never have recognized you.'

'Have I changed so much?' he answered with a wry smile. 'I suppose I must have grown up a lot since we last met, but you look just as charming as I remember.'

For some inexplicable reason, Marianne felt the need to rebel. 'You were only fourteen or fifteen,' she scoffed. 'I hardly think you would have taken any notice of what I looked like.'

'Oh, but I did.' Michael gave an easy smile now, and Marianne considered that perhaps he was not as shy as she had initially thought. 'When you're that age and the only child among a group of adults, you notice a lot of things.'

Marianne blinked at him, for a moment, taken aback. Yes, Michael was quiet, but she could imagine those sharp, shrewd eyes taking in everything about him. Not a bad asset, she supposed, if you wanted to captain a ship for a living, but she found it quite disconcerting. All at once she was anxious that she should look and act perfectly over the weekend if Michael was likely to be silently observing her all the while.

'It's a pity your mother and father couldn't make it,' she said, desperate to divert the conversation.

'Yes. Dad should just have docked in Boston and much as she wanted to come, Mum's in London looking after a good friend who's unwell.'

'I know. Pity, isn't it? It's lucky you have Sarah and Misha to stay with in Plymouth, though.'

'Yes, and they spoil me something rotten. With no children of their own, they always treated Dad like a son and me as a grandson.'

'That must be nice for you.'

'Yes, it is.'

Michael said no more, and thrown into some unwanted state of confusion, Marianne, to her annoyance, was tongue-tied, too. She was not sure if she was relieved or even more disorientated when the young man gave her that devastatingly handsome smile again, his strong teeth a white slash in his weather-browned face. It sent goosebumps down her spine, rooting her to the spot.

'I'd better bring in the luggage,' Michael said positively as if he had made a sudden, momentous decision.

'I'll help you.' Marianne sprang forward, astounded that she was grateful the conversation had come to an end – she who could normally chatter for king and empire.

'Goodness, it would be most remiss of me to allow a lady to carry anything.'

'But I'm not just any lady,' she retorted, and pushing past him, yanked the biggest suitcase from the back of the car. And yet why she had reacted so rudely, she really didn't know.

Michael's eyebrows shot up towards his hairline as he watched her carrying the heaviest item of luggage towards the house. 'I'll bring the rest in, then, shall I?' he muttered under his breath, and picked up his own small case and his great-aunt's feather-light hatbox.

Being the three members of the younger generation present, Hal, Marianne and Michael were thrown together for the rest of the day. Brother and sister proudly showed their young guest around the stud-farm. Michael displayed an intelligent interest in the horses, and Marianne unexpectedly found herself delighting in exhibiting her equestrian prowess.

'We're breaking in a lovely colt at the minute. He's going to make someone a super ride before too long. Would you like to come and watch?'

'I'd be fascinated,' Michael grinned back. 'Only don't ask me to come too close. I've never been too confident around horses.'

Marianne's spirits soared. Michael was admiring her and she was wallowing in it. Not because she was showing off – she had always taken her skills for granted – but because she … she wanted Michael to be attracted to her.

'How do you get around when you're on shore, then?' she asked him.

'I hire a cab. Or I drive my father's car if I'm at home.'

Marianne pulled a grimace. 'He trusts you to do that, then? You lucky thing! I'm desperate to drive, but the Napier's actually Hal's here, and he won't let me,' she pouted, throwing a disgruntled scowl at her brother. 'You'd think if I can break and train a horse,

I could be trusted to drive a car. It can't be *that* difficult.'

Hal threw up his head with a laugh. 'But if you crashed it, a motorcar's a pretty expensive thing to repair, and you could be badly injured. No, you stick to horses. You'd never injure one of them, and you never come off and hurt yourself.'

Marianne glared at Hal, annoyed by his backhanded compliment. And, of course, no one knew that she had been thrown just a week or so earlier when Pegasus had reared away from the adder. She must hide the colour that flared into her cheeks and turn Hal's comments to her advantage.

'Praise indeed from my brother who's such a brilliant horseman himself,' she said with jovial, mock sarcasm, and was thrilled when Michael chuckled at her little quip.

That evening, Marianne found herself taking great care when dressing for dinner. Normally she would merely tie back her riot of black hair in a ribbon and throw on the first thing to hand in her wardrobe that wasn't a riding habit. But now she picked out a dress of floating pink and grey muslin that gave her a distinctly feminine air, and carefully piled her tresses on the top of her head. She considered her reflection in the mirror, smoothing down the bodice of the dress over her tiny waist. Goodness, she was the image of her mother in the stunning portrait her father had commissioned many years ago by a Mr Tilling, an artist Rose was acquainted with in London. The painting hung in the drawing room, mesmerizing everyone who ever gazed at it, but for the first time in her life, Marianne was overjoyed that she might match her mother's beauty.

And why was that?

She frowned, chewing on her bottom lip. She wasn't succumbing to the charms of the polite, striking young man staying in one of the rooms along the landing, was she? Her thoughts went back to that distant day when Philip had announced that he and Kate were getting married because she was pregnant, and Marianne had taken a silent vow never to fall in love. She had kept faithful to that vow all these years. She was nearly twenty-five now and possibly in danger of being left on the shelf. Not that the idea bothered her in the slightest. But she had to admit that Michael Bradley had set her heart a-flutter in a way she had never experienced before. He was all but five years younger than her, but did that matter? When his father, Toby, had married Chantal Pencarrow, she had been several years his senior. And another marriage between these families who were all such good friends couldn't be bad, could it?

Marriage! What on earth was she thinking

of? She hardly knew Michael, but her heart began to race at the thought that her mother was bound to seat her and Hal by their young visitor at the dinner table.

She was not disappointed. And she found herself shining like a star, leading witty conversation, asking Michael about his training and his travels, and admiring all the tales he related of the places his burgeoning career had taken him to. His great-grandfather had been a wine and spirits merchant in London, a business Grandfather Adam had continued for some years, even though he was slowly building up his small fleet of ships. Adam had eventually sold the business in favour of developing the shipping company further with his stepson Toby's assistance, as the young man followed in his footsteps as a sea captain. It had put Michael in a privileged position of course, but his eyes sparkled as he spoke of the sea, and it was clear to Marianne that he was as enthusiastic about his career as were his father and grandfather before him.

'What about the Herefordshire estate?' Marianne enquired, wanting a reason to keep looking into those lively, shrewd eyes. 'Did that never interest you?'

'Not really. Of course, it's my family home and it's always a delight to go back there between voyages or my stints at college. But Uncle James always loved running the estate for Grandad. No. I've never wanted to do anything other than master a ship.'

'I know how you feel,' Marianne told him with an empathetic bob of her head. 'I've never wanted to do anything other than breed and train horses. Except for driving a motorcar!' she declared, shooting a meaningful glance at Hal, which to her glee, made Michael chuckle aloud.

She went to bed that night floating on a cloud, and dreamt only of a handsome young man with dark hair and eyes, and a smile that made her heart flip over. In the morning, she hurried downstairs, anxious to see him again and assure herself he was not just a figment of her imagination. But he was real, and her heart sang as she busied herself in the kitchen and with helping to carry out onto the terrace all the sumptuous savoury dishes, cakes and desserts that had been prepared for the celebration. But she took advantage of every opportunity to speak to Michael and flash him her most dazzling smile as he helped to set up the tables and carry chairs and parasols outside.

It was a pleasant day, Sunday 28th June 1914. When all was ready, Marianne charged upstairs to change into the outfit she had chosen for the occasion, once again praying that Michael would find it appealing. The other guests began to arrive, and Marianne felt she could fly with excitement as they congregated on the drive in front of the house.

'Kate!' she cried as her beloved sister hopped down from the horse and wagonette in which the Pencarrow family had driven up from Rosebank Hall.

'Marianne!' Kate hugged her tightly. 'I'm so looking forward to today. I expect you've all been busy preparing a fantastic spread!'

'Yes, Patsy's done us proud, and we've all helped as well. But we'll all be like giant dumplings by the end of today if we eat everything that's on the tables!'

'There's going to be plenty of people to eat it all, though, isn't there? Oh, isn't this fun? So lovely to have everyone together. Oh, Mum! Happy birthday!' Kate called, running over to Rose as she emerged through the double front door.

'How are you, Philip?' Marianne turned to her brother-in-law, giving him a kiss on the cheek. 'Richard and Beth, how lovely to see you again!' she addressed his parents with a warm smile. 'Adam and Becky have told us to stop calling them auntie and uncle, so I hope that's all right with you, too?'

She saw the elderly couple exchange bemused glances and then Beth beamed her homely smile. 'But, of course! Now, where's your mother? I do so want to wish her a happy birthday. Ah, there she is. Rose!'

Marianne realized that in their enthusiasm,

the family had left young Adam standing alone. Children weren't really Marianne's cup of tea, but the boy looked so overwhelmed that she went over and smiled down at him.

'Shall we put your lovely horse in one of our stables? It's a she, isn't it?' This said ducking down in a most unladylike way to glance under the animal's belly. 'She must be tired and thirsty after that long journey and all uphill.'

Little Adam nodded and to Marianne's surprise, apprehensively placed his hand in hers. Well, she was his auntie, she supposed, but she had never had much to do with him, at least not in the last couple of years. Whenever she rode over to visit her sister, she would always say goodbye to Kate outside the village school and leave her to wait for her son alone. Now, Marianne felt almost as nervous as the child himself, but his hand felt so small and vulnerable in hers that it triggered some instinct to look after him.

'What's her name?' she asked, clicking her tongue and leading the mare around the side of the house towards the stable yard.

'Clomper. Because she clomps along,' the child told her solemnly.

Marianne could not help but smile at little Adam's serious face. She brought Clomper to a stop and then began to unharness her from between the shafts. Adam at once began to help with practised hands, and Marianne tipped her head. Kate was definitely not into horses and Philip was a reluctant farmer, so young Adam must take after his grandfather, Richard, he seemed so adept and at home around the big mare.

'Aw, Marianne, let me do that!' Joe hurried up to them. 'Ruin that there beautiful outfit, you will.'

Oh. Marianne pulled herself up short. Yes, she supposed she should be acting the lady today. And she didn't want to spoil her dress with Michael around, did she?

'Shall we let Joe look after Clomper?' she found herself asking Adam. 'Thanks, Joe.'

'Only doing my job,' the groom grinned back.

As Joe took over, Marianne gazed down into Adam's earnest little face. Goodness, what next? She trawled her brain for an answer, but to her own astonishment, found the solution in seconds.

'You must be thirsty, too. We've got all the refreshments set out on the terrace. I'm sure we can find some nice cold lemonade for you.'

'Oh, yes, please, Aunt Marianne,' the boy replied with gratitude clear in his wide eyes. 'I'm gasping.' He smiled up at her and she took his hand once again. Perhaps children weren't so bad, after all!

CHAPTER FOUR

'Look, there's William!'

Little Adam's face lit up for the first time and Marianne followed his gaze along the terrace. Stepping through the French doors from the dining room were her parents' other close friends, Dr Elliott Franfield and his wife, Ling, with their two younger off-spring, Mary and William. Mary was a young woman now, but at thirteen, William was the nearest to Adam's age out of everyone present.

'Do you know him well, then?' Marianne asked her young charge, relieved since she was beginning to wonder what to do with Adam next – particularly as she wanted to spend as much of the party as possible with Michael Bradley!

The child nodded. 'You know Grandma delivers all the babies in our village? Well, she sends for Dr Elliott if she needs him. Sometimes he comes to the farmhouse and if he's not at school, William comes too. He wants to be a doctor as well.'

'Yes, I know. They come here too, quite often. Elliott's our family doctor as well as a friend, you see. Now, off you go then.' Marianne smiled down at little Adam. 'We got the croquet things out of the tack room this morning. You and William could set them out on the lawn if you want to play.'

'Oh, yes please, Aunt Marianne! Thank you!'

The boy shot away towards his friend. At least he was happy now and Marianne could go off in search of Michael. First though, she must add her own welcome to her parents' greeting of the Franfield family.

'Elliott, Ling, how good to see you!' she greeted the doctor and his wife.

'Haven't we got a good day for it?'

'At least it's not raining!' Marianne grinned back. 'Do help yourself to food and drink. I think you know most of Mum's friends, but there are a few people from Princetown you might not have met before.'

'Don't worry, we can introduce ourselves,' Ling answered with a friendly smile. 'We might know more people than you think. I was brought up on the moor near here, remember.'

'And I can see one or two of my patients from Princetown as well,' Elliott put in. 'So don't worry about us. Have a chat with Mary. I see Will's setting out the croquet equipment with young Adam.'

'Yes. The lawn's not very flat, but it's only for fun. Oh, Mary, you look lovely!' she cried as the girl appeared behind her parents.

'What a beautiful dress!'

Marianne liked Mary. They always got on well whenever they met, and Marianne wished the Franfields lived a little closer than Tavistock so that they could see more of each other. As the crow flew, it was probably the same distance away as Rosebank Hall where her sister, Kate, had lived since her marriage to Philip Pencarrow. Possible on horseback in one day, but quite a trek. She could get to Tavistock by train, of course, but even that took an hour allowing for the connection at Yelverton. And there were only a few trains a day between Princetown and Yelverton which restricted journey times as well. No. Once again it would be so much easier if Hal would allow Marianne to drive his precious motorcar!

'Do you like it?' she realized Mary was asking a little bashfully. 'I designed and made it myself.'

'Did you really? Goodness, you are clever! Mum's brilliant at sewing, but I've never had the patience. But your dress looks quite perfect!'

Mary Franfield indeed looked extremely fetching. Like her mother, she was tall and willowy with a halo of bouncing tawny curls and lively chestnut eyes. A small number of pale freckles dusted her button nose, giving her a cute, childlike appearance, yet there was a quiet shrewdness in her youthful face that gave the impression of being mature for her years.

Marianne linked her arm through Mary's elbow and led her down the terrace steps. 'Had any news yet about your nurses' training?' she asked.

'Yes, I have.' Mary's eyes gleamed with enthusiasm. 'I've been accepted at the Florence Nightingale School at St Thomas's in London.'

'That's marvellous!'

'It certainly is because you're supposed to be twenty-one to start, and I'm only nineteen. But because I've been helping out on the wards at the cottage hospital here since I was sixteen because of Dad, they've agreed to take me. I have to do an eight-week course at the Preliminary School – I start the week after next – and pass an exam at the end, but then I'll begin proper in September.'

'Well, congratulations!'

'Thank you,' Mary blushed. 'It's what I've always wanted to do. And it shows men that we women can have proper careers, too!'

'Of course we can!' Marianne concurred, feeling for not the first time that in a reserved way, she had a kindred spirit in her young friend. 'Men might be physically stronger in some situations, I admit, but woman can be just as strong if not stronger in other ways.'

'Absolutely!' Mary laughed.

'Shall we try and prove it in a game of croquet?' Marianne suggested. 'I'll go and find Michael and see if he'd like to play.'

'Michael?' Mary appeared mystified.

'Yes. Michael Bradley. Captain Adam Bradley and his wife's grandson.'

'Oh, yes. I think we met as children once or twice through your mother, but I don't really remember him.'

'Well, you go and help Will bang in the hoops and I'll try and extricate Michael from wherever he is.'

Marianne turned, joyous with expectation at the prospect of having Michael to herself again. Well, not exactly to herself, but she would at least have more of his attention while they were playing croquet. Ah, there he was, talking to Philip and looking incredibly handsome in a fashionable striped blazer and grey flannel trousers. She was almost breathless as she approached them and had to make a conscious effort to tamp down her excitement.

'We're having a game of croquet,' she interrupted their conversation. 'Would you like to join us, Michael?'

'Croquet? Lord, I haven't played that for years,' he frowned.

'Oh, don't worry. It's just for fun,' she assured him with a giggle. 'We won't play by all the proper rules. It can get so complicated and *so* serious. The grass is so uneven you couldn't play properly if you wanted to.'

'Well, in that case–'

'You'll need someone else to make the teams even, won't you?' Philip put in as he glanced across to where William was trying valiantly to hammer in the hoops.

'Yes, we will.' Marianne's brain whirled. She *must* make sure Michael was on her team. 'You join Mary and Adam,' she instructed Philip, 'and Michael, you can make up the other team with me and William. We'll be fairly evenly matched then. Come on. I'll introduce you.'

She danced along in front of Michael in a flurry of laughter. The introductions she made were brief, wrapped up as she was in the prospect of enjoying the game in Michael's close company. But first they must finish setting out the course.

'Should be over there, the next hoop, shouldn't it?' Mary pointed out.

'What, here?' Michael called, and began to drive the said hoop into the ground.

'Yes, it makes a sort of double diamond course,' Mary confirmed, 'with the single peg at the end. You have to hit it to complete the round.'

'I'll get the balls, then, if we're ready,' Marianne announced, brimming with happiness. 'What colour shall our team be, Michael? Black and blue or the red and yellow?'

'As I'll be hopeless at it, we'd better make it black and blue. That's what I'll be when you've finished hitting me for making us lose.'

'Oh, you!' She pushed his arm playfully, her fingers tingling at the physical contact. 'Have you got a coin to toss to see who goes first?'

'I certainly have,' Michael replied obligingly. 'Mary, you should choose as the female guest.'

'Heads, then,' the girl smiled back.

'Right.' Michael flipped the coin, slapping it down on the back of his hand. 'Heads it is. So your team goes first. Sorry, Marianne.'

'Tut, tut!' she joked with a mock frown and then laughed aloud. 'Go on, Adam, you start.'

The gentle thud of mallet on wooden ball began the game and very soon they were engrossed in the friendly rivalry it created. There was much laughter and cries of 'Oh, dear,' 'Good shot!' or 'Cheat!' as they fell about in helpless mirth. Marianne thought she had never been happier – except when she was galloping across the moor on Pegasus, of course – but for once in her life, she had put that to the back of her mind. For now, she was basking in the new and utterly delicious sensation of being in love – since she was sure that this all-encompassing euphoria that had wreathed itself about her was because she had fallen headlong in love with Michael Bradley.

The day passed in a haze of delight. Marianne flitted among the guests like a butterfly, her heart soaring on invisible wings, but always returning to rest by Michael's side.

'Can I fetch you a drink?' he asked. 'You look flushed from dashing about looking after the guests, so now I should look after you.'

Flushed? Oh, Lord, that was from being near *him!* Thank goodness he had not guessed the real reason. Or perhaps it would have been good if he had!

'Oh, yes, please,' she answered him, feeling positively effervescent. 'Some of Patsy's home-made lemonade would be lovely. I think I've had enough wine for one day, and Dad's going to propose a toast with champagne later on.'

Michael gave her such a deep, warm smile that made the corners of his eyes crinkle, and Marianne's heart turned a somersault. She watched him cross the lawn, a tantalizing thrill reaching to her fingertips so that she was almost disappointed when Mary came and sat down beside her.

'He's nice, isn't he, Michael?' the younger girl said with a shy blush in her cheeks. 'Mum knew his father quite well when they were young.'

'So I believe.' Was that a dart of resentment Marianne felt prick her side? But Mary was such a sweet girl, and as Michael walked back towards them with a glass of lemonade, Marianne felt the moment pass.

'Thank you, that's so kind.' She gave Michael her most winning smile. Their fingers touched as he handed her the drink, and a glorious sensation sizzled up her arm. She saw his eyes lift from their hands to her face, the moment not lost on him either, it seemed. Her heart melted for the umpteenth time that day so that it was almost like blancmange.

'When are you coming over to the farm next?'

Her sister Kate's voice drew Marianne from her dreamlike state. 'Soon. Once Adam and Becky have gone home.'

'Don't make it too long. Adam breaks up from school soon. He loves being around and about on the farm, with his grandad especially. But we can go up onto the moor for a picnic or something, just the three of us. It'll be lovely. Like old times.'

Marianne forced a smile to her lips. Like old times? No, it wouldn't! In the old days, it would have been just the two of them, and they wouldn't have taken a picnic. They were always too excited to bother about food, although in August, they would have picked wild whortleberries, their fingers and lips stained purple from the bittersweet juice. They would try to wash their hands and faces in Dartmoor's clear streams or fast-flowing manmade water courses called leats that wended across the moor. But their attempts to clean themselves usually ended in a game of launching water over each other until they were both drenched. Or they would remove their boots and socks, and hiking their skirts and petticoats about their waists, paddle in their drawers. Marianne was sure they would never do that again, and she supposed, with a sigh, that it would be inappropriate now they were grown women. What a shame. But, oh, what memories!

Her father was calling for silence now as Patsy whisked among the guests with a tray of glasses charged with bubbling champagne. Seth proposed a toast to his wife and slices of cake were distributed to be enjoyed with the sparkling drink. The June sun was sinking in the rose-hued sky and in the evening light, the shadowed folds of the moor took on dusky shades of grey and lavender. Guests began to take their leave as the day drew to a close, satiated with happiness and yet reluctant for the party to end.

Marianne was borne along with the general drift to the front of the house. The Pencarrows, Kate and young Adam with them, of course, had already left as they had a long journey to cover in the wagonette pulled by Clomper, but others either did not have so far to go or were travelling by motorcar. Among the departing guests, the Franfield family were making their way towards Elliott's shiny black vehicle.

'Thank you for a wonderful day, Rose,' Marianne overheard Ling say as she kissed her mother goodbye. 'I do hope you enjoyed it yourself.'

'Oh, it's been perfect!' Rose still radiated with delight. 'Thank you so much for coming.'

'Wouldn't have missed it for anything,' Elliott put in. 'You must all come to us for Sunday lunch soon. Can't promise I won't be called out to a patient, mind. Goodbye, Seth, and you, Hal. Take care of yourselves.' Elliott shook hands with Marianne's father and brother, and then gave her a paternal peck on the cheek. 'In we get, then. Oh, we're missing Mary. Where's she got to?'

He glanced around and Marianne, too, turned her head. A cold blade of steel touched against her heart. Under the portico, Michael and Mary were facing each other, holding hands and gazing earnestly into each other's eyes like star-struck lovers. Then Mary evidently heard her father calling and began walking towards the family motorcar – still holding hands with Michael.

The dreams that had woven about Marianne's heart all day crashed to her feet. Her muscles stilled and only her eyes had the power to move as she watched Michael open the car door for the pretty young girl.

'You will write to me, Mary, won't you?' Marianne heard him implore.

'Of course I will!' Mary answered equally as fervently, her cheeks blushed an excited peach. 'But where should I send a letter to?'

'I hope it'll be letters in the plural. But send them to the estate in Herefordshire. Grandad will always know where I am and send them on.'

'I'll do that. But do take care on that ship of yours, Michael.'

'They're all the family company's ships and Grandad wouldn't be too pleased if I sank one of them, so yes, of course I'll take care. And I hope I'll see you before, but if not, good luck when you start your nursing course.' And with that, he lifted her hand to his lips.

Marianne rocked on her feet. Her mouth uttered appropriate words of farewell to all their guests, but she knew she was speaking by instinct alone. Michael was standing next to her as they waved off the last vehicle, and slowly Marianne regained painful control of her senses.

She might have known. Michael was a pleasant young man who had been polite and friendly towards her. But she was older than him by several years and Mary was of a much more suitable age. And Mary was more like him in character, reserved and gentle but with an underlying determination – whereas Marianne knew herself to be self-confident and outward-going. *Too* outward-going at times, she supposed. So, though it broke her heart, she could understand why Michael had found her young friend more appealing.

Ah, well. It had been nice while it lasted, this daydream of hers. But that's all it could ever be. She had lived by that secret, solemn vow all these years, and it was right for her, after all. It came back to claim her now like an old friend, a pair of worn, comfortable slippers. She snuggled back into its warm familiarity where she felt safe and protected. And swore never to leave it again.

'My God, look at this.'

It was the next morning and the family and their house guests were taking breakfast together. Marianne was helping herself from the dishes of hot food on the dresser, her mental shield comfortably in place again, sealing her mind to further hurt. Michael and his great-aunt and great-uncle were catching the mid-morning train to return to Plymouth. Marianne would restrain herself until they left the house, but she would not go to the station to say goodbye. The instant the Napier turned out of the gates, she would scurry out to the horses, saddle Pegasus and streak out across the moor in the opposite direction to cleanse her heart of its agony once and for all.

Now though, like everyone else in the room, her attention was drawn by the quiet shock in her father's voice as he lifted his glance from the newspaper headlines. He always read the paper in his study after breakfast, but Patsy delivered it to his place at the table each morning.

'What's that, Seth?' Adam took the newspaper from his old friend and everyone waited, instinctively on tenterhooks, while he took out his spectacles. His face immediately stiffened, as Seth's had done, as he scanned the lead article, and then he raised his head with a profound sigh. 'Archduke Ferdinand of Austria and his wife were assassinated in Sarajevo yesterday by some Serbian students or some such. Well.' He paused to rub his hand over his mouth before he went on, 'With the situation in Europe as it is, I can't see that going without serious repercussions. And I mean serious.'

'You mean ... it can only lead to one thing?' Michael said hesitantly.

'Yes.' His grandfather gave a solemn nod. 'It might not be immediate, but it'll force a chain of events, I'm sure. My friends, I believe that war is now unavoidable.'

A tangible silence slithered menacingly

about the room. Marianne had a horrible sinking feeling in her stomach and she put down her laden plate. She suddenly wasn't hungry any more.

'So ... all that was going on yesterday while we were having such a wonderful time here?' she murmured.

Her father answered her with a dark nod, but nobody spoke, everyone locked in a private maelstrom of thought. What would it mean for the world? For them, as family and friends? For the second time in less than a day, Marianne was shaken rigid. Her father had considered for some time that the situation was tinderbox dry and only needed one small spark to explode into a conflagration. Would this assassination be that spark?

Suddenly the events of the last few days paled into insignificance. What did it matter that her heart had risen on a crest of expectation only to be smashed to pieces almost at once? What mattered was that, if war broke out across Europe as now seemed inevitable, there would be lives lost. Young men like her brother Hal or Michael who both sat at the breakfast table now. It was unbearable. Marianne no longer cared that Mary had appeared to have captured Michael's heart from under her nose. All she cared about was that Michael would not be involved in any war, and that nothing should happen to him or to Hal or any of the other young men she knew. She felt ashamed at the hurt resentment she had felt the previous evening and would make up for it in any way she could. Do whatever was in her power to help her country if it indeed went to war. She didn't know what or how, but she would. And in that instant, she made the second secret vow of her life.

CHAPTER FIVE

Seth's warm eyes smiled into his wife's face on the pillow beside him. 'That was a lovely way to start the day. I'm glad we're still able to do it.'

'Oh, you!' Rose chuckled. 'We're not *that* old!'

Seth gave an amused grunt but then his expression changed. 'Rose, the chap from the army's coming tomorrow to choose some horses. It might be a good idea to have Marianne out of the way. Could you take her on a shopping trip to Plymouth, do you think?'

Rose bit her lip. 'It's such a shame we have to do this.'

'We're at war. We have no choice. And we also have to survive ourselves.'

'It's sacrilege, though,' Rose sighed mournfully. 'It isn't what we've bred and trained our horses for.' And she snuggled against her husband for comfort.

'What's up, Ned?' the wizened fellow in the stained and threadbare jacket smirked as they moved along the busy Plymouth street. 'Look as if you've seen a ghost.'

Ned's white lips were too numb to snap at

him for using his real name. Indeed, the reprimand scarcely flitted across his mind. Jesus Christ, he *had* seen a bloody ghost, emerging from the shop opposite. Hair like ravens' wings cascaded down to her slender waist from beneath a jaunty boater, and he recognized at once that stunningly beautiful face with the violet-blue eyes that snapped with vivacity.

It was *her!*

But it couldn't be. This girl must be in her twenties, but Rose Chadwick would be sixty or so by now. Ned blinked his eyes. He must be seeing things. But then, following the apparition out of the door, came a second figure, identical but for being that much older and with silver streaking the dark tresses piled beneath a fashionable hat.

Ned's eyes bolted from their sockets.

'I'll have the package delivered to the railway station, Mrs Warrington,' the shopkeeper smiled as he saw the older woman out of his shop.

So, it was Mrs Warrington now, was it? The shock was already being driven out of Ned's heart by the age-old, simmering bitterness. So it was her, after all. She must have re-married and the ghost must be her daughter, the resemblance was so strong. But ... Rose Chadwick, as was, standing in front of him. Well, well, well...

All those years since he had returned to

Plymouth, he had resisted the temptation to trace what had happened to her. But now, seeing her again, all the jealous resentment rushed at him like a bullet, wounding, making his soul bleed. Was she still living at Fencott Place, cocooned in luxury? If she hadn't thrown him out when she was widowed, he might have been able to worm his way into her affections, and all that wealth would have been his. And he had *loved* Rose! But it was astounding how close love could be to hatred when it was rejected. And wouldn't he love to get his hands on that daughter of hers!

As Ned dragged himself away, the cogs of his scheming mind began to turn.

'So ... do you think you'll enlist?' Marianne dared to ask.

The balmy September day was dying and Marianne was leaning on the field gate, arms crossed on the top bar. Beside her, Hal too was staring at the colt they had been training together that afternoon. But Marianne could see that her brother was not really watching the animal's antics. He was lost in thought and she had a shrewd idea what those thoughts would be.

It was a moment before he brought himself to speak and Marianne waited patiently. She knew her elder brother well. He wasn't one to open up his heart readily.

'I'm not in any hurry to join up, no,' he answered at length, his words slow and pensive. 'Or to get myself maimed or killed. They're fools who rush off to the recruitment centres to see a bit of the world as they put it, expecting it all to be over by Christmas. If they had any sense, they'd realize it's going to drag on for God knows how long. The battles of Mons and the Marne and now the Aisne were hardly walkovers, were they?' he concluded with bitter irony.

Marianne let the silence settle, watching the young horse grazing contentedly before she continued, 'Are you... afraid to go and fight?' There was no criticism in her voice. Hal was the most gentle, kind fellow, and she sensed he was troubled. She only wanted to help, and talking might do just that. And somehow the time and the place seemed right, swathed as they were in the calm, Dartmoor evening.

Hal glanced at her sideways. 'I'd be a liar if I denied it,' he admitted truthfully. 'And so would any other man, I'm sure. It's all very well going down to the recruitment centres with your mates, egging each other on. But when it comes to it, out on the battlefield, you're on your own and it must be terrifying.'

'Yes, I imagine it must be,' Marianne agreed quietly. 'Dad liked being in the cavalry because he was working with horses all the time, but he always says he was glad he was never involved in any real fighting out in India, doesn't he? That was why he resigned his commission or whatever it was you did in those days. He'd been forced into the army by his family but he really didn't like the idea of having to kill someone.'

'And the officers' way of life wasn't for him. Drinking and playing silly games in the officers' mess because they were bored stiff.' Hal paused, his mouth pressing into a thin line. 'The situation's pretty different now, though, isn't it?'

'So ... don't you want to do your bit for your country?' Marianne prompted him after several moments' silence. 'That's what they're calling it, isn't it?'

'Yes.' Hal raised an agonized eyebrow. 'And of course I want to defend my country. What Germany's doing is so wrong, and I'll go and fight if I have to. Only I'd rather do my bit in other ways. Like with the horses.'

'With the horses?' Marianne frowned. 'I don't understand.'

'Well...' Hal hesitated, chewing his lip, and Marianne saw the pain in his expression as he turned to her. 'We wanted to keep it from you as long as possible, but you had to know sooner or later. You see ... the last batch of trained horses we sold, they ... they went to the army. And so will the next lot, this chap included,' he finished, jerking his head at the glorious young colt. 'We've always been on the military register, of course. The subsidy we receive from that is what's kept the stud-farm a viable business. And now we're going to be stepping up our breeding and training schedules for the army as well.'

'What!' An icy coldness trickled through Marianne's veins, chilling her to the marrow. 'You mean...?'

'I'm afraid so, sis. And I'm really sorry.'

Marianne felt the muscles of her chest contract as a horrific thought came into her head. 'And what about Pegasus? And Hermes?' she cried out.

'Ah, well, you and Mum are lucky there.' Hal turned to her with a sombre expression in his eyes. 'Dad told them in no uncertain terms that they're our champion studs, so we really need them if we're to keep our stock going, especially if we have to draft in more brood mares. The army chap wasn't interested in Hermes so much as he's getting on a bit, but I have to tell you he was seriously interested in Pegasus for himself.'

Marianne gawped at her brother as a shard of pain sliced into her breast. Oh, dear God, the idea of her beloved Pegasus being injured or even worse was ... was simply intolerable. Marianne realized she was trembling even though she managed to swallow down her sudden panic. 'B-but D-dad definitely said they couldn't have him?' she stammered.

'Absolutely. So you don't need to worry.'

Marianne nevertheless felt slightly faint as a hot sweat surged through her body. 'Thank God for that,' she mumbled in relief. 'But it still means that all our other beautiful horses are destined for the battlefields. Oh, the poor things.'

'The hunters, undoubtedly. But those that go in harness will be needed for other things, transporting supplies and bringing back wounded men, for instance. They're sending out all sorts of motor vehicles converted into ambulances, but I'm sure horses will play their part as well.'

'But badly-wounded horses will be shot on the spot, won't they?' Marianne's nerves jangled with fury, but what could she do? The horror of the images that her mind conjured up overwhelmed her with anger and sadness, making her feel unbearably useless. 'And you said we'll be increasing our breeding programme,' she said, battling to keep her frustration in check. 'So that must mean the government thinks this war could go on for years.'

'Not necessarily. But we'll need to replenish our stock anyway, if the military are going to take every available horse from us in the short term.'

'Oh!' Marianne stamped her foot in poorly suppressed rage. 'How could Dad have possibly agreed to all this?'

'We were on the register, and they'd have

found us soon, anyway. And you might not have noticed but business has slumped since the war started, and the scheme gave us a good price. Believe me, it hurt Dad as much as it does you and me. Hadn't you noticed he's been a bit quiet recently?'

Marianne paused to consider, feeling a reluctant acceptance take the place of her shock. 'Yes. Come to think of it, I suppose he has. But ... what about Mum? Does she know?'

'Yes. But, you know, she can be remarkably realistic sometimes. She gave a deep sigh and said that if it helped some of our brave lads stay alive, that was more important. And that's how we must all look at it.'

Marianne bit on her lower lip. This wretched war! 'Yes, I suppose so,' she conceded grudgingly. 'If our horses can help, well... It just seems so awful. Poor innocent creatures.'

'And we'll be doing even more than that,' Hal went on cautiously, trying to gauge his sister's emotions. 'There are plans afoot to ship in wild horses from North America. If they do, Dad's agreed to take some of them on for breaking in. A few dozen at a time, so we'll have our work cut out. That's what I meant by doing my bit without going off to fight.'

'Well, I suppose if it keeps you here, that's one advantage.'

'And we'll be paid reasonably for our services. I know the whole thing is so awful, but we *are* at war. And the other thing is that we need to make the horses pay, now more than ever. With the Stock Exchange being closed, our broker can't make us any money buying and selling shares. And dividends have plummeted since war was declared.'

'Unless you happen to own a factory that can be turned over to ammunition production, I suppose,' Marianne scoffed with bitter sarcasm. 'Then you'd be laughing.'

Hal glanced darkly at his sister. She had taken the news fairly well for her, and it really did mean that he could do important war work without enlisting. After all, much of the responsibility for turning the wild horses into reliable mounts and particularly draught animals would fall on his shoulders, since neither his father nor Joe were getting any younger. His mother and Marianne were bound to be involved as well, seeing as both were such superb horsewomen. But Hal was the youngest male and the one with the greatest strength and stamina, and so the major part of the work would fall to him.

He noticed now that Marianne had pursed her lips in thought.

'I suppose that until the government decides to reopen the Stock Exchange, you'll have no excuse to go up to London to see Louise again,' she said with her usual directness. 'Or will you go to see her anyway?'

Hal felt the colour rush into his face, but his sister had never been anything if not blunt. To her, it was a straightforward question that demanded a straightforward answer.

'Not that it's any business of yours,' he replied levelly, 'but yes, I'll go anyway. At least, if it's possible. If we do have all these horses coming in, I won't have much time. And who knows how long this war will go on for, or what it's going to mean for any of us.'

Marianne met his gaze for a moment or two, and then downcast her eyes. Hal was absolutely right. The future was uncertain for everyone. She just prayed that at the end of it all, everyone would be together again just as they had at her mother's party. Ah, that fateful day. While her soaring heart had been shot down in full flight, the world was being turned upside down…

She brought Pegasus to a halt as they trotted into the farmyard at Rosebank Hall. It was a glorious late October day, and the ride across the moor had been uplifting, the sun shining brilliantly from a clear, powder blue sky and turning the autumn vegetation to burnished gold. It was inconceivable that the country was at war, and yet it most definitely was. Only last week, thousands of

Canadian troops and horses had unexpectedly been put ashore at Plymouth because a German U-boat had been spotted near Cherbourg, and it had been deemed unsafe for them to continue their journey by sea. So the convoy had been taken on to its destination of one of the army training camps on Salisbury Plain by road and rail instead.

First, though, they had paraded through the main streets of Plymouth. It must have been a magnificent sight, and under other circumstances, Marianne would have gone to witness the proceedings. But she still could not bear the thought of such noble creatures being taken into battle, and so she had stayed at home, restless and unhappy.

The ride across the moor to visit her sister, however, had refreshed Marianne's spirit. It was a school day so that they would not be hindered by young Adam's company. Marianne had nothing against the child. Indeed, she thought him rather sensible for his age, if far too serious. But without him, she was hoping to rekindle the carefree times she and Kate had enjoyed before he came along. Now that he was getting older, Kate might not be so mentally absorbed with him even while he was at school!

'Good morning, Marianne! Did you have a good ride over?'

'Hello, Richard!' Marianne beamed at the elderly man as he strode across the yard.

'Kate is expecting me, isn't she?'

'Yes, she's in the kitchen with Beth. Why don't you go straight in? I'll see to Pegasus for you.'

'Would you? Oh, that's terribly kind.'

'It'll be a pleasure. But then Philip and I need to go up on the moor and drive down some more sheep for sorting. Josh has taken some of the last lot off to market today.'

'I guess it's time to start putting the ewes in with the ram, isn't it?'

'Not brought up on the moor for nothing, were you?' Richard chuckled as she swung one leg over the horse's back and landed lightly on her feet. 'You go on in, and I'll see you later.'

Marianne gratefully left Pegasus with him and crossed to the back-door of the farmhouse. She was soon met with the tantalizing aroma of fresh baking as she went into the kitchen with its massive old table in the centre. From the drying rack above, hung bunches of various herbs that gave Beth Pencarrow's domain a particular smell, and the open shelves were lined with jars containing concoctions of all different colours from deep purple to green and brown. It was always a mystery to Marianne, but Beth was held in high esteem for her herbal remedies which were sought after from far and wide. Even Dr Elliott Franfield recommended their use when there was no other medicine available for certain ailments.

'Marianne, you're nice and early!' Kate jumped up from the table and came to give her a hug.

'Good morning, my dear. Expect you'll be ready for a cup of tea.'

'Yes, please, Beth. It's a beautiful morning, but it is quite chilly. We should be able to have a lovely walk across the moor, Kate,' she finished, burning with enthusiasm. 'We can spend all day, can't we? Especially as Adam walks home from school on his own, now, doesn't he? Although I mustn't leave it too late with the evenings drawing in. I do wish Hal would let me drive his motorcar, and then I wouldn't have to worry.'

'Oh, you're not still grumbling about that, are you?' Kate laughed. 'One day the poor chap will give in, just to shut you up!'

Marianne pulled a face at her and then turned to take the cup of steaming tea from Beth. 'Oh, thank you. That looks lovely.'

'It's on the weak side, I'm afraid,' the older woman apologized. 'You know how people started panic buying when war was first declared, but living up here, I didn't get a chance to stock up on anything and our little village shop could get hold of so little.'

'They say supplies are getting back to normal now, though, aren't they?'

'I sincerely hope so because I'm running low on tea. Josh was going to try and get some in Tavistock for me today, mind, so we should be all right again soon.'

'But what if those German U-boat things start to attack our merchant ships?' Kate asked grimly.

'Well, from what I've read, the government seems to think we'll still hold supremacy over the sea. But if you think about it, with so much of our food being imported, it'd be a good way of bringing the country to its knees.' Beth gave a concerned sigh. 'The idea makes me worry about the Bradleys. I know dear Adam doesn't go to sea any more, but there's their son, Toby, and their daughter Charlotte's married to one of their sea captains as well. And, of course, there's young Michael. It'd break Adam and Becky if anything happened to any of them, and then there'd be the financial loss if any of their ships were lost.'

Marianne's heart had missed a beat at the mention of Michael Bradley. She had managed to drive him out of her mind for the most part, but there was still a twinge of pain at times. Such as when she had received a letter from Mary Franfield telling her about her new life at the London training hospital, but also mentioning that she and Michael had been exchanging correspondence. It was not, though, the quickly stifled spurt of jealousy that set Marianne's pulse racing with dread so much as the thought that he could be in danger.

'I'm so relieved that we're a farming family.' Kate unwittingly twisted the knife in her sister's side. 'Farmers are going to have a jolly good excuse not to join up, if the government's going to want them to produce as much home grown food as possible so we're not so reliant on imports. So Philip's going to have work harder than ever, especially with Josh running Hillside now. And they're going to do as much as they can with Moor Top as well.'

'And Richard's not as young as he was,' Beth put in with a wistful lift of one eyebrow. 'He's pretty fit for seventy-four, but he doesn't have quite the same energy as he used to.'

'Is that what he is?' Marianne marvelled. But then, Adam Bradley was remarkable at a similar age, too, although he had that problem with his heart, of course. Marianne wasn't sure if Beth knew about it, so she decided she should keep quiet on that score. 'Well, come on, Kate,' she swiftly changed the subject. 'Let's get off on that walk, if it's all right with you, Beth?'

'There's always work to be done on a farm, but all work and no play, as they say. So you two enjoy yourselves for a few hours, and forget about this horrible war for a while. And don't forget those sandwiches we made earlier,' she reminded her daughter-in-law, since she knew how woolly headed the two girls could be once they got together.

'Thanks, Beth. So, where do you suggest we go?' Kate asked, grabbing her coat as she and Marianne passed through the rear hallway.

'If it was summer, with the sun out like this, we could've gone to swim in the old millpond in the coombe.'

'Like we did with Adam during the school holidays!'

Yes, like they had with Adam. And Kate had spent all the time with one eye on her son so that he didn't drown. It was fair enough, since the locals had dug out the pond to act as a swimming pool and it was quite deep. But it would have been so much more fun if they hadn't had to worry about him at every minute. Marianne forced a smile to her face.

'Yes. That was great, wasn't it?' she lied. 'But we could go up to Tavy Cleave. Might be the last chance we get before winter sets in.'

Marianne's soul took wing at the thought. The nascent River Tavy cut a dramatic cleft through the granite hills of the high moorland. Wild and exposed, its savage beauty always seemed to release her from any worries, enthralling her with its spectacular loneliness. It was a place for contemplation down by the shallow, fast running waters that tumbled over boulders worn smooth over millions of years, but also of exhilaration and excitement. It would be exactly what she craved just now to put her turbulent emotions in order.

'Oh, but that's miles!' Kate objected. 'I'm not sure I fancy walking that far today.'

Marianne felt her enthusiasm deflate. 'Why not?' she demanded. 'We always used to walk all day.'

Kate shrugged evasively. 'Don't forget the military are up that way and could be practising manoeuvres. Why don't we go down and cross over the brook instead and then climb up to Cox Tor and make a circle around there?'

Marianne clamped her jaw. It was very close to the route she took to reach Rosebank Hall in the first place, but it was still high up on the open moor with stunning views down towards Plymouth Sound and the sea which would be clearly visible on such a fine day. And she supposed she didn't want any reminders of the war, which was something she wanted to put out of her mind for the day.

'All right, come on then!' she cried, and danced out of the door and across the farmyard.

They chatted about this and that, matters of little consequence, as they made the steep ascent towards the higher part of the moor. Kate told her sister about Adam's progress at the village school and how Philip was not looking forward to the long winter, but was happy to take over the increased paperwork running the farm now entailed. In turn, Marianne related a couple of gallops she and their mother had enjoyed, and made her sister laugh with the tale of one of her own disastrous attempts in the kitchen when Patsy had been unwell. The conversation inevitably though, turned to the war.

'So neither Philip or Josh have any plans to join up, then?' Marianne asked as they reached the summit of Cox Tor and paused to admire the magnificent view.

'No. The country's still got to be fed and farming isn't something you learn overnight. I mean, there's a certain amount of labouring anyone can do, but when you're mainly dealing with livestock, that's skilled work. And they'll be working three farms between them so it won't be easy. But what about Hal? Won't he feel he ought to enlist?'

'Fortunately our brother has his head screwed on,' Marianne told her. 'Did you know we're training *all* our horses for the military, and we might be having wild horses from across the Atlantic coming to us for breaking in for the army, as well?'

'Really? Rather you than me. They'll be real handfuls, won't they?'

'And the poor things will probably have been terrified cooped up on a ship for over a week. Some of them might be impossible to train. *And* we won't have that long to do it in, either.'

'Good job you're all so brilliant with horses, then.'

'And I hate the idea of sending them off to war. Men choose to fight, but horses don't. So I'm hoping I can find something else to do to help, instead, although I'm not sure what yet.'

'You could go and work at one of the new munitions factories they've opened in Plymouth, making shell cases, I think.'

'I'm not sure I fancy that,' Marianne grimaced. 'I don't think I could do anything where I was shut indoors all day, and I'd rather be doing something to help our troops as opposed to killing the enemy. Making weapons is too, I don't know, *direct*, somehow.'

'Yes, I know what you mean. And I'd hate working in a factory, too.'

'Maybe there's something else we can do together, then. I mean, now that Adam's more or less off your hands, you're free to do whatever you want.'

'Oh. Er...' Kate stuttered evasively. 'I'm afraid I won't be doing too much for the war effort. You see, I'm expecting another baby.'

Marianne's heart plummeted to her feet. Oh. Just as she had begun to think she and

Kate could go back and pick up their hare-brained, tomboy existence where they had left it eight years ago, her sister had gone and got herself pregnant again!

'Congratulations!' she exclaimed, hoping it sounded genuine. 'You must be thrilled.'

'We are. But I'm afraid it means you and I won't be able to go off doing things together for a while.'

'Oh, never mind about that.' Marianne flapped her hand dismissively. But she did mind. Dreadfully. She shouldn't, of course. And she was racked with guilt that she did. She should be delighted for her sister. After all, it was the natural thing for a happily married couple to want a second child. It was just that... Oh, she had so longed to be close to her sister again. And now that old emptiness had opened up inside her like a bottomless chasm. Twice in the last few months she had allowed that shield she had drawn about herself to crumble, first over Michael Bradley and now with her sister. She really must stick to her guns – and to her pledge. Never fall in love and instead devote herself to the Fencott Place horses.

Nevertheless, she felt tossed on an ocean of uncertainty as she rode home later that day, unnerved, resentful and yet torn with guilt. She really must put this new disappointment behind her. She would surely find other opportunities for fulfilment. Normally, she would have relished the challenge of the wild horses. If only they weren't destined for the battlefield.

She was still lost in thought as she and Pegasus clattered up the driveway to Fencott Place. The sight of a strange motorcar parked outside drew her from her ponderings. Her resolution dissipated as she wondered if it might be Michael...

She hurriedly saw to Pegasus and then raced indoors. She could hear male voices coming from the drawing room and sprang across to the door. But then she paused to take a huge, calming breath. If it *was* Michael, she must curb her feelings, however powerfully they overcame her.

She opened the door. Her father and Hal were seated on the couch facing a man in one of the chairs which had its back to her. On seeing her enter the room, all three got to their feet.

It was not Michael. The stranger was tall, in military uniform and incredibly handsome. So handsome, in fact, that Marianne's pulse accelerate wildly and she could not take her eyes from the broad forehead, kind grey-blue eyes and well-shaped mouth that broke into a hesitant smile. Marianne melted on the spot and had to force herself to look towards her father for an explanation.

'Major, this is my daughter, Marianne,' Seth introduced them. 'Marianne, this is

Major Albert Thorneycroft. From my old regiment. He...' Seth paused, and Marianne instinctively filled with dread. Was ... was Hal going to enlist, despite what he had said? 'The major saw Pegasus when he was here before,' Seth went on in a low voice. 'And, well, he would like to buy him.'

Marianne swayed as the blood drained from her head, and she would have fallen had not the major rushed forward to catch her in his arms.

CHAPTER SIX

'Oh, my dear Miss Warrington, I should never have suggested such a thing had I known it would provoke such a reaction. Your father said you would flatly refuse, but I hadn't expected *this.*'

'Nor had I. I thought she'd just fly off the handle and prove to you once and for all that you can't possibly have the horse. I would have put it more delicately if I'd known this would happen.'

The concerned voices, one dear and familiar and the other unknown but soft and lilting, swirled in Marianne's brain. Her eyelids were as heavy as lead and she had to force them open. The grey shroud that had dulled her senses gradually lifted as her mind clawed its way back to reality. Something appalling had just happened that she would prefer to blank out of her mind, but she just had to remember what it was so that she could fight against it.

The room slowly swam back into focus and she realized that she was lying on the couch. Her father and Hal were looking down at her, both their faces etched with worry, but kneeling beside her, very close, was the handsome stranger she had met a few moments earlier. She had been vaguely aware of him sweeping her off her feet, holding her close as he carried her across the room, her face pressed against the rough material of his uniform. Ah, uniform. Now it all came flooding back. He wanted Pegasus. Well, he couldn't have him. But it was no reason to dislike the man.

'I'm so sorry,' she muttered. 'This is most impolite of me–'

'No, I'm the one who's sorry,' the gentle voice came again. 'Don't get up until you feel better. Perhaps a glass of water…?'

He turned questioningly towards Seth and Hal, and Hal at once set off towards the kitchen. The stranger turned back, and beneath his mop of sandy curls, the grey blue eyes searched her face earnestly.

'I can only apologise again, Miss Warrington,' he repeated. 'Please do forgive me.'

'Marianne, please,' she answered, although it was still as if her lips were speaking of their own accord. 'I should only be flattered that you admire Pegasus so much, but I'm afraid he's not for sale.'

'And I fully accept that. Your father told me last time, and it was really presumptuous of me to have asked again. I could requisition him, of course, but I wouldn't want to cause you such distress. So, I shall take my leave and drive back to Longmoor in Hampshire where my regiment is based.'

'You've come all the way from Hampshire?' Marianne's brain snapped into gear. She couldn't possibly let this attractive young man out of her life so soon! 'Well, it's getting late, and you can't possibly drive all that way in the dark. He could stay overnight, couldn't he, Dad?'

Seth gave a surprised shrug. It was the last thing he had expected from his daughter, but he supposed it was the civil thing to do. 'It's your mother you need to ask. I think she's in the kitchen–'

'Oh, Marianne, what happened?' Rose blustered into the room, followed by an anxious Hal carrying the glass of water.

'I was a little shocked, that's all.' Marianne was sitting up now, her embarrassment fled in her desire to have the handsome major stay the night. 'Major ... sorry, I didn't catch your name?'

'Thorneycroft, but do call me Albert–'

'Albert, then.' She flashed her winning smile at him. 'Albert was after buying Pegasus, but he quite accepts that I won't sell him. But he's come all the way from Hampshire and we can't expect him to drive back home tonight, so I've invited him to stay if that's all right with you.'

Rose blinked at her younger daughter. Oh, she was so like herself at that age, words tumbling out of her mouth all in a rush if she had some scheme up her sleeve. So she nodded regally at the stranger.

'You're most welcome, Major. I'm afraid you'll find us a little rustic here, though.'

'That really is most kind of you.' Albert Thorneycroft's smile revealed a pleasing set of white, even teeth. 'I have a few days' leave after a minor wound to my arm and sadly no family to return to, so a night in the peace and quiet of the countryside would be an absolute delight. Especially after the mayhem of the battlefield,' he added under his breath.

'You've been in action, then, since the war began?' Seth asked him gravely.

'Yes. Which is why I am hugely grateful for your offer of a night utterly away from the military.'

'Then you must treat this like your own home,' Rose invited him. 'Marianne will show you up to what we call the blue guest room. And I'll have Patsy bring you up some hot water so that you can freshen up.'

'We can lend you a nightshirt and anything else you might need,' Marianne put in, jumping to her feet and taking Albert's arm as she led him out into the entrance hall and up the grand staircase.

'Is your family always this hospitable?' he asked, somewhat overwhelmed.

'Oh, absolutely! We quite often have guests to stay. There's invariably something interesting going on here.'

'I can imagine,' Albert answered, one corner of his mouth lifted in amusement. 'It must be the love of animals. Your father shooed two dogs out into the garden, but I have to say I would have no objection to their company.'

'They can be a bit boisterous with strangers. There, will this room do?' Marianne said, opening the door and striding across to the tall casement window. 'There's a lovely view over the moor and you can see the horses in the fields from here. You can help us put their blankets on before you freshen up if you like. There could be a light frost again tonight.'

'I should be delighted. And, well, I know it's rather forward of me, but if I can't buy him from you, I should love to have a ride on Pegasus. He's one of the finest horses I've ever set eyes on.'

Marianne puffed out her cheeks. 'Unfortunately he's had a long ride today, but if you don't need to leave too early in the morning, I'll take you on a ride over the moor. He has a very soft mouth, though, so if you're not used to–'

'My dear Miss Marianne,' Albert chuckled, 'I was practically born on a horse. And as I say, I have a few days' leave and nothing specific to do with them, so a ride over this beautiful moor before I leave tomorrow would be, well, you don't know how good that would be.'

'I'm sure you could stay more than one night if you wanted to.'

Albert blinked at her in astonishment. He didn't think he had ever met anyone, let alone a young woman and a stunningly beautiful one at that, with such direct but natural charm. He couldn't stop himself breaking into a grin. 'Well, if your parents agree, I can hardly refuse, can I?'

'That's settled, then. Now come along. We need to get blankets on all the horses while it's still light enough to see, and there are quite a lot of them.'

Marianne flitted out of the room, across the landing and down the staircase leaving Albert to follow behind or not, as he chose. The day had certainly taken an unexpected turn for the better. She might have sworn never to allow her heart to be broken again in the same way as she had let it over Michael Bradley. Although to say her heart had been *broken* was somewhat of an exaggeration, she supposed. But Major Albert Thorneycroft was different. He was clearly not involved with any female, and was more of the right age for her, about thirty she judged. And he was almost as horse-mad as she was.

Her soul spiralled heavenward as she heard his light footfall on the stairs behind her.

'That was wonderful!' Marianne heard

Albert exclaim as he brought Pegasus to a halt beside her. 'So exhilarating!'

'The ride or the view?' she quizzed him, her body moving easily to accommodate the vigorous shake of his head that Hermes gave to show his annoyance at having his head-long gallop interrupted.

'Both,' Albert declared with a grin that made his moustache curve pleasantly upwards. 'Pegasus is a joy, so spirited and strong, yet so obedient. I certainly agree with you that it would be a crime to risk him on the battlefield. He'd be a huge asset with his speed and surefootedness, but better to pass those qualities on to many more. I just feel privileged that you've allowed me to try him out.'

'Only because you obviously know what you're doing. I wouldn't trust him to just anyone.'

'Well, I'm honoured. A perfect ride, an amazing landscape.' Albert turned in the saddle to gaze about him. 'And a beautiful companion. What more could I ask for?'

Marianne knew she blushed to the roots of her hair, and prayed that Albert would think it was merely the effect of the wind rushing into her face. 'In a minute you'll see something less attractive,' she said, swiftly changing the subject. 'The prison. It's pretty formidable but it does have a certain character. It's built of local granite though, so I suppose it fits in with the landscape.'

'It must feel a miserable place to be incarcerated in,' Albert agreed as the said building came into view. 'I mean, the moor is a fantastic place on a day like this, but it must feel desolate in the depths of winter.'

'Not if you love it as I do. It's so wild and free...'

She saw Albert glance at her sideways and a smile played on his lips. 'Just as I believe you are, Marianne. And with Pegasus to bear you away...'

His voice lifted on a romantic crest and Marianne tossed her head with a merry laugh. 'What a lovely picture you create! A bit like a fairytale.'

'If only life could always be like that, rather than the pickle the world has got itself into at the moment,' Albert grimaced. 'I would so much rather be here with you without having to think that in a few days' time, I'll be back in France fighting against the enemy.'

'But you're a regular soldier. That's what you signed up to, isn't it?'

Albert's shoulders lifted in a shrug. 'It was more or less expected of me and I didn't see any reason not to. My mother died having me, and my father was a cavalryman so he was away most of the time. An elderly spinster aunt brought me up. I had my first pony when I was three, but I led a fairly claustrophobic life with my aunt. So when I was old enough, it seemed like a huge adventure to join the hussars myself. I served with my father for a few years before he died. Entirely natural causes, I must add. Perforated appendix. And then my old aunt died and there was no one else, so the army became my family. Of course, I didn't have a crystal ball and had no idea a conflict such as this would ever erupt.'

'You think it really is going to be bad?'

'It already is. You only have to look at what's happened so far. The Hun's forces are pretty formidable. I've been there, remember. This situation isn't going to resolve itself overnight.'

Marianne saw the grim expression on his face. 'Were you at Mons, then?' she asked quietly.

'No, not Mons. My regiment was, but I was part of regimental HQ which had remained at Longmoor, and I'd been sent down here to procure more quality horses as so many were unhappy with their remounts. But as soon as I got back to Longmoor, I was sent out to take command of A Squadron. Officially the regiment's there mainly for reconnaissance duties for the first three infantry divisions. That might not sound quite so dangerous, but we're really just as vulnerable and can be in the thick of it as much as anyone. A Squadron had virtually been wiped out at Mons.'

'Thank goodness you weren't there, then.'

Albert shrugged ruefully. 'I was at the Marne, though, and the Aisne. They weren't as easy as some people think, believe you me. And I'll be back out there before the week's out. But at least I'll have some happy memories to take back, even if I won't have this magnificent beast with me,' he concluded wryly, patting Pegasus's hairy neck.

Marianne felt a dagger of guilt stab beneath her ribs. A horse with Pegasus's speed could be invaluable for reconnaissance. Could even save its rider's life. Could save Albert's life. She groaned inwardly. How could she suddenly be put to such torture? Her heart had been touched by Major Albert Thorneycroft in the short time they had known each other, and he appeared to be attracted to her, too. But look what had happened last time she had allowed herself to have feelings for a member of the opposite sex. Could she risk the life of her beloved Pegasus for the sake of a virtual stranger, when all was said and done?

'Well, I expect you'd like another gallop on him, then,' she said enigmatically, and squeezed her heels into Hermes's sides.

'Goodbye, Major.'

'Goodbye, Mr and Mrs Warrington. And thank you so much for letting me stay. You don't know what your hospitality has meant to me.'

'I can imagine,' Seth replied sombrely. 'Take care of yourself.'

'I'll do my best. And goodbye to you, Marianne. Thank you for some wonderful rides across the moor.'

He held out his hand, and Marianne took it, hoping he couldn't feel her trembling. 'I'm ... so sorry I couldn't let you have Pegasus,' she faltered, even now wondering if she shouldn't change her mind.

But Albert gave a compassionate smile. 'I fully understand.' He bowed his head with a slight jerk, letting go her hand, and a few moments later, was turning his motorcar out of the driveway.

'God speed,' Marianne mumbled almost inaudibly.

Her father turned back into the house, but Rose remained beside her as the noise of the engine faded into the distance. 'Best not to know what happens to him, my dear,' she whispered to her daughter.

Marianne nodded, not turning her head since she didn't want her mother to see that her eyes were glistening with unshed tears. If Albert was killed on the battlefield, would it be her fault because she didn't let him take the horse whose speed might have saved him? No. Her mother was right. Although her soul had ached to ask Albert to write to her, let her know he was all right, it was better that she didn't hear from him again. That way the guilty wound would slowly heal. Nevertheless, as she stared blindly down the empty driveway, she felt a piece of her heart tear.

CHAPTER SEVEN

'Happy Boxing Day!'

'Welcome! Come in, all of you. Richard and Beth and everyone are already here. Elliott picked them up in the car.'

'It was a bit of a squeeze, mind,' Elliott grinned as he joined his wife, Ling, in the hallway of their home in one of the opulent Victorian villas along Tavistock's Plymouth Road. When he had inherited his parents' residence in Watts Road, he had sold both it and his own little house in Chapel Street and bought this fine abode instead. Being near the centre of the town, it was more convenient for the majority of his patients, and its spacious rooms made it perfect for social gatherings. All the same members of the Pencarrow and Warrington families who had been at Rose's party had come to visit. Only Adam and Rebecca had not made the long journey from Herefordshire.

'I was so pleased I managed to wangle Christmas off,' Mary told Marianne when after all the boisterous greetings, they found themselves seated together on a sofa in the drawing room. 'Not everyone did, of course.'

'Still enjoying your training, then?'

'Absolutely! It was definitely the right choice. I love every aspect of it, but best of all is when patients are well enough to go home.'

'That must be so gratifying,' Marianne agreed. 'Like when we've finished breaking a young horse and know we've turned it into a reliable mount. Mind you, when we start getting these wild horses from North America to train for the army, I'm not sure we'll achieve it with every one of them. But we'll do our best.'

'Yes, the war's putting all sorts of demands on people,' Elliott put in. 'If I were a few years younger, I might've volunteered for the Medical Corps. But as it is, some of my younger colleagues have gone, so I'm working twice as hard here to cover for them instead.'

'That's happening everywhere as more and more men enlist,' Richard concurred, joining in the conversation. 'They say women are stepping into the breach all over the country.'

'I wish there was something more I could do for the war effort,' Marianne declared with a frustrated sigh. 'I'll be helping to train these horses, of course, but I'd like to be more directly involved.'

'Perhaps you can be.' It was Beth who spoke now as everyone was drawn into the discussion. 'Have you heard about the healing properties of sphagnum moss? It's antiseptic, and it can hold twenty times its own weight in liquid, such as blood. So the army are starting to use it as a wound dressing.'

'So you're suggesting we could collect it from the moor?'

'We could set up a centre in Princetown!' Rose declared, effervescent with enthusiasm. 'I could appeal to the Prince of Wales himself through the Duchy Office, because we'd need somewhere to store it, and presumably it'll need processing of some sort.'

'It'd certainly have to be dried,' Elliott confirmed. 'It also needs thorough cleansing before it can be made into dressings, but whether or not that could be done at a collection centre is another matter.'

'I'll go into the Duchy Office tomorrow if it's open,' Rose announced. 'Marianne and I can organize a work force. Get local people involved, advertise in the *Gazette*. We'll need people who know the moor intimately. The moss grows best in the great bogs and they can be dangerous if you don't know them. You couldn't possibly start collecting it until the spring, but it'd take that long to set it all up anyway.'

'I'm afraid I won't be able to help, then, with the baby due in April.'

Marianne glanced across at her sister. Kate didn't appear *too* mortified at the idea of not spending her days knee-deep in the smelly moorland mires gathering sack-loads of lustrous sphagnum. Marianne could understand that it wouldn't be many people's idea of fun, but in their younger days, Kate had relished romping over the moor in all weathers as much as she had. But Kate had changed since having Adam. She still had a zest for life and was almost as outspoken as her younger sister, but her enthusiasm was channelled in a different direction nowadays.

'You can sit at home knitting socks and balaclavas for the troops instead, then,' Marianne retorted scathingly. 'I'm sure we can manage without you and find plenty of volunteers elsewhere.'

'Well, I think it's a splendid idea,' Mary put in brightly, sensing the tension between the two sisters. 'We can all do our bit, no matter how small. If I hadn't already enrolled for professional nursing, I'd have volunteered as a VAD.'

'I'm not sure I could do anything connected with nursing,' Marianne grimaced. 'All those bodily functions would make me heave.'

'VADs can do all sorts of things, though. But it looks as if you're going to have your hands full with this moss project. Look! Your mum's engaged Dad in an animated discussion on it!' Mary chuckled, jabbing her head at Rose and Elliott deep in conversation. 'And you'll be helping with those horses. When will they start arriving?'

'Soon, now. Hal will be pleased to be doing something at last. Otherwise I think he'd have enlisted by now.'

Mary lowered her eyes. 'Mum and Dad don't know it yet,' she whispered, her gaze flicking across to where her elder half-brother was talking to Richard. 'But Artie's going to enlist in the New Year. You know he took over the antiques business when Grandad died, but trade has plummeted since the war started. He has a trusted assistant who's too old to join up, so he's going to leave it in his hands until he comes back. *If* he comes back,' she finished under her breath.

Marianne shuddered involuntarily. The war slithered its evil tentacles into every nook and cranny, even a happy gathering such as this. 'And how is Michael?' she couldn't stop herself asking. It wasn't exactly changing the subject since he could well be in danger, too, but she was sure her friend would want to talk about him.

'Very well, thank you.' Mary couldn't prevent the glow that came into her cheeks. 'He was docked in London for a few days recently, and we were able to see each other a couple of times. It would've been nice to see him over Christmas, but you can't have everything. Not when there's a war on.'

No, Marianne thought glumly to herself. Not when there's a war on. It was enough that all those she held dear were safe. For now, at least. Her romantic feelings for Michael were long buried, but it was still a relief to know he was all right.

As she smiled back at Mary's flushed expression, the handsome face of Major Albert Thorneycroft slipped, unbidden and unexpected, into her mind.

Joe Tyler stood beneath the archway in the wall that separated the terrace from the stable yard at the side of the house, and nodded approvingly. The family had all gone down to celebrate Boxing Day with the Franfields in Tavistock, and he was about to set off for Princetown to spend the day with his daughter Henrietta, her prison-warder husband and the grandchildren. He was indescribably happy that Henry had produced three little tykes. His darling Molly had only given him the one daughter before she began to have problems down below that had eventually led to her death in her mid-fifties. Heart-broken though he was, Joe was hugely relieved that it didn't appear to be a condition their daughter had inherited.

Other than losing Molly before her time, Joe considered he had led a charmed life. A workhouse foundling, he had been rescued from the cruel, livery-owner master he had been apprenticed to by a vivacious and beautiful young girl little older than himself.

The memory of the accusing tirade Rose had launched at his astounded master brought a smile to Joe's face even now. He had served her with unquestioning loyalty ever since, but for a few years when she had married and moved to Fencott Place, and her first husband had employed that sly reprobate from Princetown, Ned Cornish, as their groom instead.

Joe already had his job at the Cherrybrook Gunpowder Mills the other side of Princetown where Rose's father had been manager. So it wasn't as if he had been put out of work. But he had never trusted Ned, and of course he knew exactly why Rose had dismissed the devil the moment she had buried that equally untrustworthy husband of hers! But before too long, she had taken Joe on as her new groom, and insisted that Molly and Henrietta came to live in the comfortable rooms over the tackroom as well.

And there Joe had remained, caring unfailingly for the family's horses until Rose and Seth had established the stud farm which, with them all working together, had mushroomed into the fine affair it was now. All their trained animals had gone to the army back in the summer, with the next batch to follow shortly, poor beasts. But before long, they would have those wild creatures to tame, which was at least a chal-

123

lenge Joe was looking forward to.

Now, satisfied all was secure, he went into the house to collect Patsy. She too, had served Rose most of her life. She'd never had any family of her own, and so she was going to Henrietta's with Joe. Nobody could ever replace Molly in Joe's heart, but Patsy made a very pleasant companion.

As they walked the rutted road, hard with frost, that would lead them into Princetown, neither of them saw the figure crouching on the other side of the field wall. He had found the spot again instantly on his first sortie out onto the moor to check out Fencott Place. For hadn't he met his dairymaid lover there on numerous occasions in his youth, since no one could see what they were up to there. The thought of her eager, open thighs sent a delicious shiver down his spine even now.

But he had more serious matters on his mind at the minute. With no friends to celebrate the Yuletide with, in a moment of malicious loneliness, he had decided to book into Princetown's Duchy Hotel – wearing his disguise, of course, just to be safe. At least he could indulge his passion for seeking a way to bring down Miss Fancy Breeches – or Rose Warrington as she was apparently called now.

Using the best binoculars money could buy, he had ascertained on his previous spying trips all the members of the household. To count them out one by one and find the place deserted was the best Christmas present anyone could have given him. As soon as the groom and the housekeeper were out of sight, he scaled the wall with an agility that belied his sixty-two years and scuttled along the road to the grand, isolated house that had once been his home – at least, the cosy rooms over the stables had been – until the bitch had thrown him out. His heart was thumping with the delightful prospect of wreaking some revenge.

He was out of luck. Every single downstairs door and window was firmly locked or bolted. Damn. Perhaps he should smash a window pane, but whenever he went up close to peer in, he was met by two dogs on the inside, growling at him suspiciously. They must be loose in the house, and although they were a breed known for its friendly nature, he didn't want to risk being bitten any more than he did cutting himself on broken glass.

Perhaps he'd have better luck at the back of the house which he could get round to via the stable yard. But, oh, bugger! Since his time, a wall had been built across the entrance with a pair of solid wooden gates – locked, of course – so that he couldn't even see through! Burglary wasn't his forte. He had always been the boss, employing lockpickers and safe-breakers for that sort of thing. He would need to find someone he could trust implicitly, and that would take time. But then, he smirked, he had plenty of that commodity, and the wait would make his vengeance so much the sweeter when it came.

It would also give him the chance to plan that much more meticulously how he would make the bloody vixen suffer.

CHAPTER EIGHT

'Got a couple of sacks of the stuff outside, I has.' The elderly man, trousers drenched to above the knee in oily, malodorous water, doffed his cap wearily. 'Where does you want it, missus?'

'Could you take it round to the prison officers' tennis court, please?' Rose gave him a grateful, sympathetic smile since the poor fellow looked exhausted. 'You'll find a group of volunteers spreading it out to dry in the sunshine. Thank you so much.'

'Sunshine? What bloody sunshine be that, then?' he grumbled, turning towards the door. 'Proper bloody sodden it is.'

'Was that sod*den* or sod*ding*, do you think?' a voice whispered in Rose's ear.

'Marianne!' Rose turned to her daughter, eyes wide with shock. But when she saw the suppressed amusement on Marianne's face, she couldn't help but chuckle. She wasn't sure Seth would have approved, but the war was drawing women into a man's world, and when news of renewed bitter fighting near Ypres had just reached them, a word of un-savoury language seemed pretty insignificant.

'Better not let your father hear you talk

like that,' she warned nonetheless.

'With him being in the army all those years, and then, well, you know?' Marianne puffed out her cheeks and then dropped onto the hard chair beside her mother, pulling off her white cap.

'How's it going in there?' Rose jabbed her head towards the rooms of the Imperial Hotel which had been given over to the project by the Prince of Wales.

'It's like an oven in the drying rooms, and so humid. I'd say they're marvels, the women working there, spreading out the moss on the grills. As for the boiler man, I don't know how he can stand it.'

'Well, if we can recruit more volunteers, they can all do shorter shifts,' Rose replied, consulting the timetables among the ocean of paperwork on her desk in the hotel foyer. 'But I think we should all be very proud. We've only been going a couple of weeks, and we've already got a hundred sacks of dried moss ready for our first consignment to leave tomorrow, and nearly, let me see, five hundred prepared dressings. You've done so well to oversee that side of things, you know.'

'I can't take all the credit. The women are brilliant, picking over every little shred to remove every speck of grass or dirt. I'd be bored stiff. And then there's weighing out exactly two ounces each time to put in the muslin bags.'

'And how about the chaps putting them through the sublimate? They are adhering to all the safety rules, I hope.'

'Don't worry, Mum. Yes, thick rubber gloves and everything. They'd soon have problems if they didn't. And the workers in the sterile room wrapping and packing the dressings are keeping to all the cleanliness rules. I've made sure of that.'

'Well done.' Rose presented her daughter with a proud smile, but then sucked in her lips. 'I just wish it all weren't necessary. All those young men wounded or giving their lives.'

'Well, I reckon as a family, we're doing our level best to help. We've already trained dozens of horses as well as setting this up.'

'I know.' Rose released a heartfelt sigh. 'All the same–'

'Ah, Mrs W!' Princetown's postmaster pushed his way through the door, beaming broadly. 'I thought you'd be here. I've just had a telegram come through, and with its happy contents, I thought you'd like it here rather than waiting till you get home.'

'A telegram? Oh, it's not from Philip, is it?'

The postmaster answered Rose with a grin, and Marianne watched her mother tear open the telegram, suddenly aware of her own warring emotions. They had been so pre-occupied with all the wild horses the

Remount Service had delivered to them for training, and setting up the collection centre, that she had scarcely spared a thought for her sister's expected arrival.

'A little girl!' Rose cried joyfully. 'Isn't that marvellous? Among all this horror, a new life! And a girl, so now they have one of each.'

'Yes, how wonderful!' Marianne replied, startling herself with a sudden rush of elation. 'And everyone all right?'

'Yes, look! *Mother and baby doing well*. When your father comes to fetch us in the motorcar when we finish here, we can drive straight over to Rosebank Hall!'

Marianne knew her face split into a huge grin that she was helpless to suppress. All the resentment she had felt over this second child of Kate's had miraculously disintegrated, and when she searched inside herself, Marianne realized that she was indeed delighted for her sister.

But why should she feel so differently?

'Oh, my little sweetheart,' Rose cooed over the miniscule, crunched up bundle in her elder daughter's arms. 'Don't you forget how absolutely tiny they are!'

Beth Pencarrow smiled back serenely from the foot of the bed. 'I know. Even though I deliver almost every baby in all the local villages, I can never get over how small they are. 'Tis their fingernails that always fascinate me.'

Rose nodded in agreement. 'Come on, let me have a hold.'

Kate relinquished her new baby daughter into Rose's practised arms. Rose instinctively began to rock the infant gently and was soon engrossed in conversation with Beth over the babe's head. Watching them, Marianne knew they would be chatting for some minutes, so she drew a chair up beside the bed.

'You look tired,' she sympathized with her sister.

Nevertheless, Kate's eyes danced in her face. 'But very happy,' she sighed in utter contentment.

'Was it a long labour?' Marianne surprised herself by asking. 'Weren't you scared?'

'I knew what to expect, didn't I?' Kate chuckled. 'And Beth's so brilliant, so, no, I wasn't scared. A bit apprehensive, I suppose, but mainly because you hope the baby'll be all right. Elliott's coming later to check us both over, but Beth's sure everything's fine.'

Something soothing she couldn't explain wrapped itself around Marianne, and she found herself squeezing Kate's hand. It seemed that in the euphoria of the moment, all their differences had been swept aside.

'Look at those two.' Kate used her head to indicate her mother and mother-in-law still marvelling over the baby. 'It must be hard for Mum sometimes, don't you think?' Kate whispered. 'I know it was nearly forty years ago, but she must sometimes think about the little girl she lost, our half-sister. Just a babe-in-arms, wasn't she?'

Marianne gazed at her sister, and her heart gave a strange lurch. She had been thinking exactly the same, and it filled her with joy that she and Kate seemed to be as one again.

'Dad's wetting the baby's head with Richard downstairs,' she said to cover her emotions. 'He said there was no point coming up straight away as he wouldn't get a look in with all us women flocking round the baby. Expect he'll be up in a minute, though.'

'Well, you'd better have a hold afore he does, then, Marianne,' Rose declared, catching the end of their conversation as she turned back to them. And she slid the tiny scrap of life into Marianne's arms.

Oh. She couldn't get out of that now, could she? Marianne expected to feel uneasy, but her heart instantly melted and she found herself instinctively supporting her little niece's head. With a sudden, all-encompassing wonderment that utterly astounded her, she gazed down on the button nose and rosebud mouth with enchanted reverence. The child was beautiful, sleeping peacefully, though her fairy fingers twitched as if she couldn't wait to discover what life held for her.

'What colour are her eyes?' Marianne asked eagerly, overtaken by the desire to know everything about the miracle that lay in her arms.

'I'm not sure,' Kate replied. 'A sort of grey, but I can't decide if it's bluish or brownish.'

'They're more likely to turn brown or at least hazel, given her heritage,' Beth told them. 'But then Adam has Kate's blue eyes, of course, though I reckon that could only be because both Richard's father's and my father's were blue. It were like you and Seth, Rose, having both the girls with blue eyes, although Hal's are hazel, of course, aren't they? Did one of Seth's parents have blue eyes, has he ever said?'

Marianne had been listening intently, all the time praying that the infant wouldn't start crying and she'd have to hand her back to Kate. She almost wished... But, no, she mustn't. Even to consider motherhood would break her vow, and she couldn't have that! All the same, in the deep recesses of her mind, a little voice asked her to recall what colour Albert Thorneycroft's eyes had been.

Oh, that was ridiculous!

'You'd better have her back now, Kate,' she said tersely, and handed the helpless being back to its mother as if it were a red-hot coal.

Marianne drove the horses around the edge

of the school, dusty in the August heat, and brought them to a halt next to where her father and brother were watching them. Although the animals were harnessed as a pair to drag the heavy log behind them, Marianne was astride the one on the left, just as the Remount Service had explained they would be driven in the army. She reined them in and both creatures responded obediently by coming to an immediate halt.

'They're looking really good,' Hal praised her. 'And when you think they were virtually wild a couple of months ago.'

'They always looked the most promising pair, though. And they seemed natural friends.'

'Doesn't mean to say they'd pull well together, mind,' Seth put in. 'But you'd think those two had been working together all their lives. We could use them to help train others. The army often need teams of a dozen or more to pull the really heavy guns. We'll get them pulling the wagon tomorrow, and if that goes well, we'll hitch them up as the lead pair in a foursome.'

'Sounds like a good plan,' Marianne agreed. 'But if I take them round one more time, can you let off one of those detonations when I'm over the other side, and we'll see how they react?'

'Better let me take them, then, sis–'

'I'm perfectly capable of handling them!'

134

'No, your brother's right,' Seth broke in firmly. 'Now you get down, missie.'

Marianne gave a snort of exasperation, but nevertheless obeyed. A minute later, she'd forgotten all about it and was observing with satisfaction the fruits of her labours as Hal took the pair around the school again. But even he had decided to lead them rather than act as mounted driver. When Seth activated one of the small explosive devices the army had provided for training purposes, the horses shied away but only slightly. At a soothing word from Hal, they were calmly on track once more.

Seth nodded approvingly. 'Pretty good, I'd say. Well done, Marianne.'

Marianne's chest swelled with pride as she basked in praise from this beloved parent. 'Thanks, Dad.'

'You deserve a reward for your hard work. I'll go and make sure Patsy's got the kettle on the go.'

Marianne caught his wry, teasing wink, and a twinge of sadness tugged at her heart as she saw him make his way towards the house at a much slower pace than he used to. But she must put such thoughts out of her mind, and instead she waited for Hal to bring the horses round again. She sprang forward to help her brother unhitch them from the log and then opened the gate so that they could lead the animals back to their field.

'All in all, things are going well,' Hal mused. 'This last batch from the Remounts are nearly ready, plus half a dozen of our own. And several of our mares are about to foal. We're making reasonable money from the horses, at last.'

'But not nearly enough to compensate for not being able to make much on the Stock Exchange since it reopened.'

Hal glanced at her askance. 'No. We are surviving, but the sort of profits we were making so that I could afford such a luxurious motorcar as the Napier are long gone. And who knows if they'll ever return. I think Dad will need me to go up to London for him again in the autumn to have a meeting with our broker and see if there's anything to be done.'

Marianne cocked an inquisitive eyebrow. 'And will you see Louise while you're there?' she asked cheekily.

'Maybe,' he answered, narrowing his eyes. And began whistling jauntily as they walked along between the fields of grazing horses.

CHAPTER NINE

Low cloud drenched the moor in a grey, dismal shroud that seemed to seep into every crevice. From the tall window in her bedroom at the back of the house, Marianne could see for perhaps a hundred yards before the landscape evaporated into the mist. Ah, well, it *was* November, so she shouldn't grumble. There were days on Dartmoor in July when you could barely see your own hand in front of your face.

A sudden cacophony of shouts and neighing drew her attention towards the stable yard. Just beyond it, her father, Hal and Joe were driving a pair from the latest delivery of wild horses from the fields where they were being kept to the school at the end of the yard. The poor beasts had only just arrived frightened and defensive, the previous week, and the Warringtons had spent that time trying to gain the animals' trust. But this morning, Marianne knew, Hal was going to take the next step with what, by observing the herd's behaviour, they had identified as the dominant stallion and mare. If they could tame them first, the others would follow more easily.

Marianne screwed up her lips. She and Rose were going to the collection centre to close it down for the winter. The bogs were becoming too dangerous to gather moss, and all but the most experienced moormen could become disorientated in this sort of weather. Besides, the first stage of drying the moss outdoors would be impossible until spring came round again. Every ounce of gathered moss had now been processed and the final consignment was to be collected by Red Cross lorry later that morning.

But surely they didn't need to leave for another ten minutes, and she simply must watch this most critical stage with the horses. She careered down the stairs and out through the back door, pausing only in the boot room to thrust her stockinged feet into her boots and grab her old coat from the peg.

'I thought you and your mother were going into Princetown?' Seth questioned her as they collided on the doorstep.

'We are. Tell Mum I'll be along later if she doesn't want to wait.'

Seth rolled his eyes at this madcap daughter of his, but Marianne didn't notice as she scooted along to the school. Joe had obviously taken himself off to some other chore, and she was alone as she hung over the gate to watch. Hal was standing in the centre and acknowledged her presence with a nod, while the two horses were trotting nervously to and fro along the far side.

Marianne knew exactly what her brother was going to attempt, but it wasn't going to be easy with these exceptionally spirited beasts. Like so many wild animals which had little contact with man, horses instinctively saw human beings as predators, but that fear needed to be turned into trust. But there was no time to do so in the conventional way, building up that relationship over months. The theory behind this quicker method was to make the creatures see man as their protector. But these two were already the leaders of the herd, so was Hal likely to succeed?

He began by growling, not so loudly as to startle them but to make them aware that he meant business. Then he started repeatedly slapping his left hand against his thigh in a noisy, exaggerated movement, while with the long driving whip in his other hand, he gently touched their hocks. Not wanting to come any nearer to him but wary of the whip, they scuttled around the edge of the school in the direction Hal had intended.

So far, so good. Hal kept the horses going round and round, gradually making less noise so that they became less tense. The whole process slowed down until the animals were walking, their hoofs a dull, rhythmical plod on the soft sand of the school's ground, and Hal simply stood, turning round in the middle with the whip outstretched behind them.

Marianne held her breath. It must have been half an hour, and Rose had doubtless left without her, but this was mesmerizing. She knew Hal wouldn't be rushed. It was absolutely essential he didn't make the next move until he felt the horses were totally calm and relaxed. It was so peaceful, the mist that clung to her eyelashes deadening all sound, and the magnificent creatures seemed to sense that tranquillity.

At last, Hal must have felt the moment was right and he stepped briskly forward right in front of them, looking them straight in the eye. They stopped, and Marianne felt as if her heart had stopped beating. With a disgruntled snort, the male backed away and turned round, the mare following, although both appeared unhurried as they trotted around in the opposite direction and Hal took up his position in the centre once more.

Time and again, he turned them until they began to predict what he was going to do the instant he went to step forward, and they turned at once as if they understood what he wanted. Marianne knew she should go to join her mother, but this was too good to miss. These wild creatures were beginning to obey Hal, to see him as their superior. They were learning that he had no intention of harming them, but that he had the upper hand. And as their leader now, they would look to him for protection.

Marianne knew what the next stage was. Would Hal feel these two were ready? Evidently he did. He leapt in front of them now, waving his arms to drive them away, just as the dominant animals of the herd would reprimand naughty foals. Taken aback, the two horses shied away, and Marianne bit her lip in anticipation. Would it work? Would Hal's patience be rewarded?

Marianne watched, on fire with excitement, as Hal turned his back and slowly walked away. After a moment's hesitation, the two chastized animals wanted to return to the safety of the herd and their new protector, and walked up to stand behind Hal.

He winked at his sister as he walked towards the gate, followed by the horses. The lesson was over, and with any luck the pupils would go calmly along the drove and back to their field. Marianne quietly opened the gate, as the last thing they wanted was to disturb the trusting relationship Hal was building with the animals.

'Let's hope they remember their lesson tomorrow,' Hal whispered as he passed, but they went determinedly back to their field without the slightest problem and settled down to grazing within no more than a minute or two.

'You're a marvel, Hal,' Marianne praised him as they walked back towards the stable yard. 'It never seems to work for me. I don't know what we'd do without you.'

'Perhaps you're physically too small, or they sense you're not dominant enough.'

'You mean I'm too soft.'

'Yes. But that's no criticism. You can just *love* horses into obedience. It just takes longer and sadly we don't have the luxury of time. But you'll soon find out. How to manage without me, I mean.'

Marianne stopped in her tracks as his words sunk in and she pulled her brother round to face her. She thought she had detected a certain flatness in his tone. Now she was proved right and a cold dread suddenly pumped through her veins.

'W-what do you mean?' she quizzed him.

Hal's eyes shifted about them as if to make sure no one could hear, and dropped his voice further. 'I've got something to tell you, sis. Only it's a secret. You must promise not to say a word to Mum and Dad, or anyone else for that matter.'

Marianne blinked at him, the jubilant triumph over the horses utterly crushed. For once in her life, she could think of no words to answer the pain in his expression. 'I don't understand,' was all she could muster.

'When I was in London last week, Louise turned me down.'

'What?' Marianne's shoulders sagged in relief. 'Is that all? Well, there are plenty of other–'

'No, listen to me, Marianne.' Hal's face was set as he took her by both arms. 'She said she couldn't marry a coward who wouldn't enlist, and that no other girl would want to either.'

'Oh, that's ridiculous. There are plenty of men who haven't joined up. And if she *really* loved you, she wouldn't want you to. It's not like it was a year ago when so many people said it'd be over by Christmas. The fighting this summer in France has been horrendous again, and look at the carnage that's been going on at Gallipoli and the Dardenelles.'

'I know. And that's precisely why I feel I'm needed.'

Marianne was gripped with panic as Hal's face hardened with determination. Dear Lord, she must talk him out of this! 'But your skills with the horses are needed *here*,' she insisted.

'And they're needed where I'm going. I've joined Dad's old regiment.'

'What!' Marianne's world seemed to crash at her feet. 'The 15th The King's Hussars?'

'Yes.'

'Oh, Hal.' Her voice sank, landing with a thud. 'Why?' she groaned.

'I've told you why. Only it's not all.' Hal lowered his eyes sheepishly. 'I want to leave before Mum and Dad find out what a complete and utter fool I've been. How I've let them down.' He hesitated as if summoning up his courage. 'Louise's father strongly recommended we sell some shares that were about to fall, so I agreed and put the money in the business account for safe keeping. But then Louise turned me down and I went out and got drunk. And ... oh, God, sis, I can't believe what happened. I gambled the lot away. Every last penny.'

Marianne's gaze locked on her brother's face in appalled disbelief. 'You? But you've never bet a farthing in your life!'

'That's not strictly true,' Hal admitted guiltily. 'I've gambled the odd pound here and there before, but... I don't know what happened. I completely lost my reason. And then I suddenly realized how much I'd lost, and I had to try and win it back. But all I did was lose far more.'

'Oh, Hal.' Marianne's stomach was churning viciously. 'But running away isn't going to help. And it'd be the cowardly thing to do.'

'Would it? When you consider what I'm running away *to*? And it's not just because of Louise and the money. It's because I need to prove to myself, too, that I'm not a coward.'

'But we all know you're not! You go right in among these wild horses when even experienced horsemen would run a mile. And

Mum and Dad will understand about the money. I mean, they might be cross at first–'

'Furious, more like.'

'All right, furious. But they'll get over it, even if it means we have to pull our belts in. You're their *son*, Hal. They love you and they'll forgive you. So, there you are. You don't need to go,' she rounded on him in triumph.

'Yes, I do. It's all arranged anyway. I leave the day after tomorrow. Only please don't tell anyone until after I've gone.'

'You're going to leave without saying good-bye?' Marianne was horrified. 'You can't do that! You'll break Mum and Dad's hearts! What if ... you don't come back?'

'I'll have to take that chance. But if I told them I was going, I'd end up confessing about the money as well. I'd be so ashamed, and we'd probably part on bad terms which would be even worse.'

'No.' Marianne shook her head incredulously, her brain turning circles. 'Why don't you make some excuse and pretend to be going back to London? At least you could say some sort of goodbye.'

Hal puffed out his cheeks, his eyes dark. 'All right. But promise me, not a word beforehand.'

Marianne's mouth twisted in rebellion as she met his gaze, but what could she do? Who should she be loyal to, her brother or her parents? There was no answer, and she felt as if her heart had been torn in two.

'Have a good trip, Hal,' Rose said, hugging her son. 'Take care in the capital, mind.'

Hal threw a glance at Marianne over his mother's shoulder, daring her to keep quiet. Marianne pursed her lips, her pulse rattling in her skull. Even now, she felt she should break the promise she had been coerced into.

'Goodbye, son. I'm surprised you have to go back again so soon. Got the keys to the house? And are you sure you don't want a lift to the station?'

'No thanks, Dad. It'll be good to have a lungful of fresh air before I get to London.' Hal pumped Seth's hand up and down, and Marianne thought she would break. It was on the tip of her tongue...

'I'll come out with you,' her mouth said instead. A minute later, she saw over her shoulder her parents give a final wave and turn back into the house while she and Hal crunched down the gravel drive.

'This isn't right.' She wrung the words from her throat as they came to the open gates.

'Yes, it is.' Hal's voice, nevertheless, was ragged. 'Thank you for not letting on, sis. I really appreciate it. And for letting me confide in you. Sister in a million, you are.'

'Hmm, I'm not sure about that.' She still felt angry that he had put her through such torture, but it was nothing to the agony that ruptured her heart at the thought that she might never see her brother again. But she must be cheerful for his sake. 'Maybe the Americans will decide to join in the war, and it'll all be over soon,' she said optimistically.

'If they were going to, you'd think the sinking of the *Lusitania* would have prompted them, and that was six months ago,' Hal scoffed.

'Well, maybe they're still thinking about it. It'd be a huge decision, after all. Or maybe everyone will come to their senses over the winter and sign a peace treaty before fighting begins again in earnest in the spring.'

'Perhaps.' The words were flat. Dead. They both knew they were fooling themselves. Trying to put on a brave face.

'You won't give me away before this evening, will you? Promise?'

A choking lump tore through Marianne's throat. 'I don't know how I'm going to break it to Mum and Dad,' she croaked.

'You won't have to. I've put it all in a letter. Here, sis. Just give it to them tonight. Say you found it in my room along with the house keys. And I've made a decision about the Napier. It's yours now. I've put that in the letter, too. Try not to crash it. I'll want it back after the war.'

He gave a wry smile, and the tears that had been welling in Marianne's eyes began to spill down her cheeks as she clung to him. He pulled away, lifting her chin. 'Thanks, sis. For everything.' And then he was walking away down the muddy road towards Princetown.

Marianne watched him, her vision blurred with tears, until he was a tiny speck in the distance. How in God's name could she keep the brutal sorrow hidden from her parents all day? She balled her fists, and felt her heart tighten in agony.

CHAPTER TEN

Marianne brought the Napier to a smooth halt on the gravel in front of the house, and beside her, Seth nodded in approval.

'Well done. You're turning into a good little driver. Hal will be proud of you when he comes home, I'm sure.'

Marianne's momentary pride instantly deflated. It was Boxing Day, and this year it had been the turn of Richard and Beth to host the gathering at Rosebank Hall. They had all pretended to enjoy themselves – and, of course, to a large degree, they had – but it wasn't the same. Mary hadn't been able to get home for Christmas either, which was disappointing for Marianne since they were corresponding regularly. But mostly, lurking at the back of everyone's mind, was the knowledge that Mary and William's elder half-brother, Artie, was out in Flanders somewhere with the Devonshires, while Hal was out there too, with his father's old regiment.

Marianne sensed that all these long-standing friends were putting on brave faces and attempting to buoy each other up. Besides, it was baby Valerie's first Christmas, and nobody wanted to spoil the occasion for William and young Adam either. But though Kate was twinkling in the role of happy, loving mother, Marianne could tell that her sister was just as concerned – for her brother in particular, of course – as everyone else.

Now, at the mention of Hal, Marianne caught the suppressed sigh of anguish from her mother in the back seat. When she glanced back, she could just see Rose's grim expression in the glow from the headlights reflecting back from the front wall of the house. Her own heart contracted in that horrible sensation that took hold of her whenever her brother stung into her thoughts. She still felt destroyed by guilt at never having revealed to her parents that she had known Hal was leaving. If she had, would they have been able to stop him? Or, at very least, they would have had the chance to say a proper farewell.

'Don't switch the engine off.' She was relieved when Seth's voice distracted her from her thoughts as he opened the passenger door. 'I'll go through the house and open up the stableyard gates so you can drive in.'

'All right, Dad,' she replied, and then flushed with nerves as she realized he meant her to drive through without him by her side, the first time she would have driven alone. Her mother, of course, was in the back, but Rose had never fancied learning to drive.

But Marianne would have to wait longer for her first solo drive. Before her father had reached the portico, Joe appeared from around the side of the house which led to the stable yard, running and waving his arms frantically. Seth at once turned back, and as the two men met in the Napier's headlights, Marianne could see the horror on Joe's face. Switching off the engine, both she and Rose leapt out of the vehicle.

'Aw, thank God you'm all back!' Joe was crying. 'They'm gone, an' I'm trying to round up what were left loose. An' Patsy's in the house. They've been in there an' all!'

'What do you mean, Joe? What's gone?'

'The horses!'

There was a moment's stunned silence while the news sunk in. Marianne's insides corkscrewed into a knot that made her feel sick, and she catapulted forward in utter panic.

'Pegasus?' she squealed frantically, and began racing towards the yard.

'He'm all right!' Joe called after her. 'Managed to get him back in his stable, I did, but he were proper frightened. Running about like a mad thing when I got here, but hadn't gone out of the yard even though the gates was wide open. Reckon they couldn't get him into the cattle truck.'

'Cattle truck?'

'Three of them, I reckon, from the tyre tracks.'

At hearing Pegasus was safe, Marianne had stood for a moment as the terror pulsed out of her, but now she hurried back to where the other three adults were staring at each other in total shock.

'So how many did they get?' she heard her father demand.

'A dozen, maybe twenty. They either forced or picked the locks to most of the stables an' several of the fields. I reckon they got what they could into the trucks, an' then left the rest to wander out onto the moor. I managed to drive in one or two that was near the gate, but as for the rest...'

Even in the darkness, Marianne saw Seth's eyes flash across at Rose. 'And they've been in the house as well, you say? Marianne, you'd better go inside with your mother and see what's missing. I'll help Joe secure the horses – those we've got left – and then I'll drive into Princetown and alert the constable.'

'You can tell him this were a planned job!' Joe declared in angry agitation. 'Checked every one of they locks afore Patsy an' me went off to my Henrietta's, I did. The one day of the year when the place isn't occupied, an' that only two out of three. Must've been watching us an' waiting, I reckons.'

'I think you're probably right,' Marianne heard Seth agree. 'But there's nothing we can do about searching the moor for the strays until morning. Now, go on, you two,' he instructed gently. 'Into the house.'

Marianne turned to her mother. Strangely, Rose hadn't uttered a word, but then she had been subdued ever since the shock of discovering Hal's secret enlistment. Marianne's conscience still smarted and probably would continue to do so until he returned. *If* he returned. No, *when* he returned, she reprimanded herself.

'Come on, Mum,' she smiled encouragingly, and realized as she took Rose's trembling hand that her own was shaking just as much.

The beautiful house that had been Marianne's lifelong home felt oddly hostile as they went inside. She supposed it was knowing that some stranger – or more likely strangers – had been there uninvited, searching through all their possessions. And it was evident as they came in through the entrance hall that the place had been ransacked.

'Aw, Mistress Rose!' Patsy sidled nervously from the drawing room, her face streaked with tears. 'Look what they devils have done! Take me weeks, it will, to put it all back together.' And she bent to retrieve the drawer from the elegant side table that had obviously been pulled out, the contents tipped onto the floor to be rifled through more easily, and then flung aside.

'No, Patsy, dear.' Rose had clearly been brought to her senses by the other woman's distress and laid a comforting hand on her arm. 'Better not touch anything until the police have been.'

'C-can't I even make a pot of tea?'

'Well, yes, I should think that would be all right,' Rose answered kindly. 'You do that, and Marianne and I will see what's missing.'

As Patsy shuffled off to the kitchen, lamenting miserably, mother and daughter exchanged a silent glance. Heaven knew what they were going to find, but they might as well get the shock of it over with. And so, with thudding hearts, they went into the drawing room together.

It had been turned upside down. For a moment, they just stood in appalled silence. Nothing had been left untouched. Even the upholstery of the armchairs and sofas had been slashed and the stuffing partly pulled out.

Marianne could see instantly that everything of value had been taken: the French mantle clock, the two Chinese vases and a pair of solid silver candlesticks. Thank goodness her mother wasn't a great collector of precious items. And then a wave of nausea swept through her as she turned to the mesmerizing portrait of Rose in her younger years. It was still there, but a deep slash, almost deliberate it seemed, had been gouged out across the beautiful face.

Ned Cornish put down his tumbler of whisky and leant back in the easy chair, stretching with languid satisfaction. He might be celebrating New Year alone, but he was oh, so happy. The year's planning had paid off perfectly. It had taken that time for him to find a lock and safe breaker he could trust, and three unscrupulous horse-dealers from well outside the jurisdiction of the Devonshire Constabulary, with false number plates on their trucks just in case anyone might see them and become suspicious. But Fencott Place was so isolated and people in Princetown would mostly have been indoors enjoying the Bank Holiday. The joy of it was that, as in the previous year, the house had been unoccupied for several hours. Otherwise his meticulous plans would have come to nothing, and he would have been obliged to pay his accomplices for their troubles without any gain for himself.

As it was, they would all do very nicely. Each of the horse-dealers had squeezed six valuable animals into his truck, some mares in foal – typically of Rose unbranded, since she would never put them through such an ordeal – and some ready-trained army horses whose brands would be cruelly altered and allowed to heal before they were sold back to the military. It was just a pity they hadn't been able to coax that magnificent dapple grey into one of the vehicles. It was almost as spirited as the great black nag Rose used to ride in her youth. Ned remembered only too well the agony of its teeth sinking into various parts of his anatomy. He wasn't anxious to repeat the experience with the grey. Pity. It would have fetched a tidy sum.

Oh, he was having such fun! It more than made up for the loneliness of the past nine years since he had returned from America. There was his old fence of course, who would sell on the jewellery he had stolen from the safe – shame there had been so little of it – and a few gambling cronies, but he couldn't call any of them friends. But at least, having paid off the safe-breaker with half the cash in the safe, spending the rest himself would give him huge pleasure. But the greatest joy had been breathing in the perfume on Rose's underwear – and then drawing the blade of his pocket-knife across her face in the painting.

'So, how much do you think we've lost, Dad?' Marianne dared to ask a few days later.

They were standing by a field gate, watching the horses they had rounded up from the moor. There could well be others, but they might never know. Dartmoor consisted of over three hundred and sixty square miles, and although some of the army animals might turn up in the annual drift the following September and be identified by their branding marks, others might never be seen again. All they had was a list of those that were missing, Hermes among them, which had left Rose bereft. But they might never know which animals had been stolen and which were still roaming wild on the moor.

'Fortunately our own horses were insured, as was your mother's jewellery,' Seth informed his daughter grimly, 'although you never get the full value of what they were worth. Thank goodness your mother was wearing the amethyst necklace and her ring. But the cash wasn't covered and it was a substantial sum, and neither was the vandalism. We'll have to repair or replace all that. And I'll send your mother's portrait back to Mr Tilling to be restored, and God knows what that will cost.'

'I wonder why they didn't take it,' Marianne pondered. 'Surely it would be worth a lot.'

'Too easily identifiable, the inspector said. But he reckons the whole attack was part malicious, damaging the furniture and everything like that, as if they wanted to get at us personally.'

Marianne was all but dumbstruck. 'Y-you mean, it was deliberately against us, not just a robbery?'

'Don't say anything to your mother, but possibly, yes.'

'But who on earth–?'

'We have no idea. But if the culprits are ever caught, the authorities will come down on them like a ton of bricks, stealing horses that were essentially government property in a time of war.'

'Treason, you mean?'

'Possibly, I suppose. I don't really know. What I do know is that the Remounts are deciding whether we will have to reimburse them the value of their horses, or even if they'll trust us with training any more for them. Besides, Hal isn't here anymore, and he did the lion's share of the work. And his misdemeanour, shall we call it, cost us a great deal, too. All I can say, my dear, is that we need to make some drastic economies after all this. So enjoy the Napier while we still have it. You know it's a hugely expensive motorcar, and it's a luxury we can do without. If I can find a buyer, it'll fetch a good price.'

Marianne's already crumbling spirit dropped to her feet as the gravity of the situation hit home. 'We won't have to sell Pegasus, too, will we?' she asked in sudden panic.

Seth turned to her with a wistful smile. 'I'll hang onto him with my last breath. It's bad enough your mother grieving over Hermes. I couldn't stand two weeping women around me all day. Besides, I'll need his services as champion stud as soon as we get going again.'

But Marianne knew he had no need to voice his final thoughts. *If* we ever get going again, he should have concluded.

CHAPTER ELEVEN

Marianne chewed the end of her pen for a moment before going on with her letter to Mary. It was strange how her friendship with the younger girl had deepened since Rose's party, when her thwarted feelings for Michael Bradley should have driven them apart. As it was, Marianne found she could make confessions in her letters to Mary that she could never reveal to anyone else, as if she were talking to some absent confidante. She would always receive a sympathetic, sensible reply. Mary had a head on her shoulders far beyond her years, and Marianne recognized that her friend was having a steadying influence on her own erratic nature. It was no wonder Mary was so suited to nursing.

Marianne's hand went down to the paper again almost without her telling it to.

We're opening up the moss collection centre again tomorrow now the better weather's coming. And this new Daylight Saving business should help as well. It'll be good to feel I'm doing something useful again, although I've been helping with the horses all winter, of course. After that dreadful business at Christmas, Dad came to an agree-

ment with the Remounts. We're training a number of horses for free to make up for the losses they incurred over the ones that were stolen. I think Dad could have fought it, but he doesn't have the same energy as he used to, and it makes him feel he's making a personal contribution to the war. But it means we won't be making any money for a while. We lost all our brood mares, too, and trying to replace them when the army have requisitioned so many animals is proving a nightmare.

What with all that and making so little on the stock market, we're really down on our uppers, as they say. Dad's put the Napier up for sale and is hoping for a good price provided he can find someone to buy it, of course. It really has all been a terrible affair for us, and the police haven't had any leads. Someone saw three cattle trucks passing through Princetown on Boxing Day heading towards Two Bridges and thought it odd, but that was all. I don't suppose they'll catch the culprits now.

Marianne paused again. How could she word what was really on her mind without revealing her true guilt? She couldn't tell even Mary that, it went so deep. But perhaps it would ease her conscience a little if she touched on the subject without showing the exact depth and nature of her troubles.

We all miss Hal so much, as I'm sure you do Artie and Michael. I was so relieved to read in your last letter that they were both safe. Pray God they all remain so until this ghastly war is over. But thinking about them has brought me to a decision. I know with the moss and the horses I'm doing my bit to help, but Mum and Dad can manage perfectly well without me. So now that I've learnt to drive – and Dad says I've taken to it like a duck to water – I've decided to volunteer as an ambulance driver in France or wherever they see fit to send me. That way I can really be sure I'm helping to save the lives of our brave young volunteers. Of course, they're not all volunteers now conscription has come in. And somehow that makes my volunteering even more vital. But please don't breathe a word to anyone else yet. I won't disappear off as Hal did without saying a proper goodbye, but I want to wait until it's all settled before I tell my parents.

There, it was said. The only person in the world to know. But it was only half the story. It would be a terrifying adventure, one which filled Marianne with both excitement and dread. But the main reason was that it would provide her with some sort of penance for keeping Hal's enlisting a secret and the awful hurt it had created for their parents.

Ned Cornish drummed his fingers on the table next to him and his mouth twisted into a restless curve. He was bored. Bored, bored, bored, his mind chanted silently. Nothing to do all day. Or the next. Or the next.

The previous evening, he had paid for a woman to come home with him for the night. She wasn't particularly young or pretty, but she had been willing to let him take her in several different ways until his desire was spent. His entire body had oozed with lasciviousness. He had felt aroused just holding the woman's nakedness against his between each bout of lovemaking and talking to her about normal matters. So he had conjured up some vision of her becoming a friend, too, to ease his loneliness. But in the cold light of day, he had seen her for what she was, a common whore. She had taken his money and tucked it into the cleavage of her blouse with a casual, 'I'll want twice that next time, my lover,' and slammed the door behind her.

Had she been worth the wad of pound notes he had parted with? It had seemed so at the time, but now it seemed a total waste. For that sort of money, he wanted class. Someone like Rose Maddiford as she had been before her marriage to that toff from London.

Ah, Rose. His heart still twirled at the thought of those far off, halcyon days when she would pay him sixpence to look after that brute of a horse in the stables where he worked while she went to visit her friend Molly. She would tease him, knowing she had him wrapped round her little finger.

And then, when she had married and her husband had employed him as groom at Fencott Place, she wouldn't even give him a kiss for old times' sake. She had rejected *him*, and yet she had gone on to help that bloody escaped convict hide in the stables for weeks, right under his nose!

That had hurt him more than anything, tricking him as if he were a bloody idiot! Even more than when her husband had died and she had immediately dismissed him. The convict had been proved innocent and released – it had been in all the papers it was such an exceptional case – so there must have been someone of huge influence on his side. It was for that reason only that Ned had kept away and not sought his revenge at the time. Then he had got caught up in a web of crime on the back-streets of Plymouth which had led to his eventual going to America, and he had scarcely thought of Rose since.

That was until he had seen her in Plymouth, and the need for vengeance had frothed up inside him and burned into the core of his being. To top it all, he had later discovered that it was that damnable bloody convict she had taken as her second husband. The knowledge had ripped Ned's heart from his chest. Well, he would have revenge on the pair of them!

What he had done at Christmas had brought him satisfaction at the time, but was it enough to satisfy the jealous rage that had been eating into him like a cancer all those years, a dormant lion within him? Surely he could find a way to hurt them far more deeply than that? So, what would be more precious to them than the few trinkets and the horses he had stolen? He didn't take long to come up with the answer.

At the sound of the post dropping through the letterbox, Marianne dashed out to the hall, almost colliding with Patsy who was on her way to collect the mail herself as part of her morning duties.

'You'm always rushing to get the post afore me these days, Miss Marianne,' the elderly housekeeper declared as a twinkle came into her eye. 'Expecting a letter from someone special like, are us?'

'No, nothing like that,' Marianne smiled innocently. 'I keep hoping there'll be something from Hal.'

That was true enough. But the exact truth was that she didn't want her parents to see if she had a reply from the FANY as it would surely come in an official envelope. She would only tell them once she had been accepted and there was no going back. Unlike Hal, she wouldn't be in any real danger, but even so, she would wait until the right moment to tell them.

'Go on, then, cheel,' Patsy chuckled. 'The

sooner I can get off to the shops the better, afore all the best food's gone. Starting to get harder to get exactly what you want, it is.'

'I'm sure you'll make a super meal for us whatever you can get!' Marianne grinned, and deposited a kiss on Patsy's cheek that made the older woman colour with pride and affection.

Marianne picked up the post, her face still lit with a smile. There was nothing official-looking, but oh, there was a letter in Hal's handwriting! She danced into the dining room and handed it to her father at the breakfast table since it was addressed to her parents. Seth opened it at once and then passed it to an excited Rose to read to them aloud.

The letter began with the news that Hal was in the best of health. As he'd told them in previous letters, for the last few months, the regiment had been well behind the lines. Conditions weren't at all bad, summer had brought welcome warmth after the freezing winter, and he was perfectly safe. The only enemy was disappointment, since cavalry seemed to have become obsolete in modern warfare and they hadn't had a chance to fight properly. Nevertheless, they trained constantly, but were often granted leave to go into the nearby town. In one bar, a local chap played an accordion every evening, and they would all join in such songs as *It's a Long Way to Tipperary* and *Pack up your Troubles*, which the Frenchman had picked up by ear from the Tommies.

I'm actually serving under Major Thorney-croft, the chap who came to Fencott Place that time. Hardly a coincidence, I suppose, as we're in the same regiment. He was wounded at the Second Battle of Ypres, but I'm pleased to say was able to return to full active duty. He's a good sort and I'm happy to be under his command. It's rumoured there's going to be a huge push against the Hun, and we've had four night marches to bring us to a totally different location. If the rumour's true, it could be the end for the Boche. They're saying the cavalry will at long last be needed, so I'll be playing a part in the victory!

The letter ended with his good wishes to them all and his looking forward to being back with them at the end of the summer when the war would surely have been won.

'Do you think he could be right, Seth?' Rose cried elatedly.

'I'd like to think so,' Seth answered, but by the expression on his face, Marianne knew he didn't believe it.

'I think I'll go for a ride on Pegasus,' she announced, 'and join you at the centre later, Mum, if you think you can manage without me for a while.'

'Of course, dear,' Rose agreed, and then

her face dropped. 'I'd have joined you if I'd still had poor Hermes. It's such a lovely morning. You take care out on the moor.'

'I will,' Marianne promised, and went upstairs to change into her riding habit since she no longer wore it all the time as she used to before the war.

Out on the moor, everything was flushed with summer life. The wild grass was a luscious green, and although the full flush of spring gorse was long over, smaller bushes were dotted with fragrant canary flowers. But then it was said that gorse could be found in bloom somewhere on Dartmoor during every month of the year.

After a long gallop, Marianne slowed Pegasus to a walk and let her thoughts wander over everything in Hal's letter. He had made it all sound like a jolly romp, but was that just to alleviate her parents' fears? Mind you, she didn't like the sound of this new offensive, even if it might put an end to the war. Doubt flooded back into her mind. What if she had revealed Hal's secret? Could their parents have prevented his leaving? But that would have meant a betrayal of his trust in her. It was academic now that conscription had come in, but she still agonized over it. Although Hal's work with the horses might have been considered so vital that he would have been exempted. Oh, if only he hadn't told her about his enlisting in the first place!

The tortured thoughts still swirled in her brain as she set Pegasus's head for home. It was then that she saw the man coming towards her. He was on foot and looked like a rambler, carrying a map and using a walking stick. An older man, it struck her that he seemed fit and agile for his years, but beyond that, she scarcely gave him a second glance until he doffed his cap as he drew level with her.

'Excuse us, miss, but be this the old abbots' way to Buckfast?'

Marianne drew Pegasus to a halt. 'Yes, it is. You've a long way to go, mind, and you have to go through some difficult country, including Red Lake Mire. It isn't really sensible to go alone if you don't know it.'

'Oh, I'll be all right, miss. Can take care of me'self, I can.'

'Well, don't say I didn't warn you,' Marianne advised him, and urged Pegasus forward again past the stranger.

She didn't see the fellow swing the stick at her from behind. All she felt was the sudden, blinding pain at the back of her head, and her vision clouded with black stars. She slumped forward in the saddle and the next moment realized she was being dragged from Pegasus's back.

It only took an instant for her senses to snap back into action. The man was forcing her downwards, pulling her off balance so that she toppled sideways with no way of saving herself. But once she was on the ground, a surge of anger ripped through her that she had let the bastard trick her! He was only after one thing as he pinned her slender form beneath his own bulk, and his hand moved up beneath the folds of her riding skirt. Well, he'd have a hard job as she was wearing breeches beneath, and though she might be helpless beneath his weight, her hands were free.

His hat had fallen from his head and she dug her fingers into his hair, ready to yank it painfully from his scalp. One tug and... Good Lord, it came right away. It was a wig, and beneath it, his hair was grey and deeply receded. Marianne was so taken aback that she was unable to react to his fist that slammed into her jaw. But two could play at that game. She reached out her hand to fumble on the ground, and her fingers at once found what she was seeking. It only took a second for her to scrape the stone from the surrounding earth and she hit her assailant on the temple. At least, he moved just as she did so and as a result her aim wasn't perfect, but it was enough for him to groan and recoil with his hands to his head.

Quick as lightning, Marianne slid out from beneath him and leapt onto Pegasus's back. She kicked his flanks and, unused to such harsh treatment from her, the animal reared up in surprise, knocking flat the attacker who by now was in pursuit again. But the horse knew what his mistress wanted and streaked along the track in the direction of home.

Marianne eventually brought him to a stop and turned to look over her shoulder. There was no way the villain could catch them. Indeed, he was staggering away in the opposite direction as well he might, since she was sure to alert the constable in Princetown, wasn't she?

Or was she? A squall of indignation blasted through her chest. The devil had put her in another awkward situation, hadn't he? She knew that she ought to go to the police so that the culprit could be caught before he attacked another young woman. But as with the incident with the snake two years ago now, if her parents found out about it, they would curtail her lone rides and especially now, it was the only way she could let her taut emotions unravel. Better to keep quiet. The blackguard would surely *imagine* she had reported him, and anyway, with any luck, he would drown in the wild bogs he was heading for. Besides, she had been perfectly capable of looking after herself, hadn't she? It was proof enough to herself that she could do so out in France, too!

She set her chin determinedly and turned Pegasus's head for home once more.

CHAPTER TWELVE

The two letters and the telegram arrived at the same time.

Marianne was late coming down to breakfast and so wasn't at her usual post to intercept the mail. She had woken at dawn and the draw of yet another amazingly warm, enticing August morning had been irresistible. Pegasus had been as eager for the early ride as she had, and as she drank in the peace of the moor, it seemed incongruous that not far on the opposite side of the Channel, a vicious battle had been raging for weeks in an extensive area near a river called the Somme.

On her return from the ride, Marianne had gone upstairs to change ready to go straight to the moss collection centre after breakfast. But when she came down, the post boy was waiting by the open front door, and she knew immediately that something was wrong. The dining-room door was also ajar and Marianne hurried into the room, her stomach screwing into a sickening knot. Having placed the little silver tray on the table next to her master, Patsy had stood back, a stricken expression on her face. Marianne's glance swivelled to Seth who was opening a telegram, his jaw set like Dartmoor granite, and then she met her mother's fear-filled gaze. Oh, God. Please no. But her father's audible gulp confirmed their ultimate terror. He lifted his shocked, misted eyes and looked at his wife. Didn't speak a word. Didn't need to. They all knew.

Time fractured. Marianne's confused mind felt she was staring at a human tableau. No one moved. It could have been for seconds or hours. And when her mother finally rose up like some silent effigy and Seth moved wordlessly to fold her in his arms, he seemed to float. They clung to each other, desperate. As they faltered past her towards the door, Marianne knew their hearts were broken, for so was hers, bleeding and dying. Patsy followed them out of the door a moment later, sniffing loudly as she went to tell the post boy there would be no reply, leaving Marianne alone in the room that had so often rung with fun and laughter.

It seemed unreal, like a nightmare. She *wanted* it to be unreal, a horrible dream from which she would soon wake. Her hand moved of its own will towards the scrap of paper that held the key to her family's future. Would it crumble to dust as her eyes opened from sleep? But no. It was real enough, despite her demented pleas. The paper wasn't pure white but a mottled fawn colour, which seemed disrespectful somehow. The letters wavered like seaweed beneath the water, and Marianne had to force her eyes to focus on them, for until she read the words for herself, she would not believe them.

REGRET TO HAVE TO INFORM YOU LT H WARRINGTON OF THE 15TH THE KINGS HUSSARS KILLED IN ACTION FRANCE AUGUST 6TH

Marianne lowered herself slowly onto a chair, her vision locked, unseeing, on the telegram which still trembled in her hands. Her brother, her kind, gentle brother was dead. Blown to pieces, perhaps riddled with bullets. She prayed it had been quick, that he hadn't suffered and that it hadn't been from that dreadful gas the Germans had been using that caused men to vomit and choke on liquid that oozed from inside their own burning lungs. Suddenly the horrific vision her mind had conjured up brought reality rushing down on her, and she buried her face in her hands as the tears began to flow, unchecked, down her cheeks.

How long she sat there, she didn't know. The grand house was silent, like a mausoleum. Her parents were in another room, perhaps upstairs, distraught as she was, grieving for their only son. Never to hear his quiet, thoughtful voice, see that slow, amused grin as he good-naturedly received the butt of both his sisters' teasing. Never again.

She ran out of tears at last and sat, immobile and dry as a rock. Oh, Hal. Why hadn't she tried harder to dissuade him from enlisting? But he would doubtless have been called up by now, and it could have happened in a different way at a different time and place. But at least he had died working with horses, his passion, which might not have been possible if he had waited for conscription to catch up with him. Fate. Call it what you will. She didn't feel guilty if the truth be told. Just drowning in a bottomless void.

She had dropped the telegram on the table among the silver cutlery glinting in the morning sun that streamed through the French doors. Normally, the familiar, reassuring sight would have heralded a happy summer's day. But not now.

As she moved her head, the sunlight caught on the silver tray on which Patsy had carried in the tragic news. Two other envelopes lay there, insignificant after the telegram. Marianne picked one up, mechanically and without thought. And her heart exploded agonizingly so that her hand went across her chest. It was a letter from Hal.

Oh, Lord.

Should she open it? It was addressed to her

parents, after all. But somehow propriety didn't come into her numbed brain just now. If Hal had written them a letter, the telegram must be a mistake. Among all the chaos of the battlefield, the confusion must be immense. Marianne's heart crashed against her ribcage, driven by a surge of reckless hope as she tore open the envelope.

As always, the red shield of the Soldiers' Christian Association at the head of the page, and Hal had filled in the tiny red square with his name, rank and regiment. And, of course, just 'France'. Yes, it was definitely him. His handwriting. So he was alive, after all!

And then she read the date. 1st August. She grabbed the telegram. Perhaps ... August 6th. Her eyes moved desperately from one to the other, and then came to rest as her world splintered into a million shards. Of course. A telegram would be almost immediate whereas letters from the Front took four or five days to reach their destination.

Oh. Nothing left, then. No hope. It was true. Dear Hal had gone, buried in the sepulchre of war. This was likely his last letter home.

Should she read it? But some unidentifiable compulsion drove her to do so, she couldn't say what. Would it bring her comfort, or gouge deeper into the already gaping wound? But perhaps it would make her accept the truth, and so she dragged her gaze down to the familiar handwriting.

Dear All

I hope this finds you well, as I am. I'm sure news of our big offensive in the area of the Somme has been widely reported back in Blighty but if I write anything I shouldn't, the censor people will blank it out. Suffice to say, there have been countless attacks and counter-attacks, and we're still waiting to ride our horses through that elusive Gap in the German defences. We remain in hope that the cavalry will have its longed-for opportunity, but we are, at present, being kept two hours' march from the Front. However, we are constantly providing work parties in various capacities just behind the trenches and we can be under shell-fire then. But it makes me feel I am making some contribution to the fight. Our casualties from these work parties are negligible and when we finally ride through the Gap, it will be in victory so you mustn't worry about me at all. Meanwhile, we keep our horses in tip-top condition which gives me great pleasure and reminds me of home. I think of you all constantly and dream of our beautiful Dartmoor. God willing, that breakthrough will come soon and I will be back with you before winter comes round again. Look after yourselves and I will write again soon. With all my love, Your loving son and brother, Hal.

Write again soon? He wouldn't, would he? Marianne stroked the paper, one of the last things Hal had touched, and the tearing pain raked her throat again. But she mustn't allow herself to renew her tears. Reality must be faced, life got on with. The moss collection centre must be opened, and her mother clearly wasn't in any fit state to do so. It was vital work, was helping to save lives even if it was too late for Hal.

She was about to get resignedly to her feet when she noticed the other envelope was typewritten and addressed to her. She frowned. Who could be writing to her in an official capacity? And then her pulse accelerated as the fog of shock cleared from her brain. Of course. What she had been waiting for. A reply from the FANY.

This time, she opened the envelope carefully. She was right. The letter stated that strictly speaking, an applicant needed to be recommended by an existing member. However, from what she had told them about herself, she sounded more than suitable and so was invited to London for interview the week after next.

Oh. She could really do without this just now. She would have to write back and ask them to postpone it. Surely they would understand? She had just lost her brother. But on the other hand, it would help her to cope with her grief, throwing herself into helping to save lives so that others might not receive the same devastating news they just had. Resolve strengthened inside her before she slipped the letter back in its envelope. Yes, she would go. Hal was dead, and for his sake, she must.

But, dear Lord, how could she tell her parents she wanted to serve in the very place where her brother had just lost his life?

'I'm going to London next week,' she announced a few days later, 'to see Mary Franfield.'

She cringed at the lie – or rather the half-truth as she was indeed going to meet up with her dear friend while she was in the capital. But it seemed unfair to inform her parents of her plans when they were still so raw from the dreadful news about Hal. And after all, she didn't know that she would actually be accepted into the First Aid Nursing Yeomanry anyway, so there was no point putting them through that distress until it was confirmed.

Her mother looked up from aimlessly turning over the food on her plate with a fork, and met her with a wan smile. 'That'll be nice for you. She's proved a good friend, hasn't she? I'm so pleased. I know how I valued dear Molly's friendship for all those years.'

'You don't mind me going, then?' Marianne's relief at Rose's attitude was nonetheless tempered with guilt at her deceit.

'It'll be good for you,' her father agreed. 'But will you be all right travelling and staying at the house all alone? Do you need myself or your mother to come with you? You've never been to London on your own before.'

'Mary does the journey on her own and she's years younger than I am,' Marianne replied hastily. 'I'm sure I can look after myself.'

'You be careful, then. They say the trains are full of soldiers these days.'

'I'll be careful, I promise.'

'And when you get back, we'll start planning a memorial service for Hal.' Seth cleared his throat, glancing at his wife who gave a silent nod of approval as if they had been sharing a secret. 'This came this morning,' he said gravely, drawing a letter from his breast pocket. 'It's from Major Thorneycroft, Hal's commanding officer. You remember him?'

All at once, a shiver of excitement tingled through Marianne's veins and she instantly recalled those steady grey-blue eyes and his wistful smile. 'But of course,' she nodded. 'And Hal ... mentioned him in one of his letters recently.'

'Yes, he did. But as Hal's CO, it was his duty to write to us. Only, as he knows us slightly, it's a little more personal than you'd expect. You might like to read it in private.'

'Oh. Yes. Thank you,' Marianne faltered, not quite sure how she felt as she took the letter from her father's hand. Her guilt over deceiving her parents appeared to double at the happy surprise of hearing from Albert Thorneycroft, especially since it was only as a result of Hal's death. But surely it wasn't wrong to feel joy that someone who had briefly touched her heart had survived the battlefield for two more years? Nevertheless, she was all at odds with herself, her stomach fluttering with butterflies, as she went outside to sit on one of the benches on the terrace.

The letter was slightly crumpled, the ink smudged here and there, which was hardly surprising. The major's handwriting wasn't the neatest, either, but Marianne rejoiced that he was still alive and that Hal had spent his last days in Albert's company. But her heart tripped nervously as she wondered what she would discover in the letter, and she had to steel herself to unfold it and start to read.

Dear Mr and Mrs Warrington, Miss Marianne and family

You will by now have received the terrible news of your son's demise, and it is my duty to write to you as his Commanding Officer. It is doubly difficult for me to do so as I know you personally and will never forget your kindness and hospitality when I stayed with you for those few days what now seems a lifetime ago. It grieves me particularly deeply also to have to tell you that your son was the only officer our regiment has lost during the current offensive, since we have yet to be ordered into the expected cavalry charge. We were, however, waiting two hours' ride behind the lines when we received the order to provide a work party to return to the trenches for the sad task of burying the dead of whom hundreds had been recovered while thousands more lay out in the battlefield. Your son, with whom I became well acquainted during his time in the regiment, volunteered to lead the party and, quite simply, he was caught by a stray enemy shell and killed outright. So, although he was not engaged in any particular act of heroism in action, he gave his life giving dignity to some of those who had gone before him.

Lt Warrington was very popular among both his fellow officers and his men. Although he scarcely had the chance to show his valour on the field, he always had a good, calm head and I know would have followed any order bravely and courageously. His devotion to the horses was second to none, and he was always willing to help those whose equestrian skills were not quite up to his own. He learnt those skills, he always said, from you, his parents, and was as proud of you as I am sure you are of him. He always spoke with outstanding affection, also, for his madcap sister as he referred to you, Miss Marianne, as well as

for his married sister. I know there is nothing that can ease the pain of your bereavement, but rest assured that Lt Warrington was held in high regard by all who knew him. Please accept my most sincere sympathy for your loss.
   Your faithful servant
   Major Albert Thorneycroft

Marianne lowered the letter onto her lap, scarcely able to read the signature as her vision blurred with tears. Dear Hal. The major's thoughtful, caring words had torn open the chasm of her sorrow before it had barely had the chance to start closing, and yet she thanked him for it. There would never be an end to her grief until her soul had been scoured dry, and as she stared sightlessly out over the garden and the moor beyond, she somehow drew comfort from those rolling granite hills. For no matter what madness man made of the world, Dartmoor would always be there, cradling the souls of all those who had loved its magnificent, savage wilderness.

A few weeks later, Marianne broke the news to her parents over dinner, her pulse thundering as she did so for she knew how hard it was going to be for them. But Hal's death had made her even more determined since she felt she was doing it for him. The memorial service had been and gone, and somehow this was the next step for her to be able to come to terms with her grief.

When she had finished speaking, she gazed at her parents in silent anticipation. Oh, God, what would they say? Her mother's face had blanched, making her eyes appear to deepen to sable, while Seth stared at her, immobile.

When no one spoke for what seemed like an eternity, Marianne felt the colour flood into her cheeks. 'I know ... you might not want me to go. Not after Hal...' she stammered in a broken whisper. 'And ... I suppose I could still back out. But I originally applied long before all that. And I really want to go. For Hal's sake even more now. And they don't let the FANY anywhere near the lines. Not any more, anyway. Most of the work's ferrying the wounded from the trains to the hospitals, and then from the hospitals to the quayside when they're fit enough to be shipped home. So I won't be in any danger.'

She waited, trembling, until her father finally rose to his feet and came round to her. 'I'm so proud of you,' he said quietly.

Marianne felt his beloved hand squeeze her shoulder and she rubbed her cheek against it. 'Mum?' she dared to breathe, and watched as Rose lifted her eyes and the shadow of a smile hovered over her mouth.

'I know you must go. I've been expecting it. If I'd been your age again, I'd have done exactly the same.'

'Y-you don't mind, then?'

'Of course I mind. But sometimes in life there are things you have to do. And for you, this is one of them.'

Marianne's eyes pooled with tears and, just for a moment, she almost felt she might change her mind. 'Thank you,' she murmured. 'Thank you both for understanding.'

'When do you go?' Seth asked, and Marianne was distracted as Rose stood up and stepped out through the open French doors onto the terrace.

'Oh, I have to do two mechanics' courses and several First Aid ones in London yet,' she answered, bringing her attention back to her father. 'I have to pay for those and my uniform, but I've been saving up my allowance. But ... let me go and talk to Mum now.'

Seth nodded and stood back as Marianne followed Rose outside. Marianne was so like her mother, and he sensed they needed to be alone together.

It was a beautiful, balmy summer's night, utterly still, and Rose smiled at her daughter as she came to lean on the stone parapet beside her. The sky was a dome of indigo velvet scattered with a million twinkling stars, and below it, the folds of the moor were liquid silver in the light of a full moon.

'Breathtaking, isn't it?' Rose murmured. 'I've always loved this house, you know, and the view over the moor from here. It'll be yours and Kate's to share one day, you know.'

Marianne nodded, not wanting to think of the time when her parents would inevitably join Hal wherever he had gone. 'You don't get many evenings like this,' she muttered instead. 'Just look at that old moon up there. I wonder what he's thinking about the mess our world is in just now.'

'I was just wondering the self same thing.' Rose's voice, too, was low, almost reverent, as she spoke. 'I think he's looking down on the earth and crying. You can see his teardrops so clearly tonight. Tears for Hal and all the other thousands of dead.'

Yes. Marianne's gaze joined her mother's. As a child, she had liked to make out the face of the Man in the Moon, to pick out his features, the curve of his eyes, the nose and mouth. And tonight her mother was right. The moon was definitely crying.

She linked her arm through Rose's. 'It can't go on forever, you know. It must end some day.'

She heard her mother give a wistful sigh. 'I hope so, my dearest child. And you must take care out there.'

'Yes, I promise. If you promise to take care of Pegasus for me.'

'Of course we will.'

Marianne returned her mother's fathomless smile and together they turned back to contemplate the moon.

CHAPTER THIRTEEN

'Climb aboard then, chaps,' the giant of a woman invited them cheerily. 'Been cleaned out this morning, of course. First duty of the day, and we wouldn't want to throw you in at the deep end with a dirty ambulance, would we, what? Hear you had a damned filthy crossing. If any of you think you still might be sick, you'll find kidney bowls in the back. Pile in, then.'

She held open the back of the ambulance with a confident, welcoming grin. Since her companions appeared to hesitate, Marianne took the initiative and dived under the woman's arm. If it hadn't been for the fact that she was in FANY uniform and, close up, her skin was smooth and hairless, Marianne felt anyone could be forgiven for thinking it was a man. She must have been six foot tall with shoulders to match and a deep, masculine voice.

Inside the ambulance, they were plunged into gloom. Marianne shuffled along, negotiating the runners, top and bottom on each side, that she knew from her training took the stretchers. The smell of disinfectant was overpowering, and it wasn't so dark that she

187

couldn't make out the stains on the floor. Blood and God knew what else, she realized with a gulp. But this was what she'd come for. What the months of training had been about.

'Righto, everyone?' the big woman boomed, although Marianne couldn't imagine anyone daring to reply in the negative. 'I'm Captain Lansdowne, by the way. But everyone calls me Tanky. Built like one, don't you know. God knows what Pater would think of such a nickname. Baronet, you see. Doesn't hold with my being out here, but good old Mac persuaded him otherwise. Anyway, hang onto your hats. The old Sizzley-Beastey's a devil to drive. Has a revolving gearbox. Any of you come across one of those before? Haven't got to go far, mind. Might just take a minute to start her up.' With that, she disappeared and Marianne had to peer into the gloom to make out the shapes of her fellow troopers.

'Heavens, she's a one.' Marianne recognized the voice of Phyllis Harcourt from the opposite side.

'Bet you can rely on her in a crisis, though,' Marianne commented. 'Steady as a rock, I should think.'

'Does that make her Lady Lansdowne, do you think?' Lucy Ainsworth asked in total awe.

'Get used to it, Lucy,' Phyllis chastized her mildly. 'A lot of the FANY are from the aristocracy.' And then, 'Oh, Lordy Love, can anyone find one of those bowls? I think I'm going to be sick again. I never want to go on another ship in my life.'

'You still look green. At least you did when I could still see you. Here.' Just in time, Marianne shoved a bowl under Phyllis's chin. 'You'll have to, to get home,' she sympathized. 'Go on a ship, I mean. I think I was too scared of being torpedoed by a U-boat to feel sick. I think I could face anything but drowning.'

'It was a pretty rough crossing, though.'

'Well, it *is* December. And we're here now.'

'Thank God.'

'It doesn't make her Lady Lansdowne,' a small, hesitant voice managed to get a word in edgeways. 'But, actually, *I*'m a lady.'

'What, *you*, Stella?'

'All these weeks training together and you never said?'

'I didn't want you to think I was toffee-nosed or anything.'

'But you're the kindest, gentlest thing I've ever come across. We all think so, don't we? Oh, whoops!'

They had all heard the familiar clanking of the engine being cranked and once it burst into life, Tanky had obviously clambered into the driving seat. The vehicle lurched forward, ceasing all conversation. As her eyes adjusted to the dim light, Marianne looked about her.

Like many of the FANY ambulances, it had been converted from a normal motorcar, probably donated by some wealthy patron back in Blighty. The seats had been removed and replaced with the fittings for the stretchers with a wooden box for the driver. As was common practice, Marianne had noticed that the windscreen had also been removed to avoid reflecting light and attracting enemy fire in a raid and so that there couldn't be any broken glass to injure the driver.

'When she said Mac, do you think she meant Grace McDougall, our founder?' Ursula, the fifth recruit, drew Marianne from her thoughts. 'Do you think we'll meet her?'

'She spends a lot of time campaigning for supplies and Lord knows what else back home, from what I've heard,' Phyllis declared knowledgeably, lifting her head from the bowl.

Before anyone could say more, they hit another pothole and were all thrown whichways, grabbing whatever came to hand, which was mostly each other. They scrambled back into their places laughing, and all the tensions of the journey instantly dissipated.

'Didn't expect the roads to be this bad.'

'All the air raids, I suppose. If we'd known the Germans were going to be bombing Calais so regularly, my parents might have tried to stop me joining up. I'd have come anyway, but it was good to know I had their blessing.'

A vision flashed across Marianne's brain of her parents standing on the terrace with the tranquillity of Dartmoor spread out behind them. For a second or two, she was swamped with intense longing to be back with them in her peaceful home, so different from the bustling quayside, heaving with soldiers, vehicles and supplies, where they had just disembarked.

'Looks like we're here,' Phyllis announced as the car came to a halt and the engine stopped. 'Hopefully I'll stop being sick now.'

'Wasn't far now, was it, chaps?' Tanky's head appeared once more. 'Like to meet any new troopers off the ship if we can. I know you've had street maps to study and you'd have found your own way, but plans look different in reality. Suggest you take a few days wandering about so you know the place backwards. If you get caught in a raid, you might not be able to take your normal route and have to find an alternative, what.'

As the last one off, Marianne hadn't heard Tanky clearly but had caught the gist of her words well enough. She was used to wide, open spaces where the greatest challenge was finding the way in a swirling, disorientating mist, and she was aware of nerves fluttering in her stomach at the thought of being lost in a maze of streets. But she supposed she would soon find her bearings. To her relief, as she climbed down from the ambulance, she discovered they were parked by a huge expanse of sandy beach which seemed to stretch for miles. The sea they had just crossed had been whipped up into banks of rollers driving onto the shore, and the bracing wind stung into Marianne's nostrils with the distinctive tang of salt water and seaweed.

'Welcome to Unit Three's sumptuous quarters!' Tanky bellowed. 'Just had tents among the sand dunes when we first came here back in January but Mac got us these huts delivered in the spring. Mind you, they've already warped and are almost as draughty as the tents were, but they're sending us asbestos sheets to line the cubicles, which should help. But come inside. We've put you all together and once you've settled, come over to the mess hut. That's that one over there.'

The five recruits followed Tanky inside the large wooden hut, taking in their surroundings in silence. Marianne's heart sank. She expected the accommodation to be basic, but this was hardly even that. The conscientious objectors who were now incarcerated in Dartmoor Prison surely fared better than this! They were each allocated a tiny cubicle coming off a central passage with a communal bathroom at one end, the whole inside painted what Marianne imagined was supposed to be a cheery bright green. They had been warned to bring very little with them, and she could see why. There was room for an army-issue bed and some shelving, but little else.

Marianne lowered herself onto the bed and had to take a strong hold on herself to keep back her tears. Oh, Lord. She knew she was shaking, but was that from nerves or the arctic cold? She had to force herself to remember that she was there to help wounded soldiers, soldiers who often had to sleep in the trenches wherever they could, knowing they could be blown up or gassed as they slept. There was a continuous rotation system so that no man spent too long in a front-line trench before being pulled back to recover, but even then, they mainly only slept in barns or tents or whatever makeshift accommodation could be found. Marianne knew she flushed with shame and jumped up to unpack. Her few toiletries, the photograph of her family, a few books and her spare underclothes and uniform she put on the shelves. The rest remained in the small case, which she pushed under the bed.

'Everyone ready?' she heard Phyllis's voice from the corridor.

As ready as I'll ever be, Marianne replied in her head. As she went outside, she glanced at Hal's face in the photograph, and felt a determined strength flow back into her. She was doing this for him, but also for herself, and she mustn't lose courage now she was here.

'Hardly the Ritz, is it?' Lucy grimaced.

'Look, though,' Marianne said in sudden surprise, pointing to the open door of another cubicle. 'That one's been made really cosy. Bedside table made out of an old box with a lace doily on it and pictures on the walls.'

'And a nice warm quilt on the bed,' Ursula observed. 'Staying warm's not going to be easy.'

'We'll be given sleeping bags, won't we? But a thick quilt like that on top looks a good idea.'

'Come along, chaps.' Stella astounded them with a perfect imitation of Tanky. 'Let's find the mess hut, what ho.'

They all fell about laughing, a happy release from the qualms each of them was feeling, and Phyllis clapped Stella on the shoulder.

'That was brilliant! You're a dark horse and no mistake.'

'Well, we've got to make the most of it,' Stella replied in her normal quiet voice. 'We're here to do a job, not have a holiday.'

'Hear! Hear!' Marianne beamed back. Although she liked everyone in the group, she had felt an instant affection for young Stella in particular when they had all first met.

Tanky was waiting for them in the mess hut, handing out mugs of steaming tea and bacon butties. The newcomers were so cold and hungry, they agreed it was the best meal they'd ever consumed!

'Have a ciggie to warm you up, too,' Tanky offered, handing round a packet of cigarettes.

'B-but I don't smoke,' Stella answered warily.

'Helps the old nerves, too, don't you know,' Tanky advised, fixing her own cigarette into a long holder like the one Marianne had seen in the one and only silent film she had ever watched. 'Have a go, if I were you. Soon get used to it.'

Gingerly, Marianne accepted one, too. She had barely taken a breath on it before it made her cough and she felt dizzy. It evidently showed as Phyllis, who she had seen have the occasional cigarette before, said quickly, 'Don't breathe it in deeply. Just puff on it gently until you're used to it.'

Marianne blinked as her head cleared again. Well, she didn't think *she* would ever get used to it, and it left a disgusting taste in her mouth. But then she saw Stella and Lucy both taking their first tentative puff, and felt she should persevere for a while at least. If, as Tanky suggested, it helped warm you up, it would be worth it. She already felt colder than she ever had in her life, even when they were snowed in by ten-foot drifts on Dartmoor. She could understand why many of the other girls who had wandered into the mess were wearing fur coats over their uniforms rather than the long, navy coats with their smart red piping that were the regulation uniform.

'Expect you already know,' Tanky boomed at them, 'but I'll just run through the few rules we have. Anything you're unsure of, just ask. We're a jolly friendly lot, I'd say, and you'll soon settle in. Now, no smoking in public and you must always wear your uniform. I know it's not very flattering, and that wearing a collar and tie and puttees round your legs might feel odd at first, but it's practical and it reminds the British Army that we're a fighting force. You must all know that only the Belgians would accept our help at first, and Mac fought tooth and nail to prove to the British that they needed us. It was only this January they finally agreed to let the FANY work for them, and now they couldn't do without us. Not that the old stuffed shirts would admit it, but *we* know, don't we, girls?' she grinned, addressing everyone else present in the hut, and she was met by a cheery chorus that made the new recruits feel warmly welcomed.

'Just one more thing,' Tanky nodded more seriously now. 'We're in a civilian town and you can make the most of that. But you're not allowed to consort with any soldier, only officers, and even then never without a chaperone, except for having lunch in a public place. And you must always have permission from a senior FANY officer.'

'Lore, can't we have *any* fun?' Phyllis groaned.

'Good heavens, yes. We're lucky, really. The VADs aren't allowed to fraternize with the opposite sex *at all*. One poor girl wasn't even permitted to go for a walk with her father who's a *general!* But *we* can!' Tanky tipped her head and gave a cheeky wink.

'That sounds more promising.' Lucy, who had surprised them all by having a string of admirers during their training, looked distinctly relieved, Marianne thought. As for herself, it would be nice to have some diversion from the horrors they would undoubtedly witness, but she wasn't fussed about the opposite sex. On both occasions she'd had feelings in that direction, she had suffered – and she had no intention of being hurt ever again.

'Oh, yes, we have some spiffing times, you know,' Tanky went on with an unexpected twinkle in her eye. 'We're always invited to the shows the troops put on. We sit in the front with the officers, of course, and more than one of us has found a husband that way. That's how Mac met hers. She was Ashley-Smith before she married.'

'Hope for us all yet, then,' Phyllis commented drily.

'You never know,' Tanky replied, flushing such a deep crimson that Marianne felt convinced the gigantic woman must have enjoyed some sort of amorous relationship through the said concerts. 'By the way, we're having a fancy dress party at Christmas, so put your thinking caps on. You need to be pretty resourceful, but it's all good fun. And if any of you have any talent – well, even if you don't – join the *Fantastiks* anyway. We put on the most diabolically unrehearsed concerts, but they're an absolute hoot!'

'Stella has a talent for impersonating people.'

'Oh, I don't know about that!' Marianne could see that Stella looked horrified.

'That would be top hole. Just the sort of thing people love! But to more serious matters. Your fleabags are in that box over there. That's sleeping bags. The other box has tin helmets in it. Always have yours with you. Take your caps off and go and pick one out that fits.'

Each trooper dutifully obeyed, removing her soft beret with the FANY emblem, the Maltese Cross inside a circle, on the band. That morning, Marianne had tamed her rebellious tresses into a bun at the nape of her neck, but now she could feel it working loose.

'Trooper Warrington,' she realized Tanky

was speaking in a quiet voice for once as she drew her aside. 'I see you're the only one not to have cut your hair short, but I strongly advise you to do so. Long hair can be dangerous and believe me, we don't have the time or the facilities to look after it. I'll introduce you to Lieutenant Grainger. She does all our hair. Come along, let's strike while the iron's hot.'

Marianne took a trembling gulp. She had hoped to retain a vestige of her femininity and her tumbling locks were very much a part of that. But she supposed that she would soon become used to it, and she could always grow her hair long again after the war.

A few minutes later, she was sitting at one of the mess tables, silently gritting her teeth against her tears as Lieutenant Grainger, a very pleasant young woman, denuded her of her crowning glory.

'Do you fancy a bob or would you like it more shaped to your head?' she was asking. 'You've such lovely hair, it'll look superb either way.'

'I-I think a bob,' Marianne faltered. 'It'll be less of a shock.'

'Don't worry. We've all been through it, those of us who didn't want to embrace the new fashion. There. Take a look. You're truly one of us now.'

The girl produced a mirror and Marianne's heart leapt nervously into her mouth. She stared back at the unfamiliar reflection, feeling for her riotous tresses that now ended half-way down her swan-like neck. But the FANY hairdresser had cut a fringe and shaped Marianne's curls around her ears, to keep them out of her eyes, she had said, but it gave a softer effect which wasn't altogether displeasing

'Oh, thank you,' Marianne muttered, pleasantly surprised.

'Not at all. If you want to try something different, just let me know. It's all on the house.'

'We all felt odd at first.' Another girl gave a friendly smile. 'Mine could do with a trim if you wouldn't mind, Sylvie.'

'Sorry, no time for that!' a voice called out. 'Message just come through. Couple of hospital barges coming along the canal.'

'You new troopers might as well pile in, too,' Tanky announced. 'See what it's all about. The worst cases come by barge. Less painful than being jostled about on a hospital train.'

Within seconds, Marianne and her four comrades were swept up in the avalanche of urgency as FANY Unit Three catapulted into action. They found themselves outside again in the bitter, dying winter's day, icy air biting into their faces as engines were cranked up and spluttered into life. Marianne's shorn hair was instantly forgotten as her new life began.

CHAPTER FOURTEEN

The soldier was staring up at her, his eyes boring into hers. Boring through her and beyond. The hastily applied bandage, heavy with congealed blood and other matter, had slipped from his head, revealing an open chasm from which something grey and unidentifiable had been oozing. Marianne answered his stare, helpless and overwhelmed.

'No good.' The haggard young medical officer shook his head and slung the stethoscope back around his neck. He pulled the filthy blanket over the mutilated head and moved on, leaving Marianne stunned with horror. There were people everywhere, orderlies carrying stretcher after stretcher from the barges that rocked on the black, icy water, army nurses and doctors, and the whole of FANY Unit Three scurrying about the canal-side, guiding stretcher poles onto the runners in the back of the ambulances and then struggling to negotiate the vehicles back up the steep, slippery slope to the road.

'You there, FANY girl, stop dithering and hold this poor blighter's guts in while I redo the bandage.'

Marianne's brain clicked back into action.

The other doctor meant her, didn't he? Everyone else was occupied, and he wasn't to know she had only just got off the ship for her first tour of duty and had never witnessed anything like this before. With every nerve stretched, she placed her hands over the thick, stained gauze, feeling the soft springiness beneath her touch, her own stomach sickened beyond belief.

'Don't worry. He's up to his eyeballs in morphine. There. All done. Thanks, private.'

He turned away, obviously bone-weary, to the next mangled body. And the next.

Marianne stood, floundering in a quagmire of confusion and pain at the sea of broken bodies which only days before would have been strong, vibrant men. Her mind whirled in circles. People were calling to each other, the rumble of the car engines rose in a drowning cacophony and the cries and screams of the wounded swirled inside her head, ringing in her ears, ringing, ringing...

Marianne dragged herself from sleep and reached out to turn off the alarm clock. She paused for just a second to rub her hand over her face. At least she had been rescued from her nightmare. Except that it hadn't been a nightmare; her mind had been reliving the trip to the canal-side on her very first day, a sight she had witnessed over and over again in the two months she had been in Calais.

'Come on, sleepy head,' Stella chastized her, rubbing the sleep from her own eyes as she put her head around the cubicle door. 'Once more unto the breach!' she declared, theatrically raising her arm as if brandishing an imaginary sword.

Marianne chuckled as she pulled herself from her sleeping bag, fully clothed but for her boots and the thick fur coat she had purchased like many of the other FANY. It was said to be the coldest winter on record, and it certainly felt like it as the small troop who were on night duty traipsed out into the darkness yet again, trying not to slide on the frozen snow.

'Every bally hour,' Phyllis complained as they crunched along, the intense arctic air blasting against their cheeks. 'Lucky Luce and the Bear are all tucked up–'

'Their turn next week,' Marianne reminded her curtly, since she didn't exactly relish the duty herself. 'We'll soon warm up.'

It was a slight exaggeration to say the least, for it seemed that each time they ventured out, everyone risked frostbite. But cranking up each engine in the fleet and running it for a few minutes to stop it freezing solid certainly lessened the cold. The temperature was so low that anti-freeze was useless, as was draining the radiator and carburettor. The girls' brains also seemed to freeze up, and they had to remind each other to be careful when winding the crank-handles and remember to jump clear when the engine caught, to avoid any backfire that could easily break a limb.

When every engine had been dealt with, the group slithered back toward the huts, managing to raise a laugh or two despite the desperate cold. Marianne hung back for a moment, since although chilled to the marrow, there was a certain magic about being out in the dead of night. There was no air-raid and, bar the fading voices of her comrades as they went inside for an hour's rest before the next round, the quiet was thick and heavy. It reminded Marianne of home when frost encrusted Dartmoor in a crisp blanket of white and she liked to stand outside alone for a few minutes. She glanced up now at the clouds scudding across the moon, and thought of it glistening down on her distant home. And it wasn't just the cutting wind that made her eyes water.

Somewhere deep in her mind, she knew she was stiff with cold, but there wasn't room for it to register. This was her fifth trip down to the station, foot down on the accelerator, peering into the ink-dark, black-iced streets by the glimmer from the small, oil sidelights. Stella was hunched beside her, the small canvas roof above giving them little protection against the piercing sleet that drove into their faces like needles, victorious since there was no windscreen to halt it.

The whole unit had been woken. A message had come through that a hospital train with over four hundred wounded was approaching Calais.

'Bet it has to stop down the line for troops going *to* the Front,' Phyllis grumbled, 'and we'll be kept waiting for hours in the cold. Again,' she concluded pointedly.

'I don't suppose the poor devils on board will appreciate any delays, either,' Marianne retorted.

'At least they're inside. But no, you're right. It's just that I've actually forgotten what it's like to be warm.'

'You'll probably complain it's too hot in the summer,' Marianne said with grim humour as she went off with Stella to crank the engine of the converted Napier which had been assigned to them. It was almost unrecognizable from Hal's, but at least Marianne felt more at home driving it than some of the other vehicles in the fleet.

They had indeed been obliged to wait for the train, although not as long as sometimes. When it finally chugged in at the platform, it was spilling over with wounded. The walking were evacuated first, to be driven either to the main British Army hospital in the casino or other hospitals about the town, while others were to be taken direct to the docks. Marianne's stomach cramped with nerves as she was given a human cargo destined for immediate shipping home. The quayside was dangerously narrow and with no room to turn round, had to be negotiated in reverse on the return journey. But with Stella outside yelling instructions at her in the pitch black, she had managed to go backwards up the icy slope without ending up in the water.

Relief overtook her when, on their second return to the station, the walking wounded had all been transported and the FANY were ferrying the stretcher cases to hospital. All they had to cope with now were aching backs, arms and shoulders as they backed the heavy vehicles up to the carriages, helped load on the stretchers and then drive as smoothly as possible through the dark, pot-holed, ice-covered streets. Again and again. For hours. Until the last soldier was safely in hospital.

Their utter exhaustion was however, always tempered with a certain excitement and sense of adventure. If it hadn't been for the fact that they were conveying seriously wounded men and that there was always the danger of skidding on the ice and having an accident, it would have felt like fun. Tonight there was thankfully no air-raid and no enemy planes flying overhead although, as ever, the silvery beams from the searchlights constantly scanned the sable sweep of the sky, making the barrage balloons glow eerily like giant, floating ghosts.

'At least it's quiet tonight,' Stella observed optimistically as they bumped along the road despite Marianne's efforts to pick out and avoid the potholes in the darkened streets.

'Don't speak too soon,' Marianne answered. 'It seems dark down here but the sky's lighter and there's no wind. Perfect for a raid. Do you want to drive on the way back, by the way?'

'I don't mind. You know I prefer being in the back with the patients, but I'll take over if you like.'

'Thanks, Stell. My arm's killing from this wretched stiff gearbox. If I can just give it a short rest, we can swap back again.'

Marianne knew that Stella was more of a natural at nursing, while she herself had more confidence as a driver. They worked well as a team, not just on the ambulance runs but with all the other fatigues they had to do: chopping and carrying wood for the boiler, generally keeping the camp clean, taking their turn in the corrugated iron shed that was the cookhouse with its temperamental primus stove, and of course the mechanical care of the ambulance itself.

'I can't wait for the better weather to

come,' Stella renewed the conversation.

'They say the fighting will get even worse again then, though, as if these operations along the Ancre haven't produced enough cas–'

She didn't have the chance to finish her words before a deafening whir shot over their heads and the next instant a blinding flash pierced the darkness before them. A roaring crash shattered the calm of the night and a horrible bang split their ears as the ambulance shook so violently that there was nothing Marianne could do to stop it slewing sideways. Both girls were thrown forward as it came to an abrupt halt, Marianne bracing herself on the steering-wheel and hearing Stella cry out as her tin hat was knocked off and her head slammed into the dashboard.

'Crikey, Stell, are you all right?' Marianne called out as Stella fell back with her hands over her forehead.

'I ... think so,' Stella managed to gasp, stifling a squeal of pain. 'You?'

'Jarred my arm a bit, but–'

'W-what h-happened?'

Stella's voice sounded weak and dazed, but before Marianne could say or do anything, another explosion ripped through the night, making the ground shake. Both girls instinctively ducked, and Marianne was shot through with fear as she realized Stella was reeling on the seat, clearly far from all right. They had driven through air-raids before, but had never come so close to disaster. It was far from over as bombs began raining down on the town, but – Marianne thanked God – not quite so close.

'Air-raid,' she answered simply since she was so shocked herself she could barely speak. 'I think we've been hit.'

'But there were no planes,' Stella mumbled through her hands which still covered her face.

'No.' Though her heart was frozen in terror, Marianne stood up and poked her head out from beneath the ambulance canopy. 'It's coming from the sea, I think. Hang on, Stell. I'm just going to check the ambulance and then I'm taking you straight to hospital.'

'No, I'm all right.'

'Let me be the judge of that. Two seconds now.'

Marianne's knees were trembling as she climbed out, an icy sweat dampening her skin. Groping in the darkness, she found a huge shard of metal, probably from the shell-case, embedded in the side of the ambulance. Good God, they must have been *that* close! A foot or so's difference and the shrapnel would have been embedded in *her!*

Struggling to hold her nerves together, she clambered back on board. The shell had exploded only yards away, blasting a crater in the road that had made it impassable. Marianne slammed the gears into reverse, her heart savage with panic as Stella slumped beside her. She managed to turn the vehicle round, setting off back towards the nearest hospital. As she peered into the shadows, she felt gripped with relief as she spied another ambulance coming towards them. She must warn the driver of the new crater, but also report her change of action.

But, just as she put her foot on the brake, a shower of sparks encompassed the approaching vehicle in a fluid, moving arc almost like a firework display. For a moment, Marianne frowned in confusion, almost mesmerized as she tried to work out what was happening. And then her heart bucked in her chest as she realized that the raid had brought down an electricity cable that was now twisting and writhing through the air like some wild, deranged serpent and was coiling itself around the other ambulance.

Dear God! If whoever was inside didn't get out, they'd be electrocuted – if they hadn't already been so! But it would be just as dangerous to get out as the heavy wire leapt and spiralled, hissing and spitting, and there was nothing Marianne could do. Saturated with horror, she put her hands to her head as her brain battled to make a split second decision as to what she should do.

The next instant, she had her answer. The

dark shape of someone in a long coat sprang from the cab and ran for its life towards her. As the cable continued its macabre dance, a flash of flame wrapped itself about the figure which faltered and then staggered forward.

Marianne was suddenly released from her own leaden legs and without further thought, she rushed towards the other FANY driver. The woman collapsed into her arms, scarcely conscious, and Marianne half-dragged her to safety, falling to her knees with her burden onto the frozen ground.

Marianne sat there in the intense cold and dark, her mind fragmented with terror. Here she was, alone in a raid, with two semi-conscious patients, cut off by the crater in one direction and the live cable in the other, so that even if another ambulance came along the same route, it might turn back and not even see them. There was nothing else for it. She would have to abandon her own ambulance and the two injured girls, and set off alone for help.

As quickly as she could, she grabbed pillows and blankets from the back of the vehicle to make Stella and the other driver as comfortable as possible. And then, with a desperate prayer and her pulse battering against her temples, she hurried down the shell-pocked road through the blackness and the falling bombs.

'You're looking much better today,' she told Stella a few days later. Her friend was propped up in a hospital bed, a bruised swelling the size of an egg on her forehead, but with a much better colour in her cheeks and looking altogether more alert. 'The sister said another week and they'll probably discharge you.'

'Poppycock,' Stella protested. 'I'm taking a bed from someone who really needs it.'

'No, you're not. You were seriously concussed and you have as much right to be in a civilian hospital as anyone.'

'Well, I'd rather not be here. The sister's a harridan. Thank goodness I speak reasonable French or it would've been even worse. *Mademoiselle, vous avez trôp d'impatience!*' Stella mimicked, and Marianne burst into laughter it was such a good impression of the hard-faced sister.

'Ssh, she'll hear you.'

'Don't care if she does.' Stella's pout softened and a translucent smile glowed in her eyes as she gazed at her friend. 'Thank you for saving me,' she said quietly.

'I didn't really do anything,' Marianne shrugged, suddenly embarrassed. 'We were incredibly lucky. If the shell had been any closer, we could've been killed by the concussion alone. And it wasn't just that one big piece of shrapnel that stuck in the ambulance. The side was pitted all over and the radiator was caved in. It's been replaced, so she's serviceable again now.'

'And what about the other FANY? Is she all right?'

'You'll never believe who it was,' Marianne replied, her eyes stretching wide. 'It was Mac.'

She waited patiently while the surprise registered on Stella's face. 'Mac? You mean Commanding Officer Grace Macdonald, our founder?'

'The very same. I didn't know she was in Calais. She'd borrowed an ambulance for some important business in Boulogne and was driving back. She heard about the hospital train and was on her way to help.'

'Was she hurt?' Stella asked, horrified to learn that her icon had been involved.

'Stunned at the time, but perfectly all right. She was wearing a leather coat and rubber boots which they reckon saved her. She didn't have a single burn and her heart was absolutely fine.'

Stella puffed out her cheeks. 'I think we all had a miraculous escape, then. It hasn't put you off, has it? I wouldn't want to go on without you.'

'Not a bit of it,' Marianne grinned. 'If the old Boche couldn't see us off that night, they never will.' And a warm sense of serenity rippled through her as Stella's mouth spread into a relieved smile.

CHAPTER FIFTEEN

'You coming down to the strand for the races?' Lucy asked. 'Should be fun.'

'I'm hoping I might be able to ride in one or two of them,' Marianne told her excitedly. 'I'm desperate to get on a horse again!'

'So am I,' Phyllis agreed. 'I was thrilled when I heard about it.'

'Jolly dee!' Tanky declared boisterously, catching their conversation as she passed where they were seated at a table in the mess. 'We could do with another couple of riders. All FANY were mounted when we were originally formed years before this ghastly war, but I'm sure you know that. But these races were spiffingly popular last year, so we couldn't wait to start them again. Not that the weather's improved much yet, but it was time we did something.'

'Well, I'm really looking forward to it. I'll bet on you both every time!' Stella announced.

'I wouldn't do that,' Marianne laughed, 'not if you don't want to lose your money.'

'Let's just hope there isn't a raid, or that we don't get a call,' Ursula – the Bear – put in, ever the practical one.

'We'd better all cross our fingers and toes, then! Are we ready?'

The merry group stood up in unison, some swallowing down the last of mugs of weak tea, before joining the general exodus. The winter had been hard. Four thousand cases had been transported by the FANY in February, and they had already exceeded that number for March, even though they were only three quarters of the way through the month. So the races along the beach were eagerly anticipated as a diversion from the strenuous toil and harsh conditions they continued to face.

Down on the sand, there was happy chaos. Marianne was amazed to see what she guessed must be a few hundred people: almost the whole of FANY Unit Three and the newly established Unit Five who were working for the Belgian Army, one or two cavalry officers who by some fluke happened to be in the vicinity with their fine horses, VADs and women from other nursing units, many other army personnel of one sort or another, and many French civilians. Several betting posts had been set up, and a course marked out on the firm, wet sand where the tide had retreated what seemed miles into the Channel.

Marianne made her way with Phyllis to the arena of horses. They were all shapes and sizes since, as in England, so many had been taken away for the war effort. There were numerous ponies, too small to be of much use to the military, and to Marianne's pleasant surprise, a fair number of fine hunters and such. But again, she supposed it was strong, carthorse types the armies needed most, not these more delicate creatures that would be worse than useless in harness up to their hocks or even deeper in mud and slime.

They made themselves known at the table of officials, and both were enlisted to ride in three races. Marianne wasn't needed until the third one, so leaving Phyllis who was in the first, she went back to join their friends. However, the crowds were so dense that she couldn't find them. Not that it mattered. She was enjoying herself immensely. Everyone was in buoyant mood, laughing and joking and calling to each other at the tops of their voices. The atmosphere was charged with excitement and Marianne felt a joyous happiness bubble up inside her. Only for a moment did she find herself wishing it was Pegasus she would be riding, but she refused to let the thought spoil her present pleasure and pushed it to the back of her mind.

She had been allocated a pony for her first race. It was a dear little mare, no more than twelve hands, but with Marianne being so light, it was able to give a good account of itself. It was just so wonderful to be back in the saddle that Marianne's whole body fizzled with delight, and she was flushed with elation when they romped over the finishing line in third place.

'Well done!' She suddenly found herself surrounded by her friends who were jumping up and down with excitement. 'I got my stake back and two francs to boot!'

'That'll make you rich! You can buy me a drink at the *estaminet* tonight.'

'When's your next race?'

'It's the sixth one. I'm riding this lovely girl again,' Marianne explained, stroking the docile animal's hairy neck. 'I'd better take her back now and you can watch Phyllis in the next race.'

Marianne's heart was rocked in contentment as she walked the pretty pony back to the enclosure and put the blanket back on her. Although the wind had dropped, it was overcast and cold, with no hint of spring in the air yet. Marianne wondered if the winter, like the war, would ever come to an end.

They didn't do so well in the next race mainly because they were up against bigger horses, including some French cavalrymen. But Marianne didn't mind. Being among horses again was soothing away the horrors she had been part of over the last few months. What she was looking forward to most was the final race in which she was to ride a beautiful Arab cross. She wondered who owned him, for most of the horses had been cajoled for the afternoon from local civilians.

A sparkle of pleasure twinkled in her heart as she mounted the magnificent beast. Their rivals were all of a similar calibre, and although *Zéphyr* as she was told he was called, wasn't the biggest, she could feel the power of his muscled haunches as they trotted up to the start. Phyllis lined up beside her on a huge liver chestnut which was champing at the bit, eager to be away.

'That one looks like a bit of a handful!'

'Certainly is, but I think I can handle him!' Phyllis grinned back. 'Bet I beat you!'

'Bet you don't!' Marianne bantered cheerfully.

A second later they were off. Marianne felt *Zéphyr's* legs explode beneath her and they shot forward. Within a few strides, he had broken into a gallop and Marianne urged him on, glorying in his speed and the cold air against her flushed cheeks. The sand beneath them flew past in a blur as they went faster and faster, the pounding of hoofs like the very life-force within her. She glanced over her shoulder. They were leading the field, ahead even of two cavalry officers. Only Phyllis's spirited mount was drawing level, and for half the course, they were neck and neck. But something jolted in Marianne's mind and she heard Hal's voice, as clear as day, shouting at her, 'You can do it, sis!'

Her soul swelled as her whole body moved with the animal's rhythm, leaning over the outstretched neck, her rear-end out of the saddle. She gripped only with her knees, taking the weight from the horse's back as if she were a professional jockey. He responded in glorious ecstasy and streaked ahead, crossing the finishing line with the speed of a bullet and galloping on so that Marianne had to fight to slow him – reluctantly as there was nothing she would have relished more than racing for miles along the sand, as if some dam had burst inside her.

When she finally brought him to a walk and turned him round, strangers were running up to meet them.

'God, that was amazing!'

'I've never seen anyone go as fast as that along the sand!'

'What's your name?' a reporter with a notebook and pen wanted to know. 'Where did you learn to ride like that?'

'I'm sorry,' Marianne answered firmly. 'I can't answer any questions. I must see to the horse.'

'Well done!' Phyllis called, setting her own steed to walk beside them as they headed back to the makeshift enclosure. 'You beat me fair and square.'

'It was a close thing,' Marianne said

modestly, jumping from *Zéphyr's* back and going in search of his blanket and something to rub him down with.

She had finished seeing to his welfare and handed him back to the ring officials. The furore had died down, thank goodness, for she had simply spilled over with the joy of the chase, and the attention was unwelcome. It was as she was walking alone back to join her friends that another voice hailed her.

'That was superb, Miss Marianne. It is you, isn't it?'

She frowned, a trifle irritated that someone else wanted to congratulate her when all she had done was to enjoy herself. Somewhere deep in her memory, the voice seemed vaguely familiar, but she turned round, ready to fob the person off with some platitude. And then her heart turned a cartwheel.

In front of her, dressed in an army greatcoat, stood the tall, slender figure she had recalled so many times. His face was gaunt and haggard, but the grey-blue eyes looked at her with the same translucent light, and when he politely removed his officer's cap, the same sandy curl fell roguishly over his forehead.

A flicker of light burst into flame inside her. 'Major Thorneycroft. Albert. Well, I never. But how on earth...?' She broke off, stunned with delight and confusion, and her fingers sizzled as he took off his glove to shake her hand.

'I had some leave to take before things start hotting up again and I thought I'd come to Calais for a change. But I never expected to find *you* here. What a wonderful surprise! I see from your uniform that you joined the FANY.'

'Yes,' she said, wondering how on earth she could contain the tide of elation that washed through her. 'I'd applied before ... well, before ... you know ... Hal...' The thought cast a shadow over her happy surprise, but she brushed it aside. 'I did my training and I've been out here since December.'

'And doing a sterling job, I'm sure.' Albert paused, and his grin widened. 'Oh, it's so good to see you again. I've thought about you so often. I mean... I was so sorry I had to write that letter.'

Marianne's mouth curved in a wistful smile. 'It was beautifully written and brought us all great comfort.'

'And your parents, how are they?'

'Very well, thank you. Grieving, of course. But I'm sure they'll be as surprised as I am when I tell them I bumped into you.'

They stared at each other, both smiling, unsure of the other, happy, hoping, yet not knowing what to say.

'Er, is there anywhere we can go?' Albert faltered at last. 'Somewhere we can sit and talk? Can I buy you a drink? A coffee, some-where?'

'Oh.' Marianne's face fell. 'I'm not allowed, I'm afraid. Not without permission. And I have to have a chaperone. Unless we go out to lunch in a public place. Although why that's supposed to be less innocuous I have no idea. How long are you here for?'

'I've only just arrived. I've got a whole week.'

The expectant look on Albert's face made Marianne's heart sing. 'I get a day off a month. I could try and take it this week. We could have lunch, and then maybe one of my friends could tag along afterwards as my chaperone.'

'I should be delighted to meet any friend of yours. If I must!' Albert said cheekily. 'Look, this is where I'm staying.' He pulled a notepad from his pocket and scribbled an address on a small square of paper. 'Send me a message. But surely we can talk for a while now, before everyone leaves?'

'Well, just for ten minutes. I'm officially on duty. So, tell me,' Marianne asked, feeling at once relaxed and yet on edge with excite-ment, 'where are you stationed at the mo-ment?'

'A Squadron's billeted at a village called Hesdin-l'Abbé, near Boulogne. We do drills and practice manoeuvres and all that sort of thing. It's all so depressing, really, that we've never had the chance to fight properly as a cavalry unit, although we've been used as infantry often enough. At the moment, it's mainly a case of enduring the appalling weather and getting fodder for the horses. With all the U-boat attacks, the authorities have cut forage supplies to a minimum, and the stabling's pretty poor, too.'

'Oh, the poor things!'

'Yes. And all for nothing, really. I'm so glad I didn't requisition Pegasus from you. We did some vital communication work at the First Battle of Ypres, but since then, we've stood to our horses so often, but nothing much has ever come of it. The nature of warfare has changed so much. More than anything, we've been used as dismounted reserves. We were in the front line at the Second Battle of Ypres, and lost a lot of men and officers.'

'You were wounded yourself, weren't you, I think Hal said?'

Albert gave a wistful smile. 'Yes, I was. Out of action for a few months, but back in time to serve at Loos, but all we did there was bury the dead. There was a vicious battle in the same area shortly afterwards and we were very much involved in that but dismounted again. But then all last year, virtually nothing.' Albert puffed out his cheeks despondently, but then the smile crept back onto his face. 'Listen to me, rambling on when we've precious little time if you're to obey the rules.' He lifted one eyebrow rakishly, at the same time jabbing his head towards where the crowds had almost dispersed.

'Rules are made to be broken,' Marianne grinned back. 'I ought to be going. But I really will try to get my day off this week.'

'Promise? Oh, it's been so good to see you again. It's been like bumping into an old friend, even though we hardly know each other.'

'We had those few days at home on Dartmoor,' Marianne reminded him. 'It wasn't long, but we did find some sort of kindred spirit.'

'Yes, I believe we did.' Albert's eyes seemed to light with a thousand stars. 'So, I'll await your message?'

'Most definitely. Until then.'

She turned, dragging herself away and forcing herself not to look back. Well, that was a turn-up for the books. In all the chaos and carnage of the war, she had met up with the one man in the world who had moved her heart. Apart from Michael Bradley, whom she didn't count anymore. But it was sheer madness to think anything might come of it. Albert had to survive the war for a start. No. As her mother had said, it was better not to get involved. And she had turned her back on that sort of thing long ago, hadn't she? Nevertheless, she found herself humming softly as she made her way back to the

FANY camp.

'Who was that gorgeous officer you were talking to?' Stella asked her enviously as they sat in the mess for dinner that evening.

'Someone I once met back home.' Marianne gave a casual shrug but somehow couldn't suppress the euphoria that frothed up inside her. She glanced round furtively to make sure no one was in earshot before continuing in a conspiratorial whisper, 'He's Major Thorneycroft of the 15th The King's Hussars, my father's old regiment and my poor late brother's as well. We got to know each other a little back in Blighty shortly after the war started. It was an amazing coincidence we should meet again.'

'Lucky you,' Stella sighed, and then she asked cheekily, 'Anything in it?'

'Well, actually...' Marianne bit her lip, trying to damp down her emotions, but it was impossible. 'I've put in for this month's leave. He's in Calais for a week, so I'm going to ask Tanky's permission to have lunch with him. And maybe dinner, if you'll agree to be my chaperone.'

Stella's face lit up. 'I wouldn't mind a jot having dinner with him even if I'm playing gooseberry.'

'Oh, thanks, Stell. You're a brick!'

'I know,' she said airily, and both of them collapsed in giggles.

CHAPTER SIXTEEN

Albert blinked his eyes wide in happy surprise. 'Miss Marianne! Oh, for a while then I wasn't sure you were coming.'

'What, after my note?'

'You could have changed your mind.'

'I don't usually. I'm just a bit late. Sorry about that. We were de-coking our engine and I couldn't leave until we had the cylinder block back in place.'

'That all sounds very technical. I'm impressed. I can drive a motorcar as you know, but I know very little about the mechanics of the things.'

'Nor did I until joined the FANY and we had to go on courses and pass them before we could come out here. To de-coke an engine, you have to hoist the complete cylinder block clear of the pistons before you can get at them and the valves. And when you've finished, you have to squeeze the piston rings back into place around each piston.'

'Well, you learn something new every day,' Albert smiled, taking her coat. 'Do sit down. What'll you have? The menu's rather limited, I'm afraid,' he grimaced.

'They are everywhere. Now let me see.

Croque Monsieur, Omelette aux Fines Herbes or *Coq au Vin*. That should be best. There might not be much chicken in it, but wine is something the French seem to have an endless supply of.'

'In that case, *une bouteille de votre meilleur vin blanc, s'il vous plaît, monsieur,*' Albert called to the restaurateur, and then turned back to Marianne with a saucy grin. 'Now tell me, Miss FANY Warrington, what's life like out here for you?'

Marianne couldn't help but giggle at his playful mood. 'In a word, cold,' she told him. 'Our huts have more holes in them than a colander, and we have to melt our washing water over an oil stove. We keep having air-raids, and we don't have windscreens so we have no protection against the wind and the sleet and the snow. Of course, it's been so icy that we slide about all over the place, and we're not allowed headlights so we can't see where we're going at night. To top it all, we don't even get proper army rations, so this meal will be a banquet for which I am truly grateful.'

The restaurateur came over with the wine, then, and nodded at Albert with a knowing wink, commenting, '*Très jolie!*' into his customer's ear in what was supposed to be a whisper. Albert and Marianne just managed to keep their faces straight long enough to order their meal before bursting into laughter the moment the old fellow had shuffled out to the back.

'I wish my pal, Stella, could have seen that!' Marianne spluttered. 'You'd think she's a little mouse, but she's actually a very good actress and a brilliant mimic. But you'll meet her later. She's going to be our chaperone.'

'I shall look forward to meeting her. But you were telling me about your work here.'

Marianne pursed her lips solemnly. 'Well, it can be pretty grim at times. Not just the conditions we face ourselves, but the appalling cases we see. Our discomforts are nothing by comparison. Gas victims, men with limbs blown off, shrapnel and bullet wounds to every imaginable part. But I don't need to tell you. You'll have seen it for yourself. Some are so dreadful I can't imagine how they made it this far. Of course, a lot of them don't make it any further. And you know how when someone's dying, they sometimes bring relatives over from Blighty to be at their bedside? Well, sometimes it falls to us to meet them off the ship and take them to the hospital. That can be absolutely heartbreaking.'

'Yes, I can imagine,' Albert said gravely, and took her hand across the table. There was nothing romantic in the gesture. It was simply comforting, as one human being to another, and it gave Marianne the strength to continue.

'Despite our name, we don't do that much

actual nursing. We carry certain dressings, but most of that sort of thing's already been done. If there is anything like that, Stella does most of it, and I do the driving. There's paperwork, of course, and sometimes we have to change the men out of their filthy uniforms when we get to whichever hospital it is, and get them into pyjamas. One of the worst things though, is cleaning out the ambulance after a run. Doing corpses isn't as bad as that.'

'Oh, dear, I wish I hadn't asked.' Albert gave a nervous laugh. 'And not the best topic when we're just about to eat a meal.'

Marianne shrugged. 'You soon get used to it. Not the appalling injuries and loss of life, but *coping* with it. And we do other things as well. Have you heard of James?'

'James?' Albert frowned doubtfully.

'Oh. Not as famous as we thought, then. Our mobile bath. We can do two hundred and fifty baths a day and fumigate all the uniforms as well. It's all rather fun and the men are so grateful afterwards. And we ran a soldiers' canteen for a few months during the worst of the winter. And, of course, we put on concerts! We call ourselves the *Fantastiks*. It's all rather fun. There's one girl who's a brilliant ventriloquist and her friend plays the dummy. She sticks red paper on her cheeks and wears a hospital gown. It really is very funny.'

'I can imagine!' Albert chuckled in reply. 'And what do you do?'

'I join in the singing, and we do a version of the can-can. It looks quite funny with us wearing puttees and army boots.'

'Oh, I'm sure you look quite fetching. And the short hair rather suits you, by the way.'

'Oh.' Marianne's hand went up to her shorn curls, aware of the sudden blush in her cheeks. But she was saved any further embarrassment as their meal was served just then and she tucked in ravenously. 'What about you, then?' she asked. 'Or is that a bit of a silly question?'

'Not really,' Albert answered, pouring out the wine and tasting it. 'That's good. Mmm.' He raised his eyebrows in appreciation and then his face moved into a sombre mask. 'I try to make sure that my men and myself stay alive. As I said the other day, we get pretty frustrated at not doing much in the way of fighting as a cavalry unit, but being constantly at the ready can be unbelievably wearing on the nerves. I reckon that's sometimes worse than when we're used as fighting infantry, and that can be indescribable. The Second Ypres was the worst, along the Menin Road. The liquid mud in the trenches was two foot deep in places, and then we had to push forward over an open plain in full view of the enemy. Altogether we lost nine killed or wounded officers and nearly a hundred and forty other ranks. But at least we felt we'd played an important part in the fighting. We didn't let the Hun take an inch of ground from us.'

'But you were wounded and didn't see the end?' Marianne asked, her forehead wrinkling into a concerned frown.

'Oh, yes, I did.' Albert's voice took on a sudden vehemence. 'I was wounded on the last day, and I held on to the bitter end. I was determined to see the German attack repelled, fired with revenge, if you like, after what they'd done to some of my men. I mean...' He broke off with a deep sigh. 'I know it's war, and most of the enemy are simply obeying orders in the same way we are, but you can't help being sucked into the "him or me" syndrome. But anyway,' he shook his head dismissively, 'I caught two bullets, in my left shoulder and arm, so it wasn't too bad and I was able to fight on to the end of the day.'

Marianne's face lengthened. 'Sounds bad enough to me.'

'Well, it took several months before I was fully fit again,' Albert admitted. 'I had Blighty leave. In fact, I wondered about going to visit a certain young lady down in Devon, but I thought it might be a little presumptuous of me.'

'Oh, Albert, you should have done! You'd have been most welcome.'

'Would I?' Marianne noticed a spasm of pleasure twitch on Albert's face and then his eyes deepened with intensity as he suddenly closed his hand on hers. 'Marianne, I've thought of you so often, even before your brother joined the regiment. Do you think, when this dreadful war is over, that there could be some sort of future for us? You and me, I mean?'

Marianne's breath became trapped in her throat. This was all so sudden, and nothing could have been further from her thoughts. She had come out here to do a worthwhile job, and had proved herself as capable as any man. Had the time now come to abandon the vow she had made as a young girl? No. This was ridiculous, yet her heart was trying to escape from her chest as she answered evasively, 'That might be difficult with you in the army.'

But Albert was not to be put off and his expression grew even more serious. 'No. I've decided that when this carnage is over, I'm going to resign. Assuming I survive to do so, of course.'

'I sincerely hope you do.' Marianne spoke with a conviction that astounded even herself.

'And if I do, I could think of nothing I'd like better than to help you and your family run your stud farm. I have some money of my own and a small house in Surrey I could sell. And if I could just be near you, even if it were no more than that.'

Marianne felt the blood rush from her head and she knew she groaned inside herself. Yes, of course she hoped Albert survived the war, but she hoped everyone did. Every time a broken, mangled body passed through her care she uttered a silent prayer for the victim. She liked Albert. More than liked him. But to feel so deeply for someone that every day became a tortured anxiety, she could do without. Her dear mother had been right in that.

'Let's just see how things go,' she muttered.

'I ask for no more than that. And,' Albert hesitated, 'may I write to you? And ... make you my person to be informed? Since my aunt died, I've had no next of kin.'

'Yes, of course,' Marianne replied, feeling her emotions twist into a tangled knot.

'Good. Then let's celebrate with another glass of wine. And you can tell me everything about yourself. The first time you rode a horse. All the adventures you've had on your wonderful Dartmoor. Your friends. Everything.'

He was smiling broadly now, making him look like a cheeky school-boy, Marianne considered. She felt her taut nerves slacken and she began to relax again. And as the conversation continued, she knew that a faint light was dawning somewhere inside her so that she didn't want the day to end.

'Oh, listen round, troops!' Tanky bellowed across the mess. 'It's just been announced on the radio. The United States of America has decided to join in the war!'

A roaring cheer rippled through the hut and every conversation turned to a discussion of this momentous, welcome news.

'About bally time,' Phyllis pronounced.

'Things are looking up, then!' Stella said cheerily. 'First the weather's suddenly improved dramatically–'

'At long last–'

'And now this. With the Americans on our side, the war could soon be over.'

'Sadly, I doubt that,' Marianne reasoned. 'If they'd come in earlier, perhaps. And they've got to get here first. Moving thousands of troops across the Atlantic will take time.'

'That's true. But this really is good news. We ought to celebrate.'

'It's enough for me that I'm not shivering like an icicle anymore. We'll be swimming in the sea and sunbathing before too long at this rate!'

'Letter for you, Trooper Warrington,' Tanky interrupted their joviality as she passed Marianne an envelope from a pile in her hand. 'And one for you, Trooper Ainsworth.

Hope it's all good news, what.'

Marianne's heart gave a little bound, but it wasn't a letter from Albert. She recognized Mary Franfield's handwriting at once. It was almost a relief as she wouldn't have to face the confusion that tweaked at her every time Albert came to mind. She opened the letter, happy with anticipation as Mary always had a wealth of interesting things to relate, not just about her training that was nearing its completion, but also about London and the sights she saw in the capital. But as Marianne's eyes scanned the unusually brief note, a crippling horror took hold of her.

'Oh, my God,' she muttered under her breath.

Her friends' conversation at once came to a stop.

'What's the matter, Marianne?' a chorus of anxious voices asked.

'It's ... my friend in London,' she stammered as a sharp pain seemed to tear through her chest. 'Her fiancé – someone I know, too – he's in the Merchant Navy and ... and his ship's been sunk.'

'Oh, no!'

'That's *awful!*'

'Oh ... poor Mary,' Marianne choked as Michael's handsome face floated into her mind. 'And all his family, too. It'll break them all. His parents. And Adam and Becky. And Richard and Beth. They're all his grandparents. Oh, this is all too much. He's ... was such a lovely young man.'

A storm of grief broke over her despite the sympathetic concern of all her pals who collectively put their arms about her. Tears coursed down her cheeks, and the tearing sorrow of her lost brother rushed to the surface and mingled with this new tragedy. Her heart cried out in despair, for who else would she lose before this appalling, godless war came to an end?

CHAPTER SEVENTEEN

They drove like bats out of hell through the slumbering town to the railway station, always in convoy or at least in pairs. The air raids were almost nightly now and they might need to help each other in an emergency. The return journey was utterly different; slow, steady, using the heavy gears to make the passage as smooth as possible for the poor souls in the back who often cried out in agony. At least the snow and ice were things of the past, but the potholes were still there, gouged out by the severe winter weather or blasted out by exploding shells. As soon as the authorities filled them in, more appeared, a never-ending battle of a different kind from the one that had been raging first about the town of Arras, and then continuing in the surrounding area for weeks now.

Marianne followed the vehicle in front, navigating the potholes and peering into the summer darkness. She glanced up at the sky, a balmy, moonlit night – perfect for a raid. They had become almost immune to the fear, to the sound of falling shells, the flash and thunder of explosions. Such things were just a nuisance now, leaving debris that was hard to spot without headlights until the last minute so that you had to swerve suddenly or slam on the brakes, sometimes reversing out if the way had been made impassable.

It had all become so routine. Marianne's gaze shifted briefly to Stella, sitting hunched beside her, tin hat firmly strapped under her chin. They rarely spoke on a run now. They were too exhausted to do anything but concentrate their strength on getting the job done. From the beginning of April when the big offensive had started, the hospital trains had been arriving almost nightly, bringing hundreds of wounded each time. No matter what hardships they endured, the young women of the FANY would not give up until every case had been safely transported, even though they were dropping with fatigue and their limbs screamed in pain from lifting stretchers and turning heavy steering wheels.

'What've we got?' Marianne asked the orderly as she reversed the ambulance up to the train door.

'Eight walking gas cases for you, miss,' came the answer.

Marianne's heart sank. Poor devils. Most would have their eyes bandaged, eyes that might never see again. Burnt skin turned green, rasping throats or lungs. It seemed to her one of the most cruel, inhuman injuries of the war to lose one's sight, as dreadful as having half your face shot or burnt away and still being able to see your monstrous reflection in the mirror. Maybe it was better to drown in the fluid the gas made your scorched lungs exude. Was death the better option? Certainly she could understand why brave young men begged for death to release them from the excruciating pain of a blown-off limb or a gaping, gangrenous hole.

'It's all right, you're safe now,' she heard Stella's soothing voice as she held the arm of the first blinded victim, and took some comfort herself from her friend's gentle words. 'One more step. Now you need to climb up into the ambulance. Lift your foot a bit more. That's it. Let me take your hand. I'm going to guide it to a strap you can pull on. Now up we go.'

Marianne turned her head away as angry frustration erupted inside her. The image of these poor devils would be seared into her brain forever. She would deal with the paperwork first, allowing herself time to take a hold on her emotions before she went to help Stella load their patients. Stella always knew what to say, a practical voice that nonetheless resonated with compassion, while Marianne wanted to burst out in a squall of rage against the perpetrators of such monstrosities.

And so she did what she did best, drive, while Stella comforted the men in the back. After delivering them, then it was the mad dash back to the station. This time, their human cargo consisted of a bad case of trench-foot and three stretcher-wounded, at least one of whom had contracted gangrene. Marianne didn't need to be told. The stench was overpowering. Nauseating.

And rumbling always at the back of her mind as she clenched her jaw against the horrors was the thought that one night she could find Albert among the hundreds of victims. Her heart had shied away from the utter confusion he had brought her, filling her head until it felt ready to explode. He had written to her twice before she had given in to the temptation to reply. But soon her pulse beat joyously with every letter that arrived. His words made her both laugh and cry, but always assured her of his safety. The regiment had been regularly stood to its horses, even for the recent attack on the Messines Ridge, but yet again the cavalry had not been needed. It was the middle of June, but how long could this false sense of security last? The damning fear trundled in Marianne's breast, ripping her soul to shreds, for with each letter they exchanged, she became more certain that, despite every rebellious fibre of her being, she was falling irrevocably in love. It was somehow so easy to express one's deepest emotions on paper, perhaps easier than being in each other's presence. With every word Albert wrote to her, he revealed a spirit that matched her own like a glove and set her heart beating in blissful rapture.

'Stella, Marianne, meet Chuck and Travis.'

It was their monthly day off, and the two girls were wandering together along the vast, sandy beach, enjoying the first lull in the stream of casualties since the conclusion of the disastrous attack on Arras and the success of Messines. Marianne had been squinting into the July sunshine when she spotted Lucy coming towards them positively glowing in the company of not just one but two big Americans. The pristine army uniforms they sported were so different from the mud-encrusted, lice-ridden, war-torn uniforms of the British Tommies the girls were used to, that these creatures seemed to belong to another planet. Marianne knew it was unkind, but she could almost feel her lip curl with distaste. They would soon learn that they weren't there to form liaisons with impressionable young women. Marianne liked Lucy, and she was a good operative. But to say that she relished the company of the opposite sex was an understatement!

'How do, ladies?' the apparitions said in polite unison.

'Well enough, thank you,' Marianne replied tightly.

One of the Americans in particular looked

241

taken aback. 'It sure is good to meet you young ladies of the FANY,' he said hesitantly. 'The most daring of the female forces out here, so I believe.'

'We're not part of any force,' Marianne corrected him. 'We work *with* the armies, not as part of them. And *everyone* out here risks his or her life all the time, including the civilians if you take the air-raids into consideration. When you've helped pull an injured old woman or a dead child from a bombed house, *then* you know you're not being daring. Just doing a horribly necessary job.'

'And I sincerely hope we Americans can help, ma'am.' The fellow doffed his cap deferentially. 'I'm Travis and this is Chuck. So which one of you beautiful ladies is which?'

'I'm Marianne and this is Lady Stella.'

'Wow, a real English lady?'

Marianne noticed Stella flush to the roots of her hair. 'I'm afraid so,' the younger girl blushed.

'My father's the mayor of a small town in Connecticut if that counts at all.' Travis directed what appeared a genuine smile at Stella, and Marianne felt herself soften towards him. She supposed she shouldn't be so prickly. It wasn't their fault the American government had delayed so long before joining the war.

'No need for that sort of thing out here,' Stella told the American with a rueful lift of her eyebrows. 'If bits of you have been blown off, it doesn't matter if you're a general or a private.'

'Come on, let's not talk shop' Lucy urged them. 'It's our day off, all three of us. Why don't we get permission for us all to go out to dinner tonight? Please?' she cajoled, linking her arm through that of the other American, Chuck. 'I need a chaperone.'

'I don't see why not.' Stella smiled, starry-eyed, up at Travis.

'Nothing personal, but count me out,' Marianne put in, somewhat relieved that she had an excuse not to be the odd one out. 'I need to write a letter to my family. My brother was killed at the Somme last year,' she explained to the two men, 'so you can imagine they worry about me so much and I like to put their minds at rest as often as possible.'

'Sure, we understand,' Travis nodded gravely.

'And I'm sorry to hear about your brother,' Chuck put in.

'Thank you. Now, if you'll excuse me, I'll be getting back to camp. You four enjoy the beach. Make the most of the nice weather. It might not last.'

'It's true, then, that the English can't hold a conversation without mentioning the weather!' Travis teased, and like a true gentleman, he made a show of offering Stella his elbow – which she took with a shy smile.

Marianne turned away, shaking her head. Stella appeared to have taken an instant liking to the American, and good luck to her. She ought to have some fun while she could, for who knew what tomorrow would bring? Marianne just hoped her friend would not become too romantically involved. She only wished her own heart had not become ensnared, since except for when she was driving the ambulance and doing her best to alleviate the unimaginable suffering of the thousands of soldiers who passed through the FANY's care, her every waking moment was filled with her fears for dear Albert.

They were calling it the Third Battle of Ypres. It had started on the final day of July, and all at once the horrors had begun afresh. Crushing fear circled constantly around Marianne's heart for somewhere out there, she knew not exactly where, was Albert. Though she tried desperately to drive it to the very depths of her mind, the thought slashed regularly across her mind that he had been wounded at the Second Battle of Ypres. Perhaps he would be again at the Third. Or worse.

The rain had returned, too. If it wasn't falling in torrential thunderstorms, it filled the air with a warm, damp drizzle, stifling souls and bodies. Marianne felt as if she could hardly breathe as she swabbed out the ambulance one morning, sweltering in her heavy overalls and rubber boots. Her hands sweated inside their rubber gloves as she washed out the pools of vomit and faeces from some unfortunate souls who had contracted dysentery in the trenches. The stench was foul, trapped in the dank, oppressive air, and it was all Marianne could do not to retch, herself. To top it all, this new offensive had been going on for weeks now, and still she had not heard from Albert.

A sudden pounding of rushing feet drew her from the grinding dread, and Stella's head appeared at the back of the ambulance.

'Just had another call, I'm afraid. Hospital train due in half an hour, although God knows where they'll be accommodated. Every hospital's already overflowing.'

Marianne's heart dropped as she slapped the mop into the bucket of disinfectant and then made one final sweep of the ambulance floor. She had only just finished in time.

Oh, Lord, here we go again, she muttered under her breath as she jumped down and carried the cleaning equipment back to the shed. She hung up her overalls and changed from the rubber boots back into her heavy lace-up shoes, and then hurried back to the ambulance.

Stella already had the crank-handle at the ready and Marianne climbed wearily into the driver's seat. It had been her turn for the disgusting task of cleaning out the ambulance while Stella had slumbered on in her cubicle. So she was grateful to the other girl for taking on the strenuous cranking of the engine. Yet again, the unit had been up half the night dealing with a convoy of barges this time and had only snatched a few hours' sleep.

'Oh, when will it end?' Marianne sighed passionately as, the engine now purring, Stella jumped up beside her and she moved the vehicle forward to join the queue turning onto the road. 'I don't know how much longer we can all keep this up.'

'We could certainly do with more people,' Stella agreed, stifling a yawn. 'But while this major offensive's going on, we can't just abandon the wounded, can we?'

'Of course not. I wouldn't dream of it. But I do wish we could have that two weeks' leave we're owed. It's well overdue.'

'Perhaps we'll get it soon,' Stella answered, throwing her a not very optimistic smile.

'We can live in hope. Right, here we go. Hold on tight.'

They swung onto the road, following the ambulance in front and bumping along faster and faster until they were almost taking off like the aeroplanes in the Royal Flying

Corps. Down the shortest route, which for once was unobstructed, and so familiar to Marianne that she scarcely had to think. Her shoulders ached from carrying stretchers heavy with men of at least half her weight again, and each gear-change aggravated the pain in her arm. Many of the bigger-built FANYs seemed to have built up their muscles, but she supposed that someone as small-boned as herself was never going to develop the strength of others, and poor Stella was even slighter than she was. But when she thought of home, of Dartmoor, it was a tantalizing, fading dream of heaven. She simply must get home soon to recharge her batteries so to speak. To be soothed and cosseted, to wallow in long, hot baths, ride out over the moor on Pegasus, to sleep undisturbed without the distant pounding of heavy guns or the fear of being bombed. The need to go home to rest rose in her like a roaring breaker so that she could feel tears welling in her eyes.

She would be back as soon as her leave was over, there was no doubt in her mind about that. Giving up was seen by the FANY as desertion, and would be by herself, too. Every injured, maimed or dying soldier that went through her care was someone's husband, son, father or brother. Another Albert. Another Hal. No. She just needed some time to recuperate, physically and mentally. Was entitled to it. She didn't want to leave her post while the battle raged – places she had never heard of before: Gheluvelt Plateau, Langemarck, Passchendaele, were now common place – but if she didn't have some respite soon, she was beginning to feel her soul would cave in.

If only she would receive another letter from Albert. His silence overwhelmed her in terror. Had something happened to him? Had he been wounded, was he sick, or missing or killed in action? Had he decided their relationship could have no future, or that he didn't *want* it to have one after all? Marianne reared away, sickened to the core at the morose thoughts that tumbled in her head. She mustn't think like that, must concentrate on the road ahead.

They had reached the station now and for once, the train was waiting. With the warm, high humidity, simple wounds were quickly becoming infected. As Marianne reversed the ambulance to the open train-doors, the stench of sepsis coming from inside hung in the air like a heavy fog.

Poor devils, she thought as she hopped down from the driving seat. She would not let them down, and her heart filled with renewed strength and courage.

Ned Cornish held his splitting head in his hands, as near to tears as he had ever come.

He had taken two doses of aspirin in as many hours, and still the pain hadn't eased. It was a year now since that wretched horse had kicked him in the head. He didn't think the girl had been aware of what had happened as she made her escape. He had been petrified that she would set the local constabulary onto him, but apparently she hadn't. He had lumbered away, disorientated, the familiar paths and tracks a confused muddle in his brain. He couldn't tell how far he had staggered before he had blacked out. When he had come round, it had been dark. Thank God it had been summer or he might have died of exposure.

Mind you, he often wished he had, the headaches were that bad sometimes. The dent was still visible in his hairline and always would be. The doctor he had consulted had told him he had been lucky to survive, never mind anything else. He had also told him he might have bouts of depression, lethargy or aggression, moods which could take years to fade away for good – if ever.

Well, he certainly felt angry much of the time. Angry that ever since, he had found himself impotent every time he paid the most appealing whore to come to his room. Angry that his stomach constantly churned with a frustration that ate into his soul. Angry that he hadn't yet found the energy to get even with the young bitch who had caused the agony that so frequently exploded in his head.

But he would one day. He had promised himself. If not this year, then next. Sometimes he thought the vicious need for vengeance was all that kept him going. And not just against the girl who bore such an uncanny resemblance to her mother, but against the mother herself. It was her fault when all was said and done.

Oh, yes. He would take revenge for all that he was suffering, even if it was the last thing he ever did.

CHAPTER EIGHTEEN

Marianne felt as light as a bird as she found a secluded spot among the dunes and sank down in the warm sand. It was the middle of September and at long last the sun had decided to shine for a few days, quickly drying out the puddles that had persisted all summer. Marianne lay back, eyes closed, feeling the sunshine strong on her face and allowing her mind and body to float as if on a light, fluffy cloud. She hugged the moment of exquisite anticipation to her breast for just a little longer, since in her hand was a sheaf of letters from Albert, all arrived together, some tattered and dog-eared as if they had been stored God knew where for weeks on end, while others were more recent. But she could resist no longer, and sat up abruptly to tear them open.

She read them in date order. She was overcome with relief to learn that while the Third Battle of Ypres had raged viciously all summer with thousands upon thousands of appalling casualties – which she knew well enough from her own work – the 15th The King's Hussars had taken no part beyond supplying large work parties for the XVIII

Corps. The dreadful weather had rendered the countryside utterly impossible for a cavalry attack, and the regiment had recently been ordered back to billets two days' march from the Front.

Oh, thank you, God! Marianne whispered to the salty breeze that wafted off the sea. Albert was safe and perhaps if she prayed hard enough, he would stay that way. Whether or not they would have a future together was a bridge they would cross at some unidentifiable point way in the distance. Just now all that mattered to her was that he was alive and well.

Albert's letters were, though, full of that wondrous time they had spent together during the week he had been on leave in Calais. The walks they had shared along the sand, exchanging life stories, silly, insignificant anecdotes that made them the people they now were. Snatched moments, since Marianne had mainly been on duty. Indulging their equine passion together, even discussing plans for the future of the Fencott Place stud farm once the war was over. They had agreed on so much, revealed trivial secrets about themselves, Marianne even admitting how she had missed her sister and soul-mate ever since Kate had become a devoted wife and mother.

What Marianne had never revealed, however, was her secret vow taken more than a decade previously. How could she tell him that their relationship was, in fact, a torture to her? She still believed fervently in her vow, and yet Albert was slowly destroying what had been the foundation of her life for so long. Just like a nun questioning her faith. But whenever she conjured up an image of him in her mind, or he popped into her head at the most unexpected moment, she felt herself fill up with the most delicious warmth which she was losing the will to resist.

She could envisage him now, tall, slender, so handsome in his officer's uniform, striding across the sand in his high, shiny leather riding boots. He had a certain confident gait, straight-backed but never arrogant, always with an enquiring tilt of his head as if he were searching for something, supremely observant.

Marianne blinked her eyes. She shouldn't let herself be carried away by her imagination, but it was pleasant enough to dream. But when she opened her eyes again, the vision was still there. How odd. And the vision had a shadow, moving with it across the sand. It stopped, looking round. Turned until it was directly facing her.

Their eyes met as if his had been drawn to hers by an invisible, magnetic thread. Marianne's heart gave a whoop of joy. It *was* Albert! In the flesh! Throwing all reserve to the wind, she stuffed the letters into one of the large pockets of her uniform jacket and careered down the beach towards him, waving wildly. She saw him start with surprise, and break into a run.

When they came together, her head was emptied of everything but the pure joy of being with him again. He whisked her off her feet, twirling her round in mid-air, and when he set her down again, it seemed the most natural thing in the world when their mouths came together in a deep, hungry kiss. Her arms were around his neck, his about her waist, pulling her against him, and she felt the fire come to life in her belly.

'Oh, my darling girl,' Albert murmured, and she pulled away, laughing to the sky, overcome with triumph that his sudden presence had chased away her demons.

'W-what are you doing here?' she stammered in utter delight.

'Your friends said I'd find you here somewhere,' he grinned back. 'They said you'd gone for a walk.'

'Yes, to read your letters!' she cried, exposing the crumpled bundle of paper in her pocket. 'A whole bunch of them had just arrived in one go. I've been so worried about you!'

'But I wrote every week–'

'Yes, I know that now.'

'And when I received yours, saying you

hadn't heard from me for so long–'

'Never mind, you're here now! In person! Oh, Albert!' Her heart was performing a waltz as she gazed up at his own dancing grey-blue eyes. 'But how did you manage it?'

'Well, my dearest.' He took her small hand in his large, strong one. 'If you've got to my latest letters yet–'

'Which I haven't.'

'Ah, well, we were stationed at Estaires most of the summer, that's about twenty-five miles from Ypres. But they ordered us back to Frencq about two weeks ago, not that far from Etaples. So, as we didn't seem to be needed for anything, I put in for some leave. Then, a couple of days ago, we were ordered to turn out to the base camps at Etaples. There'd been some dissent among the troops there, and it was thought we'd be needed to quell it. We were jolly glad when we weren't. We wouldn't want there to be any bad blood between the cavalry and the other services. Anyway, when we got back to Frencq, I found I'd been granted a forty-eight hour pass. I managed to get on a train, so here I am. But if I'm to be sure of getting back in time, I'll need to leave first thing in the morning.'

'Oh.' Marianne's heart crashed to her feet.

'So we'll just have to make the most of the few hours we have, won't we?' Albert's eyes deepened as he lifted her hand and caressed it with his lips. 'You know, I feel I know you so well now. All the letters we've exchanged–'

'Those that got through–'

'I just felt able to open my heart to you.'

'And I felt just the same,' she answered breathlessly.

'Did you?' His gaze lingered, long and slow, on her face. 'I saw Stella at the camp. She said you both happened to be off duty until the morning. Do you think she'd be our chaperone again?'

Marianne's eyes twinkled. 'I'm sure she would. I was hers a couple of times. She's sweet on an American called Travis.'

'Really?'

'Yes. I have to say he's a very pleasant fellow. He's been away in the thick of the fighting all summer, so I hope for Stella's sake he'll be all right. Very polite, the Americans, on the whole. And Travis isn't brash and pushy like some of them are.'

'I think it's good they believe in themselves so much. If you feel invincible, it can go a long way.'

'Do you really think the Americans will change the course of the war?' Marianne asked with a despondent sigh. 'We're seeing more suffering than ever–'

'Yes, I firmly believe they will. The Boche might think that with Russia having given up the fight with the revolution, they can concentrate their forces on the Western Front, but they're not reckoning with the might of the Americans. But,' he gave that winsome smile that turned Marianne's heart to jelly, 'let's forget about the war for a few hours, shall we? And talk about, I don't know, our plans for when I come to live on Dartmoor. If you still want me, that is?'

His mouth stretched in a cheeky, boyish grin, and Marianne pushed his arm playfully. 'I might,' she teased airily, then dashed away so that Albert had to run after her, laughing as he caught her about the waist again.

He was there, waiting on the corner, just as they had arranged. It was still light, and the joy of seeing him again, so strong and handsome, swept through her like a riptide. Abandoning all propriety, she raced forward and the next moment found herself wrapped in his arms. The world slipped away, and it was just the two of them, swaddled in a deep sense of euphoria.

'One whole hour we've been apart and I've missed you so much,' Albert murmured into her hair. 'How am I going to be able to stand the months or whatever until we can be together for good? But–' He pulled back sharply, scanning the street. 'Where's Stella?'

Marianne looked up at him with a coquettish tilt of her head. 'I couldn't find her,' she lied quite openly. 'And rules are made to be broken, aren't they?'

Albert gave an amused grunt, recalling at once their conversation all those months before. 'I hope you don't get into trouble.'

'You're not going to report me, are you?' she teased. 'And no one will know. That's why I wore civvies, too.'

'And very fetching you look, too.'

'It feels rather odd, actually, not being in uniform.'

'I expect it does. But it means I can imagine you as you will be when the war's over. And taking such a vision of loveliness out to dinner will give me the greatest pleasure. Now, where would you like to go?'

'How about the little place we went before? It's rather quaint and not somewhere any of the FANY usually go, so no one should recognize me.'

'Sounds good to me.'

Albert offered her his arm and she took it, almost foolish with elation. Only for a second did she question the tangle of conflict at the back of her mind. Life, the war, had changed everything, and she knew she needed to grasp whatever happiness came her way. Tomorrow might be too late.

Almost as if reading her thoughts, Albert said as they walked through the town's shell-damaged streets, 'I was sorry to hear about your friend's fiancé, the one in the Merchant Navy.'

His words, and the sincerity in his voice, sliced at Marianne's heart. 'Yes, I know,' she answered grimly. 'It must have been awful for Mary. He was such a lovely chap. I had, well, an affection for him myself once. Not that he ever knew, or Mary. And it lasted all of two days. It was Mary he was interested in. Poor soul, I can't imagine what she's going through. It was hard enough losing Hal as my brother. But to lose your fiancé must be devastating. She was almost at the end of her nurse's training, too. But she carried on. Helped her cope, she said.' Marianne paused, releasing a pensive sigh. 'She's fully qualified now and has gone home to Devon for a while. Her father's a doctor in Tavistock and he runs a shell-shock hospital there, but I don't know what Mary's plans are. But I'm going home myself in a week's time, so I should see her then.'

'Really? I got here just in time, then!'

'Oh, I'm coming back,' Marianne assured him. 'It's just that my first fortnight's leave's just come through. It's months overdue, but I suppose with all the casualties coming through from Ypres, it was felt we couldn't be spared.'

'It's far from over yet, though.'

'I know. But I guess they thought we'd

waited long enough, and we are volunteers, after all.'

'And very brave ones, too. Ah, here we are.'

The doorbell tinkled gaily as they entered the small restaurant, in contrast to the gloomy interior. Although red-checked table-cloths gave some rustic charm, the simple, dark furniture made the place shadowed and forbidding. The same old man shuffled forward and showed them to a table, hardly necessary as they were the only customers. But he sat them in a secluded corner at the very back so that he could light a candle without risk of it being seen from an enemy aircraft overhead. So perhaps there was some logic in it after all. He would have to close the shutters later on, but for now it was pleasant to look onto the dusk-lit street.

'The menu hasn't changed, I see,' Albert observed with wry amusement. 'But hopefully he has some decent wine left.'

'I expect he will. It's one thing the French never seem short of.'

'What will you have to eat then, my love?'

At his words, a little knot tightened deliciously in Marianne's breast. *My love.* It sounded so good. So right. Perhaps she had been a fool to stand by her vow for so long – or perhaps fate had simply been waiting for her to meet the right man. To meet Albert.

They ordered the meal but, as predicted,

the choice of wine was far superior. The old man left them alone with the glasses of ruby red liquid gleaming in the vacillating candle-light, and Marianne shivered with elation as Albert took her hand across the table.

'Let's make a pact,' he said with a deep smile, 'not to talk about the war tonight. For just a few hours. Let's pretend we're on holiday.'

'All right,' Marianne grinned, falling in at once. 'Aren't we lucky with the weather, seeing how wet it's been all summer?'

'September can be a lovely time of year,' Albert agreed. 'It has a sort of mellowness to it. And then the autumn colours can be spectacular.'

'Winter has its joys, too, though. The bare twigs and branches of a tree can be like intricate lace against a grey sky. And when we have heavy snow over Dartmoor and then the sun comes out, it's quite magical, as if someone has thrown a sheet of white satin over it and then sprinkled it with millions of twinkling diamonds.'

Albert raised his eyes to hers, creased at the corners, smiling. 'I can't wait to see it. Share it with you.'

Marianne dreamily met his gaze, an intense sense of harmony sinking into her spirit. They went on talking, eating, drinking the wine, intoxicated by each other's presence. Marianne knew she had drunk too much, but she didn't care. She was drowning in a tidal wave of emotion. Of love and of yearning.

When the restaurateur slipped onto the table a key with a number two on it, they blinked at each other in stupefaction. They both stared at the key, and Marianne felt herself turn a shade of beetroot. Albert was biting his lip, his face so taut that Marianne couldn't help smiling.

'Shall we?' she dared to whisper.

Albert cleared his throat. 'I can't think of anything I'd like better. But ... we shouldn't.'

A sudden, carefree desire ripped through Marianne's soul. 'This could be our one and only chance.'

'But ... only if you're sure.'

She nodded, and Albert's shaking hand closed over the key as they both stood up.

'Suivez-moi,' the old man said quietly, reappearing from nowhere. 'Et la chambre, c'est gratuite. La guerre, vous savez.'

He led them through the tiny kitchen at the back and then indicated up a winding, wooden staircase that protested under their weight as they climbed it.

'I hope the bed doesn't creak as much,' Marianne giggled as they went into a small but clean and tidy room. The shutters were closed against the now fallen darkness, a lamp was burning very low, and a single rose lay on one of the pillows.

Albert turned the key in the lock, and then

faced her across the room. Marianne's pulse was racing like a traction engine, but she was utterly entranced by a rapturous need, a *curiosity* that burned inside her like a torch of flame. The breath quickened in her throat as Albert came towards her, eyebrows lifted in questioning. But as he slipped the cardigan from her shoulders, she didn't stop him. He kissed her, then, and her lips parted in response, tasting the wine on his tongue. His hands were undoing the buttons on her blouse, slid inside to cup her rounded breasts through her silk underwear. She gasped, a tiny, strangled sound, lost in this new, enthralling wonderment, a thrill of ecstasy tumbling down to that secret place that had never before been touched.

Slowly, delicately, teasing all her senses, Albert undressed her, leisurely, taking his time. Stroking, exploring each inch of her bare flesh as it was revealed. The sensation of the cool air on her skin, of Albert's gaze on her, drew her on to some dizzying, unknown heights. When he paused to strip off his own clothes, leaving her draped across the bed in her underwear, she missed his soft, feather-light touch, but then she was drinking in his taut, muscled body, the scars from his wounds, and she knew now what she had always missed. What would make her complete. Whole.

Albert, his own excitement in clear evidence, peeled off her remaining clothes. For a moment or two, she felt utterly vulnerable, afraid. But he caressed her, kissed her, drew his tongue across her breasts and downwards until she stretched languidly, glorying in her nakedness. He found the aching, soft sweet core of her, and she almost cried out, moaning, locked in mindless passion. He held her there, until she could have screamed with hot desire, and when he entered her, her heart flew to the stars. Her fingers dug into his shoulders as she pulled him deeper into her, moving against him, led by pure, maddened instinct until some ultimate enchantment plunged into the very core of her being and exploded like a firework. She was so taken by surprise that she hardly noticed Albert shudder against her, and the next instant, he had cradled her in his arms, showering her with little kisses.

'Oh, my darling Marianne,' he muttered. 'Thank you. You were magnificent.' And then his eyes screwed up with intensity as he groaned, 'Pray God we both come through this war so we can spend the rest of our lives together like this.'

Marianne felt a cloud of doubt bear down on her at his words. Oh, yes. It was what she wanted, too. She knew it now. But would fate allow her to keep the happiness she had at long last found, or punish her for breaking her vow by destroying it for ever?

CHAPTER NINETEEN

'I'm so deeply, *deeply* sorry about Michael,' Marianne said quietly, her voice ringing with sincerity, when she judged the moment was right.

They were sitting in the garden of the Franfields' elegant, Victorian terraced-villa in Tavistock's Plymouth Road. The early autumn sun was shining pleasantly and the two girls were enjoying the peaceful after-noon. Ling Franfield was occupied in her role as VAD Commandant – or Matron as she preferred to be called – at Mount Tavy Hospital for shell shock and other wounded soldiers that she had opened with Elliott the previous year; Elliott himself was operating at Tavistock's civilian cottage hospital, and William was, of course, at school. Only the housekeeper was indoors, so Mary and Mari-anne were alone to exchange their innermost feelings.

It was a few seconds before Mary replied, and Marianne noticed the spasm of pain on her friend's face. 'Yes, thank you,' the younger girl whispered at last, clearly fighting back tears. 'It's … horrible. There's just a vast emptiness inside me and I'm not sure it can ever be filled. I am trying, though.' She threw Marianne a weak, brave smile. 'It must be even harder for his parents, though, losing their only child. And of course, his father, Toby, is still at sea so poor Chantal must be frantic. And then there are both sets of grandparents. Poor Grandpa Adam blames himself for encouraging Michael's interest in the sea. That must be unimaginable. At least I only have my grief to cope with. And I've only known Michael a short while, whereas they'd known him all his life.'

Marianne had kept quiet, knowing it was good to let Mary pour out her emotions, but now she said gravely, 'You can't compare degrees of grief, you know. I felt the same when Hal was killed. That my parents' grief must be deeper than mine. But it was just different. I'd already secretly applied to join the FANY and I felt guilty about leaving my parents, but they fully understood, and being out there has really helped me. Doing something useful to help save others.'

Mary nodded solemnly, and Marianne saw her play with the cuff of her blouse. 'What's it like, out in France?'

Marianne gave a wry grunt. 'Hard graft. Sometimes you wonder where you'll find the strength from to carry on. But you do. And you see the most appalling injuries, of course. And back here in Blighty, I don't think people realize how many of the troops simply get ill from the dreadful conditions in the trenches: dysentery, pneumonia, frostbite, infected lice bites and fevers, trench foot, the list goes on and on. We even had a measles epidemic sweep through the army in the spring. And then there are those who've been fool enough to get themselves VD.' She paused momentarily, remembering her own night of passion with Albert less than a fortnight previously. Had that been any different? But they loved each other, so she pushed the thought aside, hoping the colour she felt rising in her cheeks didn't show. 'But, you know, I wouldn't be anywhere else,' she concluded emphatically.

She saw Mary suck in her lips thoughtfully. But her friend didn't have a chance to reply before Elliott came out into the garden.

'Do you girls mind if I join you?' he asked genially, loosening his tie and undoing the collar of his shirt. 'Mrs Humphries is just making a fresh pot of tea.'

'Of course not, Dad. How did the ops go?'

'Well, thank you,' Elliott answered, dropping into an empty deck-chair. 'I'm concerned about the appendectomy, though. The op itself was a success, but the poor woman should have brought herself in earlier. She must have been in agony. We only just caught it in time, so I just hope the infection doesn't spread. If only we had a really good drug to kill infection, it would revolutionize medicine just like anaesthetics have.'

'Dr Elliott, sir!'

'Ah, here comes tea,' Elliott sighed gratefully as the housekeeper ran across to them.

'Afraid not, sir. You'm wanted urgently back at the hospital. There's been a terrible accident at Bere Ferrers Station. Seems some New Zealand soldiers got off a troop train thinking they was at Exeter. Only you knows what a little country station it is, and the platform's too short, and they got off trackside and there were an express coming through. Several was killed outright, but they'm bringing some of the injured here.'

Elliott was already half way back up the garden. 'See you later, girls,' he called over his shoulder.

'I'll come, too!' Mary called after him, on her feet in a trice. 'You might need extra help.'

'Me, too.' Marianne leapt up after her, and the tranquillity of the afternoon was shattered. The war, it appeared, could not leave them alone.

'Mrs Humphries has come up trumps again,' Elliott declared, getting up from the dinner table and wiping his mouth with his napkin. 'She can still make a delicious meal despite all the food shortages. But I must get back to the hospital.'

'But, Elliott, you've been operating all evening,' Ling protested. 'You must be exhausted. Let the others look after them.'

But Elliott shook his head. 'Two of them should recover all right, but it'll be a miracle if the other poor devil survives the night, despite all my efforts. I just feel I should be there.'

'Do you want me to come, too, Dad?'

'No, Mary.' Elliott smiled affectionately at his daughter. 'You did enough standing in as theatre sister. It was good to see you in action. I was very impressed, even if you are my own daughter. You need to start using those skills again soon, but enjoy the evening with Marianne.'

'What a dreadful thing,' Ling groaned as her husband left the room. 'Those poor young men travelled half way round the world to come and join in the fighting, only to get mown down in some terrible accident.'

'Apparently they hadn't been given anything to eat since six o'clock this morning,' Mary explained, 'but were told to send two men from each carriage to collect rations at the first station. Coming from New Zealand, they had no idea how big Exeter Station would be, and when the train stopped at Bere Ferrers to wait for the express, they mistook it for Exeter. With the bend in the track, the driver of the express had little idea of what happened. Poor man must be going through hell now he knows.'

'Nine dead, two of them decapitated and one sliced in half,' Marianne murmured under her breath. 'And another not expected to make it through the night. And there's me thinking I'd come home to have a rest from the horrors of war.'

'William, off to bed. School in the morning.'

'Yes, Mum. But there's no need to shield me. I'm going to be a doctor, too, remember.'

'Yes, I do know.' Ling smiled fondly. 'And a jolly good one you'll be, too.'

William nodded proudly. 'Good night, then, all.'

Ling followed her younger son out of the room, leaving Mary and Marianne alone together. 'What a day,' Marianne sighed. 'It was good of your mother to ask me to stay tonight.'

'After helping out at the hospital it was the least we could do, and you were able to wire your parents so they don't worry. But, this afternoon has made up my mind. I'm going to write to the Red Cross in the morning and ask to be sent out to Calais, if possible. I've been sitting around moping for long enough.'

'Oh, well done!' Marianne cried. 'You won't regret it. You'll feel that you're really making a difference. Just be careful to dodge the bombs!'

'I'll try,' Mary grimaced. 'I don't know what Mum and Dad will say with Artie out there somewhere as well, but I'm sure they'll understand. Only, aren't I supposed to be twenty-three?'

'To be a FANY you do, yes. And possibly the QAs, I'm not sure. But as far as I know, not with the Red Cross. I'm sure they'll welcome you with open arms, and anyway, you can always lie about your age. It's only one year, after all.'

Mary's solemn face moved into a grin. 'Trust you to think like that!' she chuckled, and both girls fell about laughing as the tensions of the appalling events of the afternoon were all at once released.

Marianne peered out from the mess-hut door through the driving rain that lashed in across the sea. It was only a week into November, but already the wind was bitterly cold. Marianne was beginning to wonder if they shouldn't be preparing for another biblical flood, the two pleasant weeks in the second half of September having been the only respite in the wet weather since the snow and ice of the previous winter. And now that dreaded season was approaching once more.

She recognized immediately the forlorn figure in the Red Cross uniform, looking around in bewilderment as it battled with its umbrella in the gale. Marianne dashed straight outside without a care for her own protection, and grasped the nurse by the arm.

'Mary, quickly! Come in from the rain!'

She ran with her friend back inside the hut and hung up her wet cloak for her before the two of them hugged tightly.

'How fantastic to see you! When did you arrive?'

'Ten days ago,' Mary informed her, glancing at the strange surroundings. 'They processed me quite quickly as I'm already qualified, and suddenly I was off and didn't have the chance to write and let you know.'

'But you're here now! Are you settling in all right?'

'Thrown in at the deep end, more like! They made me a sister straight away and put me in charge of two medical wards. I'd rather be in surgical, but that might come later. So you can imagine I've been pretty busy finding my way around, and this is the first chance I've had to come and find you.'

'Oh, I'm so glad to see you! And that I spotted you out in the rain, or you'd have been even more soaked than you are!'

'At least unlike you my work's indoors, if you count tents flapping and groaning in the wind as indoors. But I do sleep in a proper building.'

'Lucky you!' Marianne laughed enviously. 'We just have cubicles in a draughty hut. But come and meet Stella, my partner in crime, and my other friends.'

She quickly made some introductions and then went to fetch Mary a welcome mug of tea. When she returned, Mary was chatting away as if she had known the group all her life.

'You'll have your work cut out on a medical ward with winter coming on,' Phyllis was telling her. 'The fighting usually dies down a bit, but the men get sick even quicker.'

'The wet conditions have already been the worst ever for all this fighting around Ypres. Men sliding off duckboards and drowning in the mud. Ugh, unimaginable. Thank God we finally took Passchendaele yesterday. You had heard the news?'

'Oh, yes–'

'I think the casualties have been the worst ever, so hopefully they should start easing off now.'

'Don't you think the Allies are going to want to push on, though, now we've had such a victory?'

'Didn't your Albert say he thought something hush-hush was going on?'

'Well, he couldn't say any more than that,' Marianne answered doubtfully.

'Albert?' Mary questioned her. 'Who's Albert? What've you been keeping from me,

Marianne?' she teased.

'Oh.' Marianne felt heat flare into her cheeks. 'I'm so sorry. I never mentioned him to you ... well, because of Michael.'

'Oh, Marianne, that's so thoughtful. But it doesn't mean you can't have a sweetheart just because... So, I want to hear all about this Albert.'

Marianne nevertheless heard a catch in Mary's voice, but before she could reply, a sudden silence fell on the entire mess hut and all the FANY girls looked heavenwards.

'That's Moaning Minnie, again, isn't it?' Mary asked in a small voice.

'The air-raid siren, yes,' Marianne confirmed. 'I'll get you a tin hat, and then we all have to go and huddle in the dug-out – until we get called out. So,' she nodded with a wry tilt of her head, 'welcome to France.'

CHAPTER TWENTY

Silence.

Earth-shattering silence. Or was it? Perhaps it was rather the devastation of shock so deep that it numbs all the senses.

Every muscle of Marianne's body was locked in paralysis, her wide eyes staring blindly across her cramped cubicle. Somewhere in her brain it finally registered that her lungs had not moved for too long as if the life had been sucked out of her. In sudden response, her chest expanded in an enormous, painful effort and she saw stars as she regained her full senses.

God Almighty! There was a hole in the outer wall where a large shard of shrapnel had sliced through it and embedded itself in the mattress – just where Marianne had been sitting on the edge of the bed. The blast that had exploded the deadly piece of metal into her cubicle had also saved her life – by flinging her across the tiny room – even if she had been winded as she crashed against the door.

Slowly, she turned the handle and sidled out into the corridor, moving in some strange, silent dream. Her comrades were emerging from their cubicles, white-faced, pale lips moving without sound, shaking their heads, hands over their ears. A trickle of blood was running down Phyllis's terrified cheek. A splinter of bomb was stuck in Lucinda's door.

Suddenly Mac was there, shaking a sharp piece of metal from her coat. 'Is everyone all right?' Marianne read her lips, noticing Mac's demented frown as she clearly couldn't hear her own words. 'The deafness will pass,' she appeared to mouth. 'Follow me to the dug-out,' she beckoned, hoping they would all understand her sign language.

Wordlessly, they all grabbed their coats and metal hats, and spilled out into the darkness. Even these brave, courageous young women who risked their lives constantly had never come so close to meeting their maker. They slid outside in various degrees of shock, only to gasp at the sight that met their eyes: a small crater where until a minute earlier, their bath-house and kitchen had stood.

'Was anyone in there?' Marianne realized that she was just about able to make out Mac's horrified words, so at least the shattering effect of the blast on her eardrums was already beginning to wear off. But it didn't stop the excruciating churning in her stomach. *Had* anyone been in the two service huts at that late hour? She glanced fearfully around her. Her little group of five were all accounted for, but what of everyone else? It was impossible to tell.

More flashes cutting through the ice-black night and explosions coming faintly to her hearing but making the ground shake, made her instinctively duck. Thank God they had the dug-out to shelter in! But at that moment, Tanky appeared and as she raised her booming voice even higher than normal, everyone heard her to some extent.

'Sorry, chaps! Message just come through. Train already arrived.'

Marianne and her companions visibly drew breath. It was the last thing they needed when they had been but yards away from a direct hit and still didn't know if everyone had survived. But on the other hand, perhaps having their treacherous task to focus on would distract them. Certainly getting the reluctant engines to splutter into life gave them something to concentrate on. November had rapidly turned into the depths of winter with continuous rain and sleet, and that night, with the first clear skies all month, the temperature had plummeted further, turning the roads to ribbons of glass.

As they slid into the station, Marianne couldn't believe her eyes. News had filtered through of a new tactic being employed around the town of Cambrai. Instead of beginning an offensive with the usual intense bombardment, the enemy had been taken entirely by surprise by a sudden, concentrated tank attack. The initial advantage had been followed by a gradual chipping away of the German defences, and the Allies were slowly gaining ground. But the costs of this success had been high.

In the frosty glimmer from a partial moon, a sea of stretchers had been laid out on the platform. Glinting in the moonlight, the train itself was too obvious a target for the bombers, and it must have been decided to off-load the wounded and take the train out of the station as soon as possible. An ominous fear blackened Marianne's heart, cramping the pit of her belly. She sensed something in her bones as she turned the ambulance around, ready to load up its broken human cargo.

They each took on as many of the walking wounded as they possibly could, mainly to free up space between the rows of tightly packed prostrate bodies. Even with their uniform skirts only reaching to their calves, the FANY girls were almost falling over them as they guided the less badly wounded into the backs of the ambulances, squeezing them in and piling one or two onto the passenger seat in the open cab as well.

'Don't mind me, miss,' the soldier beside Marianne nodded as she accidentally elbowed him whilst changing gear, they were jammed together so closely. 'I'm just so bloody relieved to get here.'

Not as relieved as she was to realize her hearing was returning, Marianne thought grimly, as she squinted into the glacial darkness – although a split second later, the sky flashed like a beacon as another resounding crash heralded a further explosion.

'Cor, blimey, didn't realize you was getting raids like this. Take me hat off to you, I would, if I could.' He held up two heavily bandaged hands, his teeth flashing tombstone white as he grinned.

'Where were you?' Marianne asked as she swerved round a new crater in the road.

'Near Cambrai, miss. Beating the Hun. Slowly. Worst casualties I've seen in me two years out in this hell. Just hope these hands are bloody bad enough to get me discharged. Give both of them gladly, I would, if it meant I didn't have to go back.'

'I hope it doesn't come to that,' Marianne managed to grimace.

By the time she drove with Stella back to the station, the train had left, hopefully no longer attracting the enemy bombers. In the gloom, all they could make out was an undulating field of writhing, groaning bodies. Some cried out in agony, others were worryingly still. Heads, eyes bandaged. Some with breathing holes in a mask. Missing limbs, torsos encased in scarlet or yellow stained dressings beneath filthy, sodden blankets.

The fetid stench of mud, blood, urine and vomit. And the nauseating stink of gangrene.

'Got a bleeder here, sir!' The clerk where Marianne had been directed to park was using a dimmed torch to read the labels on the soldiers' coats, and now he called out to the nearest army medical officer. 'Double leg amputee.'

Marianne and Stella exchanged glances. Poor devil. The MO lifted the blanket wearily. Even in the deep shadows, they could see the glistening dark patch rapidly spreading onto the stretcher from the blood-soaked bandages swathing one of the stumps.

'Leave him,' the MO sighed. 'He's unlikely to make it, and he'll be better off dead.'

As he went to turn away, Marianne caught his arm, powerless to restrain her sudden rage. 'No! You can't decide that! You have no right!'

The army doctor lifted his chin. He wasn't used to insubordination. But these head-strong, lion-hearted young women were subject to no one else's rules, military or otherwise. And you had to admire them, if the truth be told.

'Get a tourniquet, Stell,' Marianne instructed as she defiantly attempted to rip open the blood-drenched remains of the trouser-leg. 'Scissors, too!' she called as her friend jumped up into the ambulance.

The MO shrugged and moved off, the

clerk in tow, as between them, Marianne and Stella applied the tourniquet, a task made so much more difficult because they were groping in the obscurity of the night. They pulled the band as tight as possible, praying it would at least stem the bleeding long enough to get him to the hospital. The patient was unconscious, whether from blood-loss, shock or a recent shot of morphine, they couldn't tell. They doubted the latter. Drugs were getting scarcer by the day, and in all this chaos, the soldier was a drop in the ocean. He barely moaned as they lifted the stretcher and staggered with him the few feet to the ambulance.

Three others joined him, crippled mounds of humanity, faceless in the terrors of pain and darkness. One cried out at every lurch of the vehicle no matter how smoothly Marianne was able to drive through the shell-pocked streets. Stella tried to comfort him, helpless, while she could hear another grinding his teeth in his efforts to control his agony. The fourth one, whose opened chest could not be held together by any amount of bandaging, was silent. He was dead by the time they reached the hospital.

'God knows how he lasted this long,' the receiving MO sighed, pulling the foul blanket over the corpse's head. 'So what else have we got?'

'Suspected multiple fractures to the left

humerus and ribs, shrapnel in the side and a double leg amputee,' Marianne heard Stella say efficiently as she joined her at the rear of the ambulance. 'We had to put a tourniquet on the right stump.'

'Let's have him first, then!' The doctor's voice rose and he clicked his fingers impatiently at the band of waiting orderlies. Two of them sprang forward with a trolley and helped heave the man onto it before rushing it into the dimly lit corridor.

'Do we have a rank?' Marianne caught the doctor's question as she turned back to help Stella with their other charges.

'Er, yes,' she faintly heard the orderly's reply as he lifted the blanket from the soldier's sleeve. 'Major. And...' He turned his attention to the identity disc around the patient's neck. It glinted like metal, so it was clearly of the aluminium type issued prior to the war or in the very early stages before they were replaced by the thick fibre lozenges sported by the majority of soldiers nowadays. The orderly obviously noticed as he went on, 'This chap must have been around for a long time. Looks like A.G. Thorneycroft.'

Marianne's world suddenly shattered into splinters at her feet. She almost dropped the next patient as they slid the stretcher off the runners, and she had to gird up her tortured mind to regain control of herself. Dear God, *Albert!* No! It couldn't be! She'd have recognized him! But would she, in the darkness, caked in mud and filth? But ... yes. She'd have *known*. She'd have felt it.

Wouldn't she?

They carried the next case inside, Marianne's head spinning in a fragmented dance. The bewilderment on Stella's face as she suddenly lowered their patient onto the corridor floor barely registered with her as she raced after the rapidly disappearing trolley. She couldn't believe it was him. They weren't using the cavalry. He was safe behind the lines with his horse, Captain. But as she caught up with him, her heart was rearing in her chest. She *had* felt it, hadn't she? That sinking sensation in her belly as they had arrived at the station.

The savage fear must have shown on her face, for the MO and the orderly instinctively stopped their headlong rush.

'Do you know him?' The doctor's voice cracked with sympathy.

Marianne's trembling hand lifted the lock of hair from the deathly white forehead. Beneath the filth, it was sandy-coloured. The finely sculptured brow, the strong jaw.

She nodded as the tearing anguish ripped at her throat.

'Then let us save him,' the MO said firmly, and Marianne was left standing in a pool of pain as Albert was rushed on, leaving a trail of crimson droplets on the floor.

'Marianne?' Stella asked anxiously at her elbow.

'Albert,' Marianne croaked. 'It's Albert.'

'Oh, good God. But, Marianne,' Stella said gently, 'there's nothing you can do now. We have the others. Come on. I'll drive. You're in no fit state—'

'No, it's all right,' Marianne insisted, but how she dragged herself through the rest of the night, her soul crumbling inside her, she didn't know. When every man had been delivered to his destination, Stella drove her back to the hospital. Dropping with fatigue, she searched dimly lit corridors littered with the injured, accosting orderlies who shook their heads and passed her on. It was utter, demonic chaos.

On the brink of despair, she found him at last, his face as grey as the pillow behind his head. They brought her a chair as she swooned beside him, let her sit by his bed. They had successfully operated to stop the haemorrhage and given him a blood transfusion. With careful nursing to prevent infection, he should live. But who knew what deadly bacteria were already in his blood despite anti-tetanus and other vaccinations?

Marianne sat there, like an effigy, staring at his ashen face in the candlelight, her heart and soul empty and withered in her breast.

'Of course I understand.' Mac's smile was full of sympathy. 'The major has no family or anyone else to look after him. Without you, he'd end up in some sort of institution for the rest of his life, and God knows there'll be enough of them who will. But I'll be sorry to lose you, Warrington. Your service has been exemplary. And,' she broke off to raise an eyebrow, 'it's very likely you saved my own life. I'd like to give you a medal if we had one to give. You've been here a year, so you've done your bit. So.' She stood up and held out her hand. 'Good luck, Private.'

'Thank you, Commandant.'

'Major Thorneycroft will be fit to travel in a few days, you say? So you'll be home for Christmas.'

'In Blighty, yes. But the major will be in a military hospital wherever they send him for a while yet. Home will eventually be Devon.'

'Of course. Your West Country burr hasn't gone unnoticed. I'll have your papers ready and waiting.'

'Thank you again, Commandant.'

Marianne stood to attention and saluted, which Mac returned. Once outside the office, Marianne drew in a deep breath. She was going to hate leaving her comrades, knowing the dangers they would be facing daily and wishing she was still part of it. But whatever the future held for her and Albert, he needed her. For a while, at least. And maybe later she would return – if this God-damned war was still raging.

Stella parked the ambulance by the hospital entrance and turned to Marianne with a watery smile. Marianne gave a jerky nod, her mouth closed in a curve. There was a lump in her throat, too.

The four patients to be transported to the docks, Albert among them, were waiting just inside the entrance. Marianne's last duty for the FANY would be to accompany them across the Channel, praying they had a safe crossing in the winter weather and weren't attacked either by sea or air. She jumped down from the vehicle, avoiding her little case containing her few personal possessions that she had crammed at her feet. But before they went to collect their charges, Stella enveloped her in a bear-hug.

'I'll miss you,' the other girl choked.

'With any luck, my replacement will be bigger and stronger than me which will make things easier for you!' Marianne attempted to joke.

'I should hope so, too!' Stella gave a forced laugh as they pulled apart. 'You will write?'

'Of course!'

'And good luck. And I'll see you *après la guerre*.' Stella stood back and they saluted each other, a tiny gesture that meant so much. The dangers they had faced, shared

together. Come through. Yes. After the war, they would meet again.

They turned towards the hospital doors, their farewells over. But just as they did so, the sound of running feet caught Marianne's attention. A figure in a Red Cross uniform was hurrying up the road towards them, quite puffed out.

'Mary!'

'Oh, thank goodness I caught you!' Mary's face was red from exertion but also alight with some other emotion Marianne couldn't identify. 'I ran all the way from my own hospital,' Mary panted. 'I just had to tell you. I've just received a letter. From Michael! He's alive! In a POW camp in Germany!'

Marianne's heart erupted and overflowed with joy for her friend, and her face broke into a huge grin. 'That's amazing!' she cried, and waltzed Mary in a circle.

'Seems he was one of the lucky ones to be plucked out of the water by the Germans who sank his ship,' Mary explained, her eyes sparkling like diamonds. 'A few others of the crew survived as well, but it's the first time he's been allowed to write and, of course, the letter went home first. So now we can write to each other and he'll be safe until the end of the war. Whenever that is.'

'Oh, I can't tell you how happy I am for you!' But then Marianne's face clouded. 'But I was the one who persuaded you to come out here, and now I'm leaving you.'

'Marianne, I wouldn't be anywhere else. And you've done your bit and it's my turn to do mine. You go home and nurse Albert back to full health. Now give me a hug, and then I must go. I'm on duty in five minutes.'

A few seconds later, Mary was dashing back the way she had come. Marianne watched her give a little skip of joy as she turned the corner. That was a miracle indeed. Marianne met Stella's beaming face. One happy ending, at least. Marianne prayed that Mary herself survived the continuing air-raids on Calais. If anything happened to her, she would feel utterly responsible.

She turned once more towards the hospital entrance, Albert waiting inside. They had a long journey to travel yet.

CHAPTER TWENTY-ONE

'Did you have a good ride, my dear?'

Albert was sat in his wheelchair on the terrace that ran along the back of Fencott Place, apparently enjoying the April sunshine. Marianne smiled across at him as she returned from the stableyard, having seen to Pegasus's needs after a long morning ride over the moor. Her face was flushed with exhilaration, her heart lifted with contentment, but she was brought up short by the forced tone in Albert's question.

'Yes, thank you, I did. But...' She broke off, frowning, and noticed the letter on Albert's lap. 'Is anything wrong?'

Albert drew in a deep breath and held it as he met her gaze, and she could see the pain in his eyes. 'Sadly, yes,' he breathed out. 'As if Bourdon Wood wasn't bad enough, A Squadron was annihilated a couple of weeks ago. It's thought just a handful survived, and they were taken prisoner.'

'Oh, no.' Marianne felt the all too familiar coldness in her breast at the arrival of more bad news. Bourdon Wood was where Albert had been wounded and so many of his comrades had been lost or injured, but this latest news was even worse. A massive German offensive had begun towards the end of March, so vigorous that they had broken the British line. It was only after the bitterest of fighting, combined with magnificent action by the Americans, Australians and Canadians, that the enemy attack had been exhausted and the conflict had died down again.

'Albert, I'm so sorry,' Marianne said with such sympathy as she absorbed the news.

Albert shook his head, eyes closed, and then his mouth curved in a bitter grimace as he looked at her again. 'So perhaps this isn't so bad,' he said wryly, dipping his head towards what remained of his legs. 'Without this, I'd probably have been dead this time along with the rest of them.'

Marianne didn't know what to say. Her own blood ran cold at the same thought. At least Albert was alive. She dropped down on her haunches beside him and took his hand, for some minutes, neither of them saying a word.

'It's so wonderfully peaceful here,' Albert murmured at length. 'Makes it hard to imagine what's going on over in France. And the poor country itself. When we were going towards Cambrai, the countryside was absolutely decimated. Villages reduced to rubble. No fields, not a blade of grass, just the occasional charred tree-stump to break the monotony. A complete ocean of black mud and water-filled shell-holes. God knows how many men and horses are buried beneath it all. I reckon they'll still be digging up bones in a hundred years' time. If this bloody war ever ends.'

'Oh, Albert, it's got to.' Marianne's voice quivered with conviction. 'With the Americans fully engaged now, the Boche won't be able to hold out for ever.'

Albert had been staring out over the moor, but now he turned to her with a wistful smile. 'I know I've said the same thing myself, but when you get news like this, it shakes your faith. But in the meantime, it's our duty to enjoy all this,' he said, gesticulating around him. 'It's what our brave lads have given their lives for. And I shall be eternally grateful to your parents for giving me such a home.'

'Well, after you saved Pegasus from the army–'

'Didn't requisition him, you mean.'

'All right,' Marianne conceded. 'But after that, it was the least we could do for you. Besides, my father rather enjoys having another man in the house. It evens up the numbers.'

Albert gave a short laugh. 'If you can call me that. But...' He paused, chewing his lip. 'I was thinking while you were out on your ride. Feeling so utterly jealous. Now that

Captain's been shipped back and you've so kindly allowed me to have him here, maybe I can do more than feed the faithful old fellow carrots. I have a knee on one side and a thigh on the other. Surely that's enough to stay on at walking pace at least. Perhaps we could build a special mounting block of some sort. What do you think?'

Marianne swallowed hard, her eyes stretched wide. Her heart was brimming with admiration and pride in this strong, brave man whose courage, it appeared, had been no more scarred by his appalling experiences than, thankfully, had his handsome face. She had the feeling that even if he had been dreadfully burned as so many had, he would have found a way to overcome the horror of it.

'Oh, Albert, that's a wonderful idea!' she grinned. 'We'll need to see what Elliott says, though, with that one leg refusing to heal properly.' She didn't use the word *stump*. It was somehow too brutal.

'I don't really care what Elliott thinks, much though I hold him in high regard as a physician. But I can't see why I shouldn't get back in the saddle. Captain's such a steady animal. To be on his back again – well, I can't tell you what that would mean to me. Just to go for short rides on the moor at a walk.'

Marianne felt she could keel over with happiness. Through all those dark weeks nursing Albert back to health, she had never dreamt that one day he would be determined to ride again. The intensity in his eyes reached down inside her, their love of horses an invisible thread tying them together, but was she ready to let it bind them forever? Her brain whirled in circles as she instinctively shied away from the confusion that Albert had unleashed in her. He had moved her heart in a way she wasn't sure she was ready to cope with, and it made her feel lost and fragile.

The tears that trickled down Marianne's cheeks glistened like silver pearls in the moonlight that shafted through the open window. The atmosphere was hot and sultry, and Marianne had tossed and turned, unable to sleep, until she had got out of bed and gone over to the window, her mind racked with the contents of the letter she had received that morning from Mary.

It was already common knowledge that a wave of influenza had swept through the troops and other personnel in the spring. Now though, in the height of summer, it had returned with vengeful force. The virus was spreading like wildfire, returning soldiers bringing it with them to their homelands, and countries all over the world were being infected. And it had become a killer. At its most vicious, it could take a life in hours. A virulent pneumonia, clogging the lungs with a thick, scarlet jelly, was a common, deadly complication. Blood could foam from the mouth and nose, some victims became incontinent, were taken by violent vomiting or bled from the ears. Skin turned blue with heliotrope cyanosis. Among the troops it was a worse killer than the enemy, and many saw it as another plague.

And Stella had died from it in a hospital bed with Mary at her side.

Dear, darling Stella whose stalwart heart had been twice the size of her petite form. Many of the FANY had been laid low in the earlier epidemic, as had Mary, and it was hoped this would have provided some immunity to this new, far stronger wave. But Stella had escaped the first round, and now the evil, vengeful strain had wrapped her in its demonic tentacles and taken her to her maker.

Marianne couldn't believe her dear friend was dead. She could see Stella's impish face as she mimicked Tanky or Charlie Chaplin with equal ease. Or serious, as she peered into the unlit night from behind the steering wheel, tin hat rammed down on her head. Despite all the air-raids, even the direct hit on the camp, the only serious injury to any of the FANY had been when Commanding Officer Pat Waddell had lost a leg in a collision with a train on a level-crossing shortly before Marianne had arrived in Calais. And now Stella was the first fatality.

Marianne tried to swallow down her grief, but the swelling in her throat was the size of a golf ball. She opened her eyes wide in an attempt to let her tears dry, and stared up at the full moon. It was crying, too, its tears falling in heavy grey clouds that drifted across the night sky.

Marianne shut her eyes as sadness overwhelmed her again and a brutal sob escaped her lungs. She let herself weep, her heart dragging in pain. At length, her sorrow grew tired but still she sat, motionless as a statue, gazing out of the open window over the moon-drenched moor.

She was just beginning to think that sleep might come now if she climbed back into bed, when something caught the corner of her eye in the direction of the stableyard. A thin mist was spreading over the sleeping moor, which struck her as slightly odd, although the atmosphere was humid and sometimes the weather over Dartmoor had a mind of its own. But as her nose twitched and wrinkled, she recognized a familiar, acrid smell. It wasn't mist, but smoke.

Horror stung her to the marrow and for several seconds, she was paralyzed with shock. The horses of a more hardy type were out in the fields, but Pegasus, Captain and their one thoroughbred brood mare were in their looseboxes overnight. And dear Joe was asleep in the comfortable rooms over the tack-room since he had refused to move into the 'big house' itself.

Marianne's brain sprang into action and she fled across the room and out onto the landing. 'Mum! Dad!' she screamed, barging into their bedroom. 'I think the stables are on fire!'

'What!' They were both awake in a trice, rubbing the sleep from their eyes.

'There's smoke in the yard!' Marianne called, but she didn't wait for a reply. She was already flying down the staircase, her heart beating like thunder. Even in all her experience of the air-raids in Calais, she didn't think she'd ever felt such panic. This wasn't some foreign land torn apart by conflict. This was the safe haven of her home and it was under attack from one of the worst enemies possible amongst the bales of hay and straw.

She pushed her bare feet into her boots in the boot-room and shot open the bolts on the back door with shaking fingers. She scarcely gave a thought to Albert asleep in the morning room downstairs, which had been converted into a bedroom for him as try as he might, he couldn't manage the stairs. Marianne knew that he would merely feel useless and alerting him would only waste time. She cursed the key that didn't want to turn in the lock but after a moment's fumbling, she was charging through the gate in the high wall that led to the yard.

She snatched in her breath, unsure for what was just a few seconds but seemed to her an eternity of tearing uncertainty. Smoke was billowing in a choking fog from the roof of the stable-block where orange flames were licking around the door. Thank God the stalls were empty, but all the buildings in the yard were of wooden construction and the fire could spread in minutes. She could hear Pegasus and the other horses stamping about their looseboxes in the adjoining block, their instinctive fear of fire triggered by the smell of smoke. But Joe was in equal danger and being a little hard of hearing, doubtless hadn't been woken by the frantic neighing just yards away.

It was without further thought that Marianne picked up a stone and lobbed it at the small window to Joe's bedroom. The glass shattered noisily, but what was a broken pane compared to Joe's life or that of the horses? She yelled at the top of her voice and to her supreme relief, Joe appeared at the window.

'Joe, the stables are on fire!' she hollered at him.

'On my way, maid!' Joe shouted back.

Marianne didn't wait for him but hurled herself across to the looseboxes. Fed by tinder-dry material, the fire had quickly taken hold of the stables and smoke was now seeping from the first loosebox. The prize mare inside was thrashing in panic, but dear Lord, ever since the theft two and a half years previously, the doors were always securely locked and Joe had the keys.

Marianne danced on the spot in an agony of frustration. But there was Joe, pulling up the braces on his hastily donned trousers, the bunch of keys in his hand. Hampered by the darkness and the veil of thickening smoke that was making his eyes water, Joe nevertheless had the padlock unfastened in seconds and Marianne dived inside while he went to unlock the other doors.

The poor creature inside was petrified. In the smoke-filled gloom, Marianne could see the whites of its wildly rolling eyes and its huge form reared up in terror, hoofs narrowly missing Marianne's head. But a flickering red tongue was darting through the wooden wall from the stables next door. There was no time to find a sack to throw over the mare's head to calm her, and as she reared again, it would have been impractical anyway.

'Go on, girl!' Marianne encouraged her, slapping her hairy rump, and the animal sprang out through the open door.

Outside, Joe was unlocking the other doors and while he disappeared into Captain's box, Marianne flew into Pegasus. She need not have worried as he bolted outside where

Seth and Rose had now arrived, hurriedly dressed, and were driving the loose horses into the drove that led to the fields. It was fully enclosed between stone walls, so while they couldn't escape, the frightened creatures would be safe and could get some way from the burning buildings.

In moments, all the buckets had been collected. Working as one, the five of them – since Patsy had also arrived on the scene – formed a chain across the yard from the stables to the water trough, which thankfully was fed by a constantly running stream. Without a word, they began passing full buckets in one direction and empty ones in the other. Seth was dousing the looseboxes in water while Joe was using empty sacks to beat back the flames that were trying to take hold of the end wall. They clearly had no hope of saving the stableblock, but if they could stop the fire consuming the looseboxes and the other buildings in the yard, it would be something.

Smoke seared into Marianne's throat and she feared for her father's weakened lungs, but they had no choice but to tackle the blaze themselves. Eyes streaming, faces smeared with sweat and grime, they carried on valiantly, muscles and shoulders strained and aching, arms feeling as if they had been wrenched from their sockets. It was all so unreal, macabre, as their dark forms scurried about like ants silhouetted against the horrific incandescent glow from the burning stables. A crash resonated through the darkness as the roof collapsed, sending a shower of sparks into the night sky. Marianne prayed to God the fire would burn itself out and they could halt its progress by drenching the looseboxes in water.

She stopped for just a second to flex her shoulders and blinked through her stinging eyes. The gate to the terrace had been left wide open and she was sure she saw movement through her blurred vision. Surely dear Albert wasn't trying to come and help? But, no. There was someone *standing* there, and Marianne's blood froze as something flared brightly in the figure's hand – and was then hurled inside the house.

Dear God Almighty! A torrent of fear and rage broke over Marianne as she streaked forward with a demented scream. Albert! Her heart kicked in her breast as she thrust the unsuspecting intruder aside with all her might.

'You bastard, there's someone inside!' she shrieked as she careered down the passageway past the boot-room, leaping over the burning rag, nostrils flaring with the smell of paraffin. She skipped over a trail of little flames that danced along into the grand entrance hall where she yanked up a heavy rug and threw it over the threatening fire.

Sweat oozed from every pore of her filthy skin, and as the man came towards her, she became aware that she was dressed in nothing more than her flimsy nightdress. Her heart exploded with unleashed strength as she ran at him, but to her astonishment, he began stamping out the remaining flames.

'Someone inside?' he croaked. 'I had no idea. I thought...'

Marianne stared at him, dumbstruck, as he extinguished the fire he himself had started. In the strange dimness, he seemed grotesquely familiar, a devil rising from the forbidden abyss of hell. And then he disappeared out through the open door.

Marianne swayed on her feet, wanting nothing but to slump down on the floor. But she instantly found herself chasing after him, down the stone steps of the terrace, across the lawn and squeezing through a small gap in the thick hedge behind which the barbed wire fence had been cut. She felt the sharp points tearing at her flesh, ripping her night-dress, but she had to catch him. They raced across the rough ground to the road, but it was too late. A car was parked there with the cranking handle clearly left in place. With two vicious turns, the engine sprang into life and the villain leapt into the driver's seat and was speeding away, leaving Marianne stamping her foot in frustrated fury as she couldn't see to read the number-plate.

CHAPTER TWENTY-TWO

'Aw, thank the Good Lord!'

Patsy dropped down into a chair in the drawing room, something she had never done in her entire working life at Fencott Place. But this was momentous news indeed. Dense, low cloud might be enveloping the moor in a dank, grey mist on that miserable November morning, but it felt as if glorious sunshine was streaming through the glass of the French windows.

'Is it really true?' Marianne breathed incredulously.

'Yes, look,' Seth answered, clearing his damaged lungs. 'It says here an armistice was signed at five o'clock this morning, and the war will end at eleven.'

'That's in two minutes,' Albert said, consulting his watch.

Patsy suddenly jumped to her feet. 'I must tell Joe!' she squealed with delight, and hurried out of the room as fast as her rotund form allowed.

The remaining four adults looked round at each other, enshrouded in some tangled emotion none of them had words to express. It was over, the horrors, the crippling fear.

They should be bursting with joy, yet they had lived with the war for so long, there was no room for relief. They shared instead a soul-weary emptiness.

'It won't bring them back, though, will it?' Rose spoke at last, breaking the silence with a trembling whisper. 'All those hundreds of thousands of men. Just boys many of them. Our Hal.'

No one answered her quavering words for some time, each enclosed in individual reflection until Seth gave the rasping cough that had dogged him ever since the fire.

'No, my dear,' he spluttered, fighting to bring it under control. 'It won't bring Hal back. Or Marianne's friend, Stella, or Albert's comrades. But we must concentrate on the good things. Artie, for instance,' he reminded them, referring to Mary's elder half-brother who had been badly wounded the previous Christmas. 'He'll never father children, but apart from that, he's made a full recovery. Young Michael will obviously be repatriated and returned to the bosom of his family. Joshua and Philip were exempt from conscription because of their particular skills in farming and the huge increase in meat production they were achieving. Marianne returned to us unscathed, and Mary, we know, was safe when she wrote just a few days ago and the air-raids had long stopped. And without the war, Albert here would never have come into our lives.' He threw a deep, warm smile in Albert's direction that was interrupted by another coughing fit. 'I think we should stand,' he managed to croak, glancing at the clock.

They did so, each adopting a tall, attentive stance. In his wheelchair, Albert sat up straight, stiff-backed. When the clock struck the hour, Albert, Marianne and Seth, as an ex-army officer himself, instinctively raised their arms in salute to the numerous thousands who had made the ultimate sacrifice or whose lives would never be the same again. Marianne felt her throat tighten as her vision misted with tears. Opposite her, Rose's face was a mask of grief.

Down in Tavistock, marines let off a series of detonations. A train in the station repeatedly blew its whistle. The town laundry and the factory let off their sirens. Across the country, church bells rang out.

But no one would ever, *ever* forget.

'So, what are we all going to do, now the war's over?' Kate asked in her usual direct manner.

It was Wednesday morning, two days after the war had ended. Kate had driven up to Fencott Place with little Valerie in the wagonette pulled by Clomper, the only horse the Pencarrows had been allowed to keep for all the land they farmed. They were gathered in the drawing room, Valerie playing quietly on the rug with her doll.

'That's a good question.' Seth puffed out his cheeks wistfully. 'Which is why I'm pleased you came over as we need to discuss some things as a family.'

'That sounds ominous.'

'It's certainly serious,' Seth confirmed, 'and we have various matters to consider. First of all, the stud-farm. Obviously we won't be selling any more stock to the army, or training any more horses for them. And to be honest, we were struggling to keep up with their demands. I'm getting too old and this chest of mine makes me worse than useless. Your mother's the most brilliant horsewoman who ever lived, but she's sixty-four and can't be expected to work like a slave, and she needs a rest after all her work at the moss-gathering centre. Marianne, I know, will do all she can, but she has Albert to care for. So that leaves Joe, who's turned sixty himself. Now I know Marianne and Albert had plans for the stables for when the war was over but that was before Albert was injured, so we need to look at the reality of the situation as it stands now.'

'Which is?' Kate prompted.

'Well, unless they turn to tractors which I can't see happening on a large scale for quite a while, farmers will be desperate to replace their horses, but we've none to sell until our young stock matures which will be at least six months. We've only rebuilt the stable-block due to Albert's generosity–'

'It was the least I could do,' Albert insisted, blushing slightly. 'I no longer needed my own house since you took me in, so I had the money from its sale.'

'It was still very good of you.'

'Well, I can't understand why the police never managed to catch that devil who burnt them down in the first place,' Kate declared, blowing out her lips like a horse. '*And* he would have set fire to the house too, if it hadn't been for Marianne. And if it *was* the same blighter who tried to attack her back along but didn't succeed, why would he bear such a grudge?'

Marianne bit the inside of her lip. She couldn't be sure, but it had slowly dawned on her where she might have seen the blackguard before. Could it have been the stranger who had tricked her and then attempted to assault her out on the moor shortly before she had gone to France? She had only caught a glimpse of him on each occasion. She felt cross with herself for not reporting the incident at the time for fear it would make her parents try to stop her joining the FANY, and it had made her utterly ashamed when she had revealed it after the fire, claiming that she hadn't thought anything of it at the time. But at least now, if it was the same villain, she had been able not only to give a description to the police, but also to tell them that he had appeared to be in disguise when he had attacked her on the moor. Nevertheless, whoever he was, he had disappeared into thin air.

'Well, although none of us can think of anyone, it would seem we've made an enemy somewhere without realizing it,' Seth continued. 'The inspector thought it could be the same person who stole the horses. Whoever it was must have known the layout of the place, finding the one weak spot we hadn't been aware of ourselves. But there's little we can do except be extra vigilant. Anyway, to get back to what I was saying, we can't look upon the horses as a source of income for some time, and then it will only be limited. And quite frankly, until this business is solved, I don't believe we should do anything further with the horses at all.'

'When it is, though, Dad, Albert and I still want to build up the stables to some extent at least, don't we?' Marianne said, smiling fondly at Albert.

'That's right,' Albert agreed. 'Train up a couple of stable lads, perhaps. Go back to breeding fine hunters as well on a small scale. It wouldn't be the same as before the war, but I'm sure we could turn it to profit.'

'Well that's up to you, of course. But that

will take time, and meanwhile we all have to live.' Seth paused to swallow some water in order to subdue the cough that kept interrupting him. 'Once again, Albert is being most kind, but it isn't fair for us to rely on his generosity. Now, as you know, the only other source of family income has only ever been the investments Rose inherited from her first husband. And together with the unfortunate mistakes Hal made, they hit rock bottom with the war. Hopefully the stock market will pick up, but I can't see that happening for some years. So, your mother and I have come to a decision.'

He turned to Rose and she nodded, taking everyone's attention. Marianne's heart was in her mouth, for what could that decision be that it warranted the formal introduction her father had given it? From what he had said earlier, surely it wasn't that they were going to sell Fencott Place? Like much of the property on Dartmoor, it was leasehold to the Duchy of Cornwall, so wasn't worth as much as might appear anyway. And it was the only home she had ever known, ever wanted, the bedrock of her life! No, they couldn't–

'We're going to sell the house in London,' Rose announced, and Marianne almost collapsed with relief. 'It's only small, of course, not like Charles's place was. But it's been a useful base for your father to stay when he needed to go to London to sort out our affairs there. But,' she sighed, lowering her eyes, 'he's not up to doing that anymore, so it makes sense to sell it.'

'Oh.' It was Kate's audible disappointment that turned everyone's head.

'Why, do you have some objection?' her mother asked in bewildered surprise.

'W-well,' Kate stammered, 'it's just that Philip and I have been talking. And we'd anticipated much of what you've been saying. And you know Philip's much more of a businessman than a farmer. I mean, he's very knowledgeable and experienced and works like a Trojan, which was why he was exempted from conscription, he and Josh both. But he doesn't *like* farming. And now the war's over, Richard's already had people asking about tenancies on Hillside and even Moor Top for when their sons or husbands are demobilized. So, if you agreed, we were thinking of going to live in the London house, for a while at least, to see if Philip could restore some of the Warrington family fortune.'

Astonishment bounced around the room and for some moments nobody spoke as incredulous looks were exchanged.

'Well, that's a turn-up for the books,' Rose declared at length.

'Not for us, though.' Kate shook her head. 'Philip and I had been thinking about it for some time as the Allies were gradually beating back the Hun and it was obvious they were going to have to capitulate. The thing is, Philip's so good with figures and he's always followed the stock market closely. If we were living in London, he could keep his ear to the ground far better. He'd get a job, preferably in the City, to support us as a family, but I reckon, with his finger on the pulse, you'd be able to dispense with your stockbroker and that would save you money as well.'

Marianne saw her father lift a considering eyebrow, but she herself felt leaden anger at the mention of her father's stockbroker. She alone knew that it was his daughter's refusal of Hal's proposal that had sent her brother off the rails the night he had lost so much of the family money – and led to his enlisting before he was conscripted. Who knew if he might still have been alive if it hadn't been for her?

'But what about the children?' Rose was asking now. 'And the house is very small. It only has two bedrooms.'

'The children can share to start with, but Philip will turn the attic into another room,' Kate said in a matter-of-fact way. 'Adam's quite happy provided he can spend the school holidays either here or back at the farm, and Valerie's too young to know any different.'

'Well, you seem to have it all worked out.' Seth pursed his lips thoughtfully. 'I suppose we could give it a trial for, say, six months. Let your mother and me sleep on it.'

It was just then that Patsy put her head around the door to announce that lunch was ready. Everyone got to their feet to make for the dining room, including Albert who had learnt to walk in a precarious fashion using crutches and one prosthetic leg. Sadly, the other stump was still refusing to heal properly, so he would have to wait until it did before he could be fitted with a second false limb.

Kate went to fetch Valerie from her position on the rug. She was a placid child and jumped up readily to take her mother's hand. Marianne had hung back, hoping to have a quiet word with her sister, and took her little niece's other hand.

'Is this really what you want?' she asked in a desperate whisper. 'To leave Dartmoor? Our home? Forget all the adventures we had together out on the moor?'

Kate merely shrugged. 'Of course I'll always love the place and look forward to coming down for the holidays. But I'm not like you, Marianne. I don't live and breathe for the moor. This will be a new adventure. Exciting. There'll be theatres and cinemas. An entire new social life. And so many more opportunities for the children as they grow up. Now, then, Valerie,' she said, bending down to her daughter. 'Do you think Grandma Rose will have your favourite for lunch?'

Marianne almost wilted on the spot. She really had lost her soul-mate, hadn't she? All those years, she had secretly hoped she might have Kate back as her partner in crime for escapades out on the moor. Just occasionally. But that hope had finally been smashed to smithereens forever. And if she hadn't been holding Valerie's hand, she might have stayed alone in the room and wept.

The horses ambled along the frost-hardened track, their necks bending in unison and blowing out clouds of warm breath into the cold air. Pegasus and Captain had become friends in the months they had been together, the spirited stallion and the stalwart gelding. They both seemed to sense that when Albert was on Captain's back, they must pick their way slowly and carefully. But whenever Rose rode him, the pair would race as fast as the uneven terrain would allow. Rose and Captain had taken to each other as soon as he had arrived, and his presence had gone a long way to ease Rose's heartbreak over Hermes who had never been found.

'It's just beginning to sink in that the war's truly over, you know,' Albert said wistfully as they sauntered along. 'At least as cavalry we didn't spend nearly as much time in the trenches as the poor Tommies did, even when we were dismounted which was so much of the time. It was awful, you know. The rats and lice. Decomposing body parts that suddenly appeared out of the mud. The stench when it was so wet that effluent from the latrines got washed about your feet. And that was without being constantly under attack or going over the top.'

'I know. But it really is over now, and we must look to the future. My main concern is for Kate and Philip and the children,' Marianne sighed dejectedly. 'I wish they weren't up in London with this new wave of flu. They say it's not quite so virulent as back in the summer, but almost. And it's hitting cities so much worse than country areas.'

'People are wearing masks, though. And many churches and dancehalls and that sort of thing are shut. And the government has instructed cinemas to open all their windows and ventilate them every four hours.'

'Much good that'll do,' Marianne scoffed. 'Manchester's been virtually closed down though, to try and prevent it spreading. I just wish they'd do the same with London. Kate says they're trapped now as travelling back here could expose the children worse than staying put and keeping indoors. And when poor Philip comes home, Kate doesn't let him see the children. She makes him have a stripped wash in the bedroom and stay there. And she sleeps on the couch downstairs. God, I do hope her precautions work. Oh,' Marianne said suddenly, her attention diverted. 'Hold Pegasus's reins a minute would you? That sheep seems to be in trouble.'

She swung her leg over Pegasus's neck and hopped down to the ground. Not far from the track, the sheep in question was trailing a hind-leg that appeared to be entangled in a loose strand of rusty barbed wire. The animal didn't appreciate Marianne's efforts to help it, and she had to straddle it backwards even then, having to avoid its frantically kicking hoofs. It took her some time to free it, and when she did, she prized up a large stone and buried the offending item safely beneath it.

'Some farmers can be so careless with their fences,' she complained as she climbed back into the saddle.

'Do you know, Marianne Warrington,' Albert declared as they set off again, 'you are the most extraordinary woman. You face life head on. If there's a problem, you'll always find a way to solve it. You rescue sheep. Waifs and strays–'

'And who might they be?' she laughed.

'Me, for instance.' Albert's voice was low and sombre. 'You train wild horses. You tackle fires and confront intruders. You take yourself off to France to drive an ambulance through constant air-raids–'

'So did plenty of others,' Marianne protested, a trifle embarrassed. 'And many have stayed on to help refugees return to what's left of their homes and rebuild their lives. Like Mary. She said she won't come home for some time, even though Michael's likely to be repatriated soon.'

'And if it hadn't been for me, *you*'d probably still be out there, too. No, don't argue. You know it's true. But it must mean that *I* mean a great deal to you. A very great deal. So, I'm hoping,' he went on hesitantly, sucking the breath over his teeth, 'that I can mean even more to you. So... I'd get down on my knees if it were possible, but, Marianne ... will you do me the honour of becoming my wife?'

He was gazing at her so intently, his eyes boring into hers, that she had to look away, afraid of what her expression might say. She was so shocked, and yet why should she be? They had grown so close, their minds always as one. But it was an easy closeness that was somehow bereft of passion, and she liked it that way. Their heady lovemaking in the little room above the French restaurant was a forgotten dream. A world away.

'Oh, Albert, I don't know,' she groaned softly, the words out before she could stop them.

She heard Albert swallow hard. 'Of course, if you don't fancy being in bed with a man who can't even call himself a peg-leg, I'll understand.'

'Oh, no, Albert, don't think that!' She whipped her head round to face him. 'It's got nothing to with it. It's just that ... I've never told anyone before, but...' She paused, releasing a tortured sigh. But the moment had come to face up to herself. 'Years ago, I made a vow. When Kate announced she was pregnant with Adam, I felt I'd lost her. Lost part of myself, we were that close. It was as if she'd renounced Dartmoor. Everything that we'd ever had together. And I vowed that I'd never do the same. That I'd never marry and have children. That Dartmoor would be my one and only love. And the horses.'

'We can love Dartmoor and the horses together,' Albert pointed out simply.

'Yes, I know.' Marianne rolled her head in anguish. 'But with Kate going to London, all that hurt has come back again. And, well, I'm just not ready.'

'I understand,' Albert nodded gravely. 'We won't speak of it again. But if you do decide you're ready, then I'll be waiting for you.'

And the smile he gave her was so full of warmth and loving devotion that her heart was torn apart.

Mild heart attack. Ned Cornish mulled the words over in his brain, his lips pushed forward in a knot. The quack had given him some pills, but what good would they do? His days were numbered.

How did he feel? Scared? A little. Shocked? Well, somewhat numbed, he supposed. But sad or devastated? He had to admit that he didn't really. His had been a lonely life. He'd never had many friends. You didn't when you existed in the murky world of distrust and criminality.

His one regret was that he had let Rose Maddiford slip through his fingers. He had loved her with a jealous passion. And she was just as beautiful now in her mid-sixties. He could have had her if he'd tried. He'd just always felt he wasn't good enough for her. He was a stable-boy, unable to do more than scrawl his own name, but it had never bothered him much. Except where Rose was concerned. But he could have learnt to read and write properly, as he had since. He could even have asked Rose herself to teach him. She was so kind, he was sure she would have done. And then she might have seen that he wasn't as ignorant as he appeared, simply lacking in education and opportunity.

It was his stubborn pride, his innate bitter jealousy that she was a *have* and he was a *have not*, that had got in the way. And now?

Well, he shouldn't have stolen the horses and burgled the house, or attacked her beautiful daughter who was so much the image of Rose as a young woman that it brought saliva to his mouth even now. Especially when he thought of her on the night of the fire, dressed only in a flimsy nightdress. He shouldn't have done that either. His blood turned at the memory. He'd been involved in gangland murders, and they'd deserved it. But if someone innocent had died in a fire he had started, he would never have forgiven himself. He gave himself that credit, at least.

He was a dying man. But was there any way, before he went, that he could get close to Rose just one last time? Touch her hand? Beg her forgiveness? He would have to think about it. And then he could die happy.

CHAPTER TWENTY-THREE

The telegram arrived part way into January as they all sat around the table having lunch.

'Oh, it's from Philip,' Seth announced, slitting it open with his knife. And then Marianne saw his face drain of its colour. 'Oh, my God,' he muttered. 'Oh, no.' His head twisted on his neck as if he were recoiling from the news contained in the telegram, and he screwed his eyes shut. 'They've all had the flu. But ... our darling little Valerie...' The breath shook in and out of his lungs and his mouth contorted into an ugly grimace as tears began to roll down his cheeks. He held out the flimsy paper to whoever had the courage to take it, unable to watch.

Marianne was at a total loss. She had never seen her father actually cry, not even when Hal was killed. Her mother's face too, had turned white, her mouth gaping open in horror.

Marianne's senses dropped away. She was all alone, trapped in her own anguish. Her father hadn't voiced the terrible words, but it was clear what was in the telegram. Marianne didn't want to believe it, and so it was she who took the note from Seth's fingers.

Someone had to. She must be the one to be strong.

Her eyes scanned the print. Rebellious. Unaccepting. It couldn't be true, but... A vicious squall of anger plunged through her body. She wanted to lash out, vanquish the truth. But there was nothing to be done.

She watched her mother's face crumple as she burst into tears with an agonized moan that grew to a crescendo. Seth sprang to his feet, encircled his wife in his arms, and they wept together, inconsolably. Marianne looked on, dry-eyed with shock, and met Albert's horrified gaze. In all the suffering and death they had seen in France, nothing had affected them as deeply as this. An innocent child. One of their own. It was indescribable.

'B-but I thought children–' she stammered, refusing to believe.

'Seem to have more resilience?' Albert finished for her, his voice soft and sympathy etched on his face.

'I must go to Kate at once.' Marianne was suddenly on her feet, instinct overtaking all else. The idea of doing something practical was a relief from her agony. And surely, despite everything, her sister, her *soul-mate*, would need her. She stopped then, realizing her mother had lifted her head from Seth's embrace and had spoken the exact same words at the same time.

Seth exchanged glances with both his wife and his daughter. 'No, Marianne. You'd be more likely... I don't really want your mother to go, either, but I know I won't stop her.'

'I'll be careful,' Rose promised. 'I'll wear a mask. Wash my hands every few minutes. I'll break my journey in Tavistock and ask Elliott's advice. But they must all ... the others must more or less be over it by now or else Philip wouldn't have been able to send the telegram. And Kate needs me. I know you want to go, Marianne,' Rose said, her tear-filled eyes meeting her younger daughter's, 'but it's best that you don't. You're in the age-group that seems to be worst affected. And I know ... I know what it is to lose a small child.'

Marianne watched in silence as her mother hurried out of the room. Rose never spoke of her lost baby, the grief too deep to bear. Marianne lowered herself back into her chair, and at the touch of Albert's caring hand on her arm, she buried her face in her hands and sobbed.

Marianne reined Pegasus in from the long canter over the moor, and heard her mother on Captain doing the same just behind her. The gorse was in its full May bloom, canary yellow in the sunshine, its sweet fragrance strong and filling their nostrils with its heady perfume. Marianne waited for Rose to draw level with her and they continued side by side at a walk, Pegasus tossing his head with a snort of disgust that they were heading back home. Mother and daughter chuckled softly at him, and Marianne felt the familiar tranquillity of the moor soothing the very core of her.

'It's beginning to feel more as if things really are getting back to normal,' she said thoughtfully. 'Do you feel that, too?'

Rose made a sucking noise before she answered. 'Yes, I do. The better weather helps, of course. And time. Life will never be the same for us. Not without Hal. But it's been nearly three years and I suppose you learn to live with it. But Valerie, she'll be harder to get over. Such a dear little soul. It's hard enough for us, but I know what poor Kate's going through.'

Marianne nodded, her lips bunched pensively. Her mother's voice had been intense, mesmerizing. It was like old times, the shared closeness, an opening of hearts.

'Mum,' Marianne faltered, her heart suddenly pattering nervously, 'do you think it's better not to have children in the first place? I mean, if you hadn't had Alice or Hal, you'd never have had the heartbreak of losing them. Or Kate with Valerie.'

She kept facing front, not daring to look at her mother, half afraid of the words that were coming from her mouth. So the vehemence of Rose's reply took her by surprise.

'Oh, no! Alice was with me for such a short time, but I still cherish the memory of every moment I had with her. And Hal. If it hadn't been for the war... And Kate would say exactly the same about Valerie. Children are a blessing. You know I'm not particularly religious, but they are a gift from God. No one can predict the future and there's nothing like the joy of bringing new life into the world. And I wouldn't have had you or Kate.'

Out of the corner of her eye, Marianne saw her mother throw her a questioning glance, but Rose didn't press her. Had she guessed what Marianne had been thinking – and had been for months? That if she and Albert were to marry, children would be bound to come along? But if there were no children, she would never have to bear the pain of losing them?

She drew air deeply into her lungs and re-leased it in a long sigh. As if it weren't hard enough agonizing over her long-ago vow which had shaped her entire adult life, her emotions were coloured by what the war and the influenza pandemic had meant to her. There was no doubt in her mind that she loved Albert with all her heart, but the other part of her was twisting her soul into a tangled jumble that she was no nearer unravelling.

They had come to the unmade road that would take them back to Fencott Place. They plodded along side by side, both lost in thought after their conversation, Marianne's mind deep in turmoil so much so that she was only vaguely aware of the motorcar coming towards them from the direction of Princetown. Normally it would have roused some curiosity in her since virtually no motorized vehicles ever came this way. But now she merely guided Pegasus onto the left-hand verge, Rose also moving to the left beside her but still just on the road itself, so that the car could pass safely. There was plenty of room as the road was wide and so uneven that any vehicles could only proceed very slowly.

Neither woman paid much attention to the situation so it completely dumbfounded them when the car suddenly accelerated and then swerved, hurtling straight towards them. There was no time for panic, let alone to take evasive action. It was the horses that reacted, their animal instincts sharper than the human mind. Quick as lightning, Pegasus bunched his haunches and scrambled up the bank at the side of the road. Marianne was almost unseated, but instantly tightened her knee grip and grabbed Pegasus's mane so that she somehow managed to stay on. She pulled on the reins, holding Pegasus back as he threatened to bolt. Fear grasped her then as she turned him to see what had happened behind her.

Horror seared into her as she held Pegasus's prancing body in check. Captain was on the ground, but at that moment, rolled back onto his belly and heaved himself upwards. He walked on a few yards, but trained as he was to cope with noise and frightening situations, he came to a stop and stood patiently, even though he was quivering and blood was running down from a gash on his hind leg. Rose lay on the ground, although to Marianne's supreme relief, she was starting to sit up. A dozen yards further along the road, the car had crashed into the bank, the front caved in. One front wheel had lodged in a ditch, tipping the vehicle at a strange angle so that the right back end was in the air, the wheel still spinning. There was no sign of any movement from within.

A vision of driving through the air-raids flashed through Marianne's brain, and she thrust it painfully aside. She was trained to keep calm, but it was difficult when her dear mother was involved. Heart hammering, she slid from Pegasus's back and dragged him by the reins to where Rose was now sitting up, her face contorted in pain.

'Mum!'

'He hit us,' Rose grated between clenched teeth, her lips drawn back in a grimace of agony. 'Give me Pegasus's reins and go and see if Captain's all right.'

'He's got a nasty cut, but I think he's all right. Wasn't limping or anything. You're the one I need to–'

'No. Captain first,' Rose insisted.

Reluctantly, Marianne took the few paces to where the bay was standing, still trembling, but he whickered as Marianne came up to him. She walked him back to where her mother was lying, but he didn't show signs of any great pain.

'It must have been just a glancing blow.'

'But enough to knock him off his feet,' Rose rasped. 'He rolled on my leg as he went down. I'm sure it's broken.'

Marianne knew she was shaking. She was trained in First Aid but this was different. She felt utterly alone, but she must pull herself together.

'Whatever you do, don't move,' she instructed. 'And are you sure you weren't knocked out, or hurt your back or neck at all?'

'No, no. It's just my leg. But you'd better take a look at the driver.'

'Hardly deserves it,' Marianne retorted.

'Go anyway,' Rose demanded, and bit her lip in another wave of pain.

Marianne twisted her mouth, but she reluctantly obeyed. Whoever it was might have killed them both and the horses and deserved whatever injuries he might have.

And she couldn't be sure but it was almost as if he had deliberately driven into them.

She went up to the car. The driver was still sitting inside, the engine still running. Marianne checked there was no petrol leaking out as she wasn't going to risk being burnt or caught in an explosion. She had been happy to risk herself for others in France, but not in this situation! But there didn't appear to be any potential danger, so the first thing she did was open the door and reach across to switch off the engine. It was only then that she looked at the driver's face.

She gasped aloud. It was *him!* The devil who had attacked her, set fire to the stables, and doubtless stolen the horses and burgled the house. Marianne could have throttled him then and there. Her fingers itched to do so, but it would be too good for him. The police would lock him up and hopefully throw away the key, and in the meantime, if he was injured, she hoped the pain was excruciating!

His eyes were open, bolting from their sockets, staring at her. There was a split across the bridge of his nose where he had been thrown against the steering-wheel, and blood was trickling down into his mouth. But his right arm was clasped across his chest, his left arm raised and tense as if paralyzed with pain. In fact, he seemed unable to move at all, his face rigid and his breath barely wheezing in and out of his lungs.

'My heart,' he croaked in a whisper, barely moving his lips. 'Pills in my pocket. Is Rose all right? I didn't mean to hit her. I just ... wanted to talk. Tell her I'm sorry. For everything.'

Marianne stared at him, flabbergasted. *Rose?* Did he *know* her mother? 'Who the hell *are* you?' she demanded, ready to shake him.

'Ned,' he rasped, scarcely audible. 'She'll know. My pills. *Please,*' he begged.

Marianne glared at him through eyes narrowed into dangerous slits. In the most appalling moment of her life, she hovered over an abyss of torment. She wanted to leave him to die. Yet she knew it was wrong and that would make her as bad as him. With shaking fingers and utterly repulsed, she searched his pockets until she found a small bottle of pills. She unscrewed the lid and closed his fingers around the bottle. If he wanted them that badly, he would have to take them himself.

She left him then and ran back to her mother, her mind staggering. 'He said his name's Ned,' she told Rose in bewilderment. 'He said you'd know. I think he lost control of the car because he's having a heart attack. He says he just wanted to talk. Mum,' she hesitated only briefly, 'it's him.

The arsonist. And it is the same man who attacked me.'

She watched, incredulous, as her mother's face lengthened in disbelief. 'Ned?' she repeated. 'Good God! He disappeared forty years ago.'

'B-but who is he?'

'Not now, Marianne.' Rose's face suddenly seemed old. 'Go and get help.'

'Yes, but be careful. If he manages to get out of the car and comes over to you–'

'Don't worry. I can handle Ned. Always could. Now go.'

Still unsure, Marianne obeyed. But it was the only thing to do. She swung herself into the saddle and urged Pegasus homeward.

That evening, Marianne sat by Rose's bedside. She had alerted her father, and while he and Joe hurried out to the scene of the accident, she rode like the wind into Princetown to send a telegram to Elliott down in Tavistock. By the time she returned, Seth was sitting on the ground, comforting Rose as they waited for Elliott to drive up to them. Joe was standing by the open door of the motorcar, his face stiff with hatred as he watched the driver breathe his last.

Now Rose was sitting comfortably in bed, her lower left leg in plaster, what was now a dull ache eased with aspirin. Marianne was amazed how calm she was, but that was her mother. So strong.

'Ned was a stable boy in Princetown,' Rose explained slowly. 'He used to look after Gospel for me whenever I went there to visit Molly. You know Gospel will always be my favourite horse, but he was a devil sometimes, especially with Ned. I used to tease Ned about it. But I could hardly say we were ever friends. Not from my side, anyway. Ned was always one for the girls, but I'd always eluded him. I never led him on, but it was a bit of a game and I suppose, looking back, he must have resented it. Then, when I married Charles, he employed Ned as our groom. I was horrified. I wanted Joe, but Charles didn't like the way Joe and I were friends. He believed servants were inferior beings and should be kept apart. He didn't know I already knew Ned, of course. When I told him I wasn't keen on Ned, he was pleased as it meant I wouldn't fraternize with him. But Ned was always trying to fraternize with *me*. I often had to fight him off, but I knew that if I said anything, Charles wouldn't believe me. He was a very jealous sort, Charles. And then it was Ned who betrayed your father to the authorities. I'd managed to trick both Ned and Charles for weeks, and when Ned *did* realize, I think that riled him even more. That I'd fooled him for so long, and right under his nose. All the rest, you know. But when Charles died, one of the first things I did was to dismiss Ned, and I'd not seen hide nor hair of him since. Until today. I can only think that his anger had been festering all those years and he decided to try and get even.'

'But all those terrible things he did to us. He could have burnt the house down with Albert still inside.'

'I know. But he always had a chip on his shoulder. And jealousy can twist a man's mind. And who knows what sort of life he'd been leading all this time, and blaming me for it. But...' Rose turned her smile on her daughter, as stunningly beautiful as ever. 'It's over now. We need to rebuild our lives. Kate seems to be settling well in London. I think a new way of life will help with her grief over our darling Valerie, and Philip does seem to be salvaging something of our affairs, for which we are exceedingly grateful. So now we need to see *you* settled, my dear.'

Marianne gave her mother a wan smile. It had all been a great deal to take in, part of her parents' lives she had never known about. After the trauma of the day, the conflict that was tearing her apart was the last thing on her mind.

A month later, Captain Adam Bradley died peacefully in his sleep at the family home in

Herefordshire, shortly after his eighty-second birthday. It should not have come as any surprise to the Warringtons, since dear Adam's health had been failing for some time. Nevertheless, Rose and Marianne both wept for the loss of their cherished friend, and Seth was stone-faced with grief. Even the dogs sensed their sadness, noses on paws as they lay on the floor, their eyes looking up dolefully. Albert put his arm around Marianne's shoulders, and she was intensely grateful for his comfort.

'I never met the man, of course,' he said gravely, 'but you all always spoke of him with such respect and affection.'

'He was,' Marianne hiccupped between sobs, 'a sort of patriarch to us all. So kind and yet fearsome in his beliefs for justice.'

'You know how he and I campaigned for raising the age of consent, and then for an appeal system for convicted criminals,' Seth went on. 'Well, he was the one with the connections, the tireless strength.'

'And now I can't even go to his funeral,' Rose moaned, 'not with this stupid leg in plaster.'

'But I can,' Seth stated adamantly, coughing painfully as he got to his feet.

'No, you can't,' protested Rose. 'Not when your chest is so bad again.'

'But Adam saved my life all those years ago!'

'Then he'd hardly want you to risk it again by going on a long journey when you're not at all well.'

'I can go,' Marianne announced, sniffing as she brought her sorrow under control. 'Sarah and Misha are bound to be going, and probably Richard and Beth, and Ling and Elliott, too, so I can travel with them. And then, didn't you say Becky mentioned having a memorial down at Morwellham?'

'Yes, that's right,' Rose nodded, glancing down at the letter in her hand.

'Well, we can all go to that. And it will be much more appropriate. Morwellham meant so much to them. And I can represent us all at the funeral.'

Seth rubbed his hand over his forehead and let out a deep sigh as he sat back down again. 'Yes, I suppose so. But it grieves me deeply.'

'I'm sure it does, Dad, but no one would have understood more than Adam himself. And the memorial will give us a more personal chance to say goodbye.'

And so it was that a few weeks later, a small group gathered on the bank of the River Tamar down at Morwellham Quay, the once bustling copper port that was now almost deserted but for a handful of farm workers living in the little cottages. The intimate ceremony had been timed to coincide with the ten minutes of slack water before the tide started running out again, something that for so many years had governed Rebecca's life.

Now she stood on the grassy bank, a small, elderly woman in widow's weeds, her face ravaged by grief and yet still dignified. Next to her was her son Toby, reverently holding Adam's captain's cap on a black velvet cushion, his wife Chantal, Richard's daughter, beside him. With them were Michael and Mary, both returned now from the war, holding hands, a diamond ring, Marianne noticed, catching the sunlight on Mary's left ring finger, and Marianne rejoiced for them.

Rebecca's sister, Sarah, and her husband, Misha, were there, too, as were Adam and Rebecca's other children, James and Charlotte, with their families. Richard Pencarrow, still tall and robust despite being only a few years Adam's junior, stood sombrely beside his wife, Beth, whose kindly face was creased with compassion for her dear friend. Elliott and Ling Franfield had also come to say their final farewell to the man they had come to know so well, and at Marianne's side, her parents, who probably had more to thank Adam for than anyone else present. Sorrow welled up in Marianne's throat, her eyes blurring with unshed tears. For this was truly the end of an era.

'My dear friends,' Rebecca suddenly spoke, clearly finding it difficult but determined to say what she had prepared. 'Thank you all so very much for coming. I know... Adam would...' She broke off, drawing in a shaking breath, and swallowed hard. 'When Adam first came here,' she went on, finding some majestic inner strength, 'I didn't want to know him. I had other things on my mind. And then circumstances changed and I turned to him as a last resort. He became my rock. And that rock became the foundation of my love for him and we had a whole lifetime of joy and contentment together, a lifetime that I could so easily have missed out on. And so, my friends,' she said, her voice vibrant with passion as her eyes travelled over everyone present, 'I say to you, grasp every opportunity for happiness that you can. If you don't, you will never know what you are missing. None of us can predict the future, so we must live for today. Enjoy every moment, just as I will treasure every memory I have of my darling Adam.'

She stopped then, and turned towards Toby, and taking up Adam's cap, held it tightly against her breast. Marianne could see the tears running down Rebecca's cheeks and the floodgate of her own grief was opened. She let the sorrow wash over her and wept also for her brother, her niece, Stella and all the thousands and thousands of unknown who had fallen to the war or the influenza pandemic.

'You came from the water, my darling.' Rebecca's choked whisper brought Marianne back to the present. 'And to the water you will return.'

Marianne looked up, her heart fractured, as Rebecca flung Adam's cap out into the river. It landed with a small splash, but was instantly swept up in the strong current as the returning tide gathered strength and bore the memory of the skilled captain out towards the sea which he loved with a passion. The summer breeze kissed the faces of all those who watched the cap grow smaller as it bobbed on the ripples and finally disappeared around the meander in the river.

They continued to stand. Respectfully. Nursing their sadness. Until Rebecca turned and began to walk on Toby's arm back towards the centre of the little village. Others followed, began to talk in low voices.

Marianne watched everyone leave, the only adult not to have someone special to lean on. But as Becky herself had said, she had shared a lifetime of happiness with Adam. A happiness she had nearly lost by not allowing Adam into her life. Was Marianne making the same mistake Becky had so nearly made, she asked herself?

Something so strong and powerful that it almost winded her made her take a step backwards. Grasp every chance. Yes. That's what she must do. Suddenly she couldn't understand why she had hesitated. A childish vow, her own stupid independence? It was time to let go.

Yes. She *would* marry Albert! She could feel his love pouring into her, soaking into every fibre of her being, filling her up and overflowing in an unstoppable tide. Joy burst out of her in a fountain, and she wanted to shout out in triumphant exultation. Couldn't wait to return to Fencott Place and run into Albert's waiting arms.

She turned her back on the retreating party, not wanting them to witness her pure elation, and instead focussed her eyes on the summer sun spangling on the water. Adam had arrived here all those years ago, setting off a chain of events that had altered the lives of everyone who had just now stood on the bank to bid him a final farewell. Marianne's lips curved in a fond, serene smile. *Thank you, Adam. For everything.*

She turned again, and followed the others as they began to leave Morwellham Quay, the place where it had all begun.

EPILOGUE

The boy was running, running as fast as his slender, athletic legs could carry him. His heart beat hard and strong beneath his flimsy shirt and knitted, sleeveless pullover, and the pounding of his feet on the moorland track had shaken his socks into bulging folds about his ankles. The pure, early morning air brushing against his cheeks had put a warm hue in his youthful skin, and a wild, ebony curl fell carelessly over his forehead.

His pace suddenly slackened and he turned in a slow circle, arms spread wide and head thrown back, laughing to the open sky with the sheer joy of being out alone on the savage, lonely moor. He spun round twice, then raced on with a whoop of delight.

He came at length to the tarmac road. He didn't stop to look. He wasn't in busy, fume-ridden London now. The road ran out to a handful of cottages, and no vehicle was likely to pass all day, let alone at that early hour. Besides, he knew his sharp hearing would detect any approaching engine in the morning silence.

It wasn't long before the child swooped in

at the open, rusty gates in a high brick wall and sped up the driveway of the old house, scattering the gravel and waving with wild abandon at the figure standing at the window. He knew she would be waiting.

Inside, the woman watching from the drawing room took another sip of the hot, strong coffee and stubbed out her cigarette, the second of the day although it was only six o'clock. A red silk dressing-gown hugged her small waist and her raven hair, interlaced here and there with silver, fell around her shoulders in thick waves. Her fine skin was faintly lined about her intense, lavender-blue eyes, yet she was as beautiful and elegant as a film star.

She waited for the boy to rush around to the back of the house and come in through the back door. She had heard him go out, but she wasn't worried. She had taught him well about the moor and its dangers. And she had known he would go. Dartmoor was in his blood.

He had arrived the previous evening, the first time he had travelled down from London alone on the train, and she had met him at Tavistock Station rather than let him go on to Yelverton and have to change onto the Princetown line. He was but ten years old, after all. By the time they had eaten, it was too late to venture out onto the moor, although he had tugged at her arm in pleading. And so it was no surprise to her that he had been up and out at dawn.

She felt the contentment swirl in her breast as she listened for his footfall through the entrance hall. Four whole weeks alone with the child before his parents and grandparents came for their annual stay. Usually, Kate and her daughter-in-law, Sheila, remained for the entire summer holidays, Philip and Adam joining them for the last fortnight. But this year, Marianne would have her great-nephew to herself for a whole month, and she could scarcely contain her jubilation.

The old rambling house was so quiet now. They were all long gone. Her father had died of pneumonia in 1922, and Rose had simply faded away without him. Rebecca, Richard, Beth, even Joe and Patsy had all passed away years ago. Marianne and Albert – ah, her darling Albert – had let the stables go, never putting their plans into action. It simply wasn't feasible with just the two of them and Albert so disabled. They had kept Pegasus and Captain, of course, until they died of old age, but after that, they simply had each other, and that was enough.

Children never came, much to their mutual regret, so they lived for themselves, not worrying as paint peeled from the windows and the roof leaked here and there. Philip had set up a small trust for Marianne from the family's restored fortunes – or at least the

modest amount he had managed to recover.
They had Albert's army pension, which
didn't go very far, and the money that was
left from the sale of his own house all those
years before. That had paid for a telephone to
be installed, and electricity from a generator
that was housed in a brick shed out in the
yard.

They had blown most of what was left in
1932 – on a Bentley! Oh, to hell with worrying about the future. Albert's longer stump
had never completely healed. It was a constant battle against infection, and twice
Elliott had needed to amputate a little
further; neither time had it been successful
despite Elliott's skills, and Albert had never
been able to walk on two false legs as he had
always hoped. So to get about, they needed
a decent car. Marianne felt the old adren-
aline coursing through her veins as she sped
over the moor, never reckless, but pitting
her skills against the steep, twisting hillsides,
sometimes imagining she was back in
France with enemy shells exploding all
around...

It wasn't long afterwards that Albert
finally lost the fight when septicaemia set in.
He was not alone in dying from war wounds
donkey's years later, apparently. Marianne
had felt as if her own insides had withered
and died. That she was a mere living and
breathing shell. But then she began to take

more notice of the boy.

'Great Aunt Marianne!'

The door slammed open and Daniel flew into her arms.

'Good morning, my lover!' Marianne hugged him to her, swooning with the feel, the scent of him. 'Been out on the moor, have we?' she teased, her eyes dancing.

'Yes, and guess what I saw?'

'No, tell me?'

'An adders' nest!' The child's eyes, the same vivid blue as her own, were as wide as saucers, his face beaming. 'They were all slithering around each other, keeping warm until the sun comes out. But don't worry. I was very careful not to disturb them.'

Marianne's expression turned to one of tempered horror, the day she had come off Pegasus because of a snake suddenly tumbling into her head. 'I should hope so, too!'

'Come on! I'll take you to see them!' And he grasped her hand, pulling her forward.

'Daniel, I'm in my dressing-gown!'

'But it won't take you long to change.'

'No. Breakfast first. What would your mother think?' she whispered conspiratorially, and the child laughed aloud.

'Have a blue fit if she'd known I was out on the moor on my own! But you don't mind, do you, Aunty? You know I can look after myself.'

'Boiled egg?' Marianne asked as they

passed into the vast, echoing kitchen.

'Yes please. And this afternoon, can we get the Bentley out and go and visit Ed?'

'I should think so,' Marianne chuckled, 'if it's all right with Deborah. I'll give her a ring after breakfast.'

'Thank you!'

Daniel clapped his hands with delight and Marianne shook her head in amusement. She might have known it wouldn't be long before he wanted to see Edwin. Elliott had only retired a few years previously, having been in practice with his son, William, for many a long year. Elliott and Ling still lived with William, his wife Deborah, and their four children, of whom Edwin was the eldest. Being of the exact same age, Edwin and Daniel had become inseparable friends during the school holidays, both dreading the time when Daniel had to return to London. Mary and Michael lived in Plymouth and had two sons, but they were somewhat older and so were never the soul-mates Daniel and Edwin had become.

'And can Edwin come and stay here with us?' Daniel's face was aflame with enthusiasm. 'Can I show him the adders, too?'

'Only if you're very careful, and let me come too. Edwin doesn't have the same feeling for the moor that you do.'

Daniel shrugged. 'All right. To see the adders, but you won't be with us *all* the time,

343

will you?'

Marianne's smile made the corners of her eyes crinkle. She would love to be with him all the time. When she was with Daniel, she didn't mind that she and Albert had never had children. Daniel was more of a son to her than any child of her own could have been, far more like herself than his own parents and grandparents. But she understood that he needed his freedom, even if it meant leading the more sensible Edwin into scrapes he would never have got into on his own.

'Can I have Marmite soldiers to dip in my egg, please? Mummy says it's bad manners, but *you* don't mind, do you, Aunty?'

Marianne shook her head. Sheila was a very good but over-protective mother and sometimes, Marianne considered, struggled to cope with a child of such intelligence and strong will as Daniel. At the rate he was wolfing down his breakfast, impatient to be out on the moor again, Marianne gulped down her own food and ran up the grand staircase, two at a time, to throw on her clothes.

A few minutes later, they had left the tarmac road behind and were striding out along the track, Daniel dancing around her like a puppy in his enthusiasm. It was a glorious summer's morning, silent and still but for the occasional call of a moorland bird. Not a cloud hindered the duck-egg blue sky. The sun was not yet up, its brilliant light casting mysterious shadows and reflecting off the crescent moon. Marianne gazed upwards. For now the silver curve seemed to be smiling.

Daniel suddenly ceased prancing and fell into step beside her, a thoughtful frown on his young face. 'Aunty?'

'Yes, Daniel?'

'You know they say there might be another war? And they're preparing to evacuate children from London? Well, if Adolph Hitler can't be persuaded otherwise and war does break out, please can I come and live with you?'

His words robbed Marianne of her breath. Oh, dear God, she had been trying to put all of that out of her mind. Another war when the horrors of the last one were still so fresh? Yet this innocent child could only see the good side of what it would mean to him. And, if she were truly honest, the idea of having Daniel to *live* with her filled her with ecstatic joy. At long last, a child of her own.

'Of course you can!' she almost cried out with glee. 'This is your home whenever you want it to be! Now, come on,' she prompted as pure, ineffable contentment settled in her heart. 'Where's this adders' nest?'

Daniel lifted his face towards her, gilded in the golden morning light. 'This way!' he grinned, grasping her hand.

Together they ran, hand in hand, out onto the savage wilderness of the moor, and, drenched in happiness, Marianne felt, at last, that her soul had been set free.

ACKNOWLEDGEMENTS

My deepest gratitude will always go to my wonderful agent, Dorothy Lumley, whose untimely death shocked and saddened all of us who knew her. She taught me so much and I owe my writing career to her.

I should like to thank also the archive section of the Royal College of Nursing for their information on nursing during the Great War, my good friend Sir Michael Willats for his input on vintage motor vehicles, and Paul Rendell, Dartmoor guide and historian and editor of *The Dartmoor News*, for his continued support and information on the Princetown moss gatherers. And I must, of course, thank Robert Hale for publishing the story.

AUTHOR'S NOTE

Princetown is described in the book as it was in 1914. There is a 'model' for Rose-bank Hall, but Fencott Place does not exist.

The equestrian information in the story was taken from various sources.

I have endeavoured to convey as accurately as possible the role in the First World War of the First Aid Nursing Yeomanry, the 15th The King's Hussars and the Princetown moss gatherers.

The tragic accident at Bere Ferrers Station was, sadly, a true event.

To discover the past and/or future of many of the characters in this novel, please read my previous stories, details of which can be found on my website at:

www.tania-crosse.co.uk

The publishers hope that this book has given you enjoyable reading. Large Print Books are especially designed to be as easy to see and hold as possible. If you wish a complete list of our books please ask at your local library or write directly to:

Magna Large Print Books
Magna House, Long Preston,
Skipton, North Yorkshire.
BD23 4ND